The Elusive Key

A Florian Fooks Murder Mystery

The Elusive Key

Shirley Arnham

This novel is entirely a work of fiction. The names, characters and incidents portrayed in it are the work of the author's imagination. Any resemblance to actual persons, living or dead, events or localities is entirely coincidental.

Shirley Arnham asserts the moral right to be identified as the author of this work.

First edition.

A CIP catalogue record for this book is available from the British Library.

Ebook ISBN 978-1-7399186-2-0

Paperback ISBN 978-1-7399186-3-7

TABLE OF CONTENTS

CHAPTER ONE

"Mary, what on earth is on this book?"

Mary, feather duster in hand, regarded her husband, Florian Fooks, reforming outlaw. He eased the pages apart. His face took on a look of disgust. Life was hard enough for him being hardware store proprietor Joseph Crane, without a saboteur in his midst.

"This is a catalog. Belongs in the store. What are my customers gonna think if it's welded shut by …?" He broke off, his face screwing up in disgust. "I don't even know what this is." He demanded an answer. "Mashed potato?"

"We're the parents of a baby learning to feed herself. Haven't you noticed? Everything is covered in food these days."

Fooks leveled a glare in her direction, watching as she continued to dust the mantle shelf above the fireplace in their living room. She stood on tiptoe to reach the top of the clock. "If the catalog belongs in the store, why is it here?"

"I brought it home to check out the latest developments." Fooks bent his head over the page, scratching at the hardened lumps of potato. "I can't have my customers see this. What will they think?"

"What's the catalog?"

Fooks grunted.

"Excuse me?"

Fooks scowled at her. "Safes."

Mary bit her lip, amusement dancing over her face. "In the four years you've sold hardware, exactly how many customers have bought a safe from you?" she asked, tongue in cheek.

He threw daggers with full force at her. "Not the point. Still part of my range," he mumbled into the book once more.

A moment later, she said, "Samuel's letter is still here."

Fooks glanced up. Mary held the envelope he'd tucked behind the clock.

"Unopened."

"Yeah, I know."

"Are you ever going to open it?"

Fooks chewed his lips. "Hmmm, when I'm ready."

His partner, Tobias Swan's desertion was still a sore point. While he and Mary were away on honeymoon, Swan'd disappeared with a mysterious woman. Fooks was devastated to find him gone on their return. Tobias Swan, or Samuel Martin, as Bronze Canyon thought of him, left a short note with the sheriff. A woman called Caroline Fairfield offered Swan an opportunity he couldn't refuse. He gave no further explanation other than he was going to Boston to take up the opportunity, telling Fooks not to worry and he'd be in touch when he got settled. At first, Fooks vowed to go to Boston but one thing and another stopped him.

Fooks bent over the book again, inspecting the page for more edible imperfections.

"You do know this might be important?" Mary said.

"Yes." Fooks kept his head down, his tone icy.

"I expect he's wondering why you haven't replied by now."

"He's aware of the hazards mail out here runs."

"I think things are improving. I get letters regularly from friends in San Francisco now."

"That's San Francisco." He added, through gritted teeth, "Nearer." He dropped his head again.

Their previous attempts to talk about this had ended in sharp words. He didn't want a repeat. *I'll open the letter when I'm good and ready.*

Tobias Swan and Florian Fooks were partners since childhood. A lot of water had flowed under the bridge since then. Including being notorious bank and train robbers. A status which would continue to define them, although both turned their backs on a life of crime. Now trying to be law-abiding citizens living under assumed names. Their experiences together meant they were closer than brothers.

"Perhaps I'll open it for you."

Her thumb found the edge of the seal and she paused.

His head flew up. Fooks bounded to his feet, precious catalog tossed carelessly aside. He crossed the distance between them in a flash and snatched the letter from her.

"I'll open it."

He took a deep breath when he read the address, written in Swan's distinctive, untidy scrawl. Aware of her eyes on him, he growled, turned the envelope over and tore it open. Mary moved aside to give him some privacy, but his hand shot out, pulling her back.

With a further deep breath, he slid out the single sheet of paper. Didn't take him long to read.

Dear Joseph. Everything is good for me here. Settled in real well. Hope you and Mary are well and married life suits you. Don't worry 'bout me. I'm doing good. Samuel.

"Here." Fooks thrust the letter at her and walked away.

"He sounds well."

"What was the point? I don't know any more than I did a few moments ago."

"He's thinking of you."

"Yeah." He wasn't convinced.

Mary hesitated. "You have an address now." She ran her thumb over the embossed picture of a mansion. Underneath it read: Ardmaddy, Waltham, Boston, Massachusetts. "You could go and find him."

"How can I leave you and Susan? Then there's the store."

"I'm sure we'll manage."

"Not the point."

"You went away before when Susan was born. I was fine." Mary smiled pleasantly at his scowling face.

"Still not the point."

She moved forward, but stopped. The conjured-up baby's cries echoed around the house. Instead, Mary regarded him meaningfully. He glared back, hands on hips. Who was going to go? Stand-off.

"Mama's the chuck wagon." He tried his double-dimpled beam, hoping the effect would work on Mary this time. *Usually doesn't. She's somehow immune.*

"Only at night now. And that's not a hunger cry. That's an I'm-awake-and-I-want-to-know-what's-going-on cry. Something," Mary swatted him with her duster. "Pappies are ideally suited to undertake." She stood on tiptoes and smacked a kiss on his cheek. He went to grab her but she skipped away. "Besides, it will be good practice for tomorrow."

"Tomorrow? What's happening tomorrow?"

"I'm going to Cheyenne to the Millinery Convention. I'll be gone all day," Mary said, ruefully. "Don't tell me you've forgotten?"

Fooks growled. Seemed such a long way off when he'd agreed to take sole charge of their daughter for an extended period. "No, I hadn't forgotten." He flashed her a false smile.

Susan cried again. This time more insistent. When Mary raised an eyebrow, he glowered. "Okay, Susan. I'm coming."

Mary's smugness as she disappeared into the kitchen didn't go unnoticed. He stalked in the direction of the baby's bedroom.

Susan was already sitting up.

Fooks chuckled. "Hello, sweetheart." She raised her arms and squealed. He pulled her out of the crib and settled her in his arms, relishing her smell and the warmth of her body. He smoothed the baby's mop of brown hair, lighter than his own. "Mama says you want to know what's going on. Is that right?"

He carried her back into the main room. Mary had left Swan's letter on his desk, and he picked it up. "This is what's going on, a letter from your Uncle Tobias." He read the few words again. "You haven't met him yet," he said, in a regretful murmur.

Susan reached for the letter, but he held it away. If this proved to be the last ever communication from Tobias, he didn't want Susan crumpling it up. Despite her protests he dropped the letter back onto the desk.

"Mama thinks I oughta go see him. How can I go and leave you and Mama, huh?"

Susan played with the lapel of his vest and remained silent.

"What d'you think? Should I go?" He kissed the top of the baby's head. "I really need to know if he's okay. Y'know how impulsive he can be. The trouble he can get himself into without me."

Fooks groaned.

"Aw, who am I kidding? He's a grown man, Susan. He's capable of taking care of himself." Fooks pulled a face. "Yeah, worked out well in the past, didn't it? Remember Denver? How he got himself arrested 'cos he tried to save a soiled dove from a beating? Got himself thrown in jail and who got him out? Me. That's who. There's me risking life and limb to rescue his sorry ass, and the woman isn't even grateful. Play acting but it looked real enough to me." He shook his head. "Wonder what play this woman Caroline Fairfield is starring in? I've heard the name from somewhere. Just won't come to me."

CHAPTER TWO

Where on earth is she? She was on my lap. "No!"

Fooks frantically searched around for Susan. He'd settled down to read the latest copy of *Scientific American*, in the wing-backed chair, waiting for Mary to come home from the Millinery Convention. She was late, he was tired and his eyes closed. Howling, he searched everywhere, even in improbable places. Under cushions, in cupboards, on his desk, under the sofa. Where had Susan gone?

"Lost something?"

Fooks' head snapped around, hair falling forward over his face. Mary stood in the doorway of Susan's room, arms folded and smiling knowingly.

"Mary..."

Mary took pity on him. "I've put Susan to bed."

"Oh, sheesh." He pushed his hair from his eyes and climbed to his feet. He sank into the wing-backed chair, leaned forward, and pressed his hands over his face. "For a moment there I thought..."

"How did today go?" Mary asked, wryly.

With a groan, he slumped back in the chair. "Easier leading an outlaw gang."

Mary crossed the room. "Is that why Susan is in a different dress to the one I put her in this morning?"

Fooks growled. His face soon changed when she slid onto his lap. "Hello," he said. Her hand went to his cheek, and they kissed gently. His arms tightened around her when their kiss deepened. When it ended, he reluctantly let her go.

She stroked his cheek. "You're tired."

"I love our little daughter, Mary, but I hadn't appreciated until today how demanding she is." Mary nodded in understanding. "She crawls away so fast. Coulda done with eyes in the back of my head."

"When she starts walking then where will we be?"

Fooks grunted. "Won't be long. She's already pulling herself onto her feet." He sighed contentedly. "She was clingy. Every time I tried to put her down for a nap, she'd cry."

He glanced at his desk where his latest Florian Fooks story, *The Fake or Fortune Mystery*, lay unfinished. Mary followed his gaze. Part of his grand plan for rehabilitation was writing the truth behind his outlaw life. When, or if, his real identity became common knowledge, he wanted public opinion on his side. Judging by the reaction to his stories, he was well on the way to achieving it. "Didn't get anything done I planned to."

"She probably missed all the attention she usually gets." As a rule, Mary took Susan with her to The Hat Shop and a procession of ladies stopped by to coo at the cute baby.

"Making do with Pappy today musta been hard," Fooks said, kissing Mary's fingers. "How was the Hat Fair?"

"It was a Millinery Convention," she said, nose in the air. "And it was great. I could have spent several days there, admiring all the new creations. I ordered far too much. At least I'll have the satisfaction of knowing the hats of Bronze Canyon ladies will be the best for miles around."

"I'm glad you had a good time." Fooks played with her fingers. "Luke stopped by. Said you'd asked him to check on me."

"I did not." Mary was indignant. "I simply told Papa you'd be on your own with Susan all day. I thought you might appreciate someone else to talk to for a while."

"Hmmm. He seemed to think I'm taking a trip back East soon."

Mary raised an eyebrow at him. "Aren't you?"

Fooks scowled. "I haven't decided yet."

Mary eyed him knowingly. "I won't hold my breath."

Fooks frowned at her. "D'you really think I would go and leave you and Susan, like that?" He clicked his fingers.

Mary put a hand on his chest. "No, but I do know how concerned about Samuel you are. Especially the way he left and the lack of explanation he offered."

Fooks grunted. "Yeah, I'm gonna have words with him." He glanced away and then back. "I don't know, Mary. I have responsibilities here. Tobias is a grown man and entitled to make his own decisions in life. He can be pretty stubborn at times, and I'm not sure he'd appreciate me going to Boston. Seem like I'm chasing after him."

"Now you have an address you can write to him."

"Yeah, I might." He pushed back a stray lock of hair from her face. "I missed you today."

"Did you miss me? Or my diaper wielding skills?"

"Your diaper wielding skills are of course unsurpassed." Fooks deepened his dimples. "But I'm pretty sure it was you I missed."

Mary kissed him. He settled her cozily, trying for something more ardent when Susan cried. He kept Mary close, chuckling. "How does she know?"

"I'll go. I should settle her properly for the night." Mary patted his chest, smiling coyly. "And then as you're tired, we should turn in ourselves."

Aware Fooks watched her walking away, Mary felt lucky. She'd lost her baby fat easily and was back to her previous trim self. In her smart business suit, she presented an image of the astute modern businesswoman she was. And had been before she met Fooks. Once they married, convention said he should have insisted she give up her business. He'd never do that to her. If anything should happen to him, she would always have her business to fall back on. She was fortunate to live in Wyoming. Here women had significantly more freedom than their sisters in surrounding states. They had the vote for one, and property rights even after marriage.

Would he go all the way to Boston? He was worried, but the decision remanded a difficult one. If he left Bronze Canyon, recognition always a constant danger. Perhaps safer to write to Tobias.

Mary turned in the doorway of Susan's room. His smile was uneasy. He couldn't go on like this. He needed to make a decision.

Sooner than either of them thought, a decision would be made for him.

Mary opened the front door early the next morning and blinked in surprise to see the sheriff of Bronze Canyon, Washington Turner, standing there. "Is he in?" Wash asked

"Yes, he's giving Susan her breakfast."

Wash followed her into the kitchen. His lips creased ruefully at the vision of domestic bliss. The notorious outlaw Florian Fooks, feeding his baby daughter her breakfast, was a sight to behold.

It was delicate work, requiring patience and guile. Patience to wait as the baby gummed her oatmeal. Guile to be alert for the opening mouth and fill it once more from the loaded spoon. Fooks appeared entirely suited to the role. He glanced around at Wash.

"Hey Wash. What brings you here so early in the morning?" He turned back to his daughter, ready for when her mouth next opened.

"This." Wash became serious and dropped a newspaper on the table in front of Fooks, tapping a section.

Fooks glanced at the small headline. Mary read over his shoulder. Time stood still as they read:

SAMUEL MARTIN INJURED IN SHOOTING

The spoon fell from Fooks' hand and clattered to the floor.

Susan whimpered at the sudden cessation of her breakfast. Her face crumpled.

Fooks snatched at the newspaper. His chair crashed back onto the floor. He swallowed hard, reading quickly.

"This paper is a month old. It doesn't say if ..." Fooks stared at Wash.

Susan's fists pounded the tray of her highchair. Mary pulled a disgruntled Susan into her arms.

"Mary, I have to go to Boston. Right now. I've really gotta go this time." He showed Mary the newspaper.

"I can see." She hugged his arm, glanced at him in concern and frowned. "This is a Boston newspaper. How—"

Wash rolled his eyes. "Craig and his easterlies. Got a delivery yesterday. He spotted it when he went through 'em. Brought it to my attention."

"I need to go."

CHAPTER THREE

The brief letter, Samuel sent saying he was all right and not to worry, had done nothing to stop Fooks worrying. Fooks tried to hide it, saying he couldn't leave Mary and Susan. Justifying to himself rather than her why he shouldn't go. The article in the newspaper now demanded he act.

"How can I go to Boston?" Fooks tossed a dismissive hand in the air.

He'd been pacing across the main room of their little house since Wash left. Rubbing the back of his neck. Muttering under his breath. He closed his eyes, attempting to stay calm. The fact he should be in The Hardware Store by now, adding to his sense of anxiety.

Mary raised her head from her sewing for a moment but quickly glanced away again when he continued pacing. The Hat Shop awaited her, but she wasn't leaving with Fooks in this undecided state.

"I mean, I have responsibilities," he pivoted on his heel, "Here. You and Susan, the store." He crept closer to her and threw another dismissive hand into the air. "Not to mention the danger of being spotted."

"Wouldn't the East be safer? Away from your...exploits."

Fooks scowled. "Not the point. Still gotta get there." He resumed pacing.

Mary jabbed her needle into the cloth and yanked the thread through. She gave her attention fully to her husband.

"Joe, he's your friend and he's hurt. He needs you."

Fooks shook his head. He came to a stop but kept his back to her. Mary unconsciously flicked her eyes to the carpet. *Was it becoming a mite threadbare?*

"How about sending a telegram. He might answer you himself and then—"

"And supposing..." He put his head down and shook it. His hands went to his hips. "I don't want to send a telegram in case... I don't want to hear bad news."

"Wash said it wasn't serious."

"Tobias was shot weeks ago. Anything coulda happened. I've seen men who look like they're recovering from being gunshot and then suddenly, they up and die. A bullet wound is always serious." He rolled his eyes at her. "Believe me, I know."

Mary pushed her lips together. She was well aware of the scars on her husband's body, several being gunshot wounds. Reminders of his previous occupation.

"Let me—"

"Nope."

"But Joe, if we send a telegram to Caroline Fairfield, she'll—"

"No!"

Mary cast her mending aside and went to him. "Not knowing is going to eat you up."

Fooks ran a hand through his hair. "I know." He shook his head. "But I can't rush off to Boston. It's the end of the world. I've never been east of the Mississippi." He fumbled for her hand. "I'd hope the first time I did go; it would be with you."

Mary smoothed his hair back from his face, noting that it needed a cut. "Joe, please be sensible about this. If you don't at least find out more, you'll drive yourself into a state. Children pick up on things, and Susan—"

"Don't lay that on me Mary." He shook his head. "This Caroline Fairfield doesn't know who I am and why I'm asking. Why should she tell me anything?"

"I'm sure Sam told her about you."

Fooks shook his head. "Not necessarily." He bit his lip. "Not the way he left," he said, quietly.

"He didn't go because he was mad at you."

Fooks grunted. "Seemed like it." He walked away, stopped, and put his hands on his hips. "I dunno Mary."

"Well, I do." Mary was firm. "Go to Boston. Go and find out what happened." He peered at her over his shoulder. She added, "I don't want any more nonsense about not being able to leave me and Susan. We were perfectly fine before."

"Sounds like you're trying to get rid of me."

"No of course not. I want what's best for you." She hesitated. "For us. You'll never settle until you do."

He scowled at her. Finally, he sighed. "I've got some things to sort out first." He ran a hand through his hair. "I'll think about it. Wash said he wasn't hurt bad. Perhaps I'll send a telegram."

Fooks finally went off to The Hardware Store and spent most of the day, first deciding he would go, then he wouldn't. He eventually made up his mind. Before he changed it yet again, he checked out the times of the transcontinental train. The 5:40 p.m. train from Cheyenne would do.

He caught the train to Cheyenne by the skin of his teeth, scrambling into a window seat as the train pulled out of Bronze Canyon station. He managed a quick wave to Mary and Susan, before the train sped away.

For who knew how long. He shook his head. Tobias could be impetuous without Fooks there to keep a lid on things. *What has he got himself into now?* If he wasn't so worried, this would be a grand adventure. A long train journey to parts unknown, and when he arrived, a city the likes of which he'd only seen in pictures. First city though, Cheyenne, a place familiar to him.

Even this brief familiar journey wasn't without difficulties. The Guardian Wall Gang had targeted the Union Pacific railroad. In particular, this section which ran through southern Wyoming. From Granger in the west all the way along to Cheyenne and beyond into western Nebraska.

Only on a few occasions, since his reformation, had he reason to journey to Cheyenne by train. Then he'd hid his face behind a newspaper or pulled the brim of his Stetson over his face, feigning sleep. Today no newspaper to hide behind. His hat, the homburg, with its slight brim, matching the suit he wore under his red and unusually green plaid Mackinaw jacket. Black being the more common other color. Might be a giveaway. Too distinctive, and described in his folk lore. He should have made the time to buy a new coat for last winter, but somehow never found the opening to get along to the men's outfitters. The best he could do on this trip was keep his face towards the window.

He watched the scenery slip by. This part of Wyoming quickly became monotonous. The softly undulating hills of sagebrush and greasewood, seemingly endless. He was cutting things fine. Delayed, the train, out of schedule, steamed more slowly than usual. *If this is what it'll be like all the way to Boston, my nerves won't stand it.*

Relieved to arrive at Cheyenne, he ran to catch the transcontinental train. Dodging around the major construction for a new depot building. He'd seen the architect's designs. It would be impressive.

But for now, barely enough time to buy a ticket through to Chicago. Not able to afford first class and a cabin all to himself, second class would have to do. At least it wasn't third class and hard benches all the way. Second offered a warm, comfortable car, with upholstered seating. With a bit of luck no one will sit in his group of seats, and he'll be able to stretch out. After his frantic departure, he wouldn't mind a sleep.

Fooks gulped when the train chugged out of Cheyenne. Now he really was on an adventure. The scenery soon became unfamiliar, and he began to relax. On the journey into Cheyenne, some of the train crew did appear familiar. He ducked his head away with a pounding heart until they passed. On this much longer journey, it was unlikely he would run into anyone he recognized. Yet he'd keep an eye out, at least until the train completed its journey through Nebraska.

When the train stopped at Denver Junction, a passenger settled opposite him. He immediately took out a book. Fooks' fellow passenger showed no signs of wanting to talk. Which was a pity. Now in Nebraska, he could do with the distraction. This was the land of his childhood, its abrupt ending with the killing of his parents, leaving him orphaned at twelve. The train would steam close to a place he hadn't returned to since, and had no wish to see again. No, Nebraska held no good memories for him.

CHAPTER FOUR

"Are you going far?" Fooks asked.

For the first full day on the train, the scenery was flat grassland after flat grassland. The only breaks, stops to water the locomotive and take on coal. Long enough to hop off and pay a dollar for something to eat. Sometimes of dubious quality and description. *I've eaten worse.*

The train still crossed Nebraska. Fooks'd be glad when they were through. Hopefully, his fellow passenger would provide a distraction.

"To Omaha. Where my firm is based. I travel in hardware."

Fooks chuckled.

"Why so funny?" the man asked, slightly put out.

"Oh, nothing against your trade, sir. Hardware is needed in any situation. I run a hardware store myself."

"Do you? My that is a coincidence. Can I ask where? I cover Nebraska and Colorado."

"Ah, my store is in Wyoming."

"We cover there too, but not me." The man rummaged into his pocket and handed Fooks a card. "Our headquarters are at this address. Had a telephone installed so you can use it to place orders now."

Fooks blanched. *Telephone?* Modern communications were the reason he'd decided to go straight. Too much risk of being caught. The telegraph had been bad enough, but now the telephone as well? *Sheesh.* "Perhaps in Cheyenne or Laramie. Not in small towns like mine."

"It'll come, mark my words. Great way to do business."

Fooks tucked away the card. "I'll bear that in mind."

Now inclined to talk, they introduced themselves and passed the time and miles in idle conversation. Until the man stood to pull down his trunk.

"Next stop is mine."

Fooks took out the railroad timetable he'd purchased with his ticket. "I'm puzzled. I'm going on to Chicago. Do I change in Omaha?"

"You can if you intend to break your journey."

Fooks shook his head. "No, I intend to go right on."

"Stay on the train across the bridge until you reach the U.P. Transfer Yard."

With a cheery wave, the man alighted at Omaha, leaving Fooks to ponder the Missouri Bridge.

The train trundled slowly between the boxy trusses. An altogether flimsy structure, 50 feet above the swirling waters. Must be the longest bridge he'd ever crossed in a train. A glance out of the window confirmed the bridge supported all the train at one point. Damaged by high winds a decade before, the repairs were alarmingly obvious. With the wind today, Fooks hoped the bridge would stay up long enough for the train to get across in one piece.

In a short while, the train slowed to a stop at the end of the Union Pacific railroad. He'd never seen this many railroad tracks in one place, some converging on the terminus building up ahead. Others, reserved for freight. A steady stream of heavily laden trains steamed up and down on the extensive marshaling yards. Further away,

Fooks made out the vast stockyards, now silent, but between July and October would house some 7,000 head of cattle, prior to their departure to Chicago.

Fooks gathered his belongings. He had a ninety-minute wait for his next train, one with Chicago in its name.

Too many folks here. Don't like it. The Union Pacific Transfer Depot was nothing like Fooks had ever seen. To get to the main terminus building, he fought through immigrants of all nationalities. A variety of languages assailed his ears, some familiar, some he made a guess at and others he couldn't determine. The adjacent track from the one he alighted onto held a rapidly filling train, a mixture of well-to-do and poor, separated into appropriate cars by brusque conductors.

Fooks pondered on the incongruous building in front of him. Red brick with sandstone moldings, topped by a gray slate roof. A central mansard attic with galvanized iron corniche and finials. The building was three sides of a quadrangle and of a size he'd rarely experienced beyond San Francisco. Out of place here in the middle of the vast railroad landscape. The whole structure reminded him of a spooky French chateau. He imagined bats flying from the forbidding windows. He shivered. He hated bats.

As he stepped across the threshold and glanced back, a sign above picked out in red tiles read *Where the West Begins*. Well, if that didn't bring it home to him that he was leaving life as he knew it, nothing would.

He moved further into the building and stopped, gazing around in awe. The interior didn't disappoint. All black walnut and white pine. The ceiling must be twenty feet high, the floor black and white diagonal tiles. Would be dizzy if there weren't all these people milling around.

To his right a steady stream of porters whisked heavily laden trolleys through doors, a sign above read "Baggage Room." An equally long stream of porters whisked luggage in the opposite direction. To his left a ticket office. He didn't need a ticket. His was valid through to Chicago. Waiting rooms behind, to the left for men and across the hall, another for women. Directions told him the hall would take him through to the hotel above.

But first he sent a telegram back to Mary and bought a newspaper. Distracted by the aromas wafting out of the dining room, he bought a sandwich and coffee.

He discovered too late the hotel offered washing facilities to passengers. Fooks happy to take quick advantage. No time for a complete wash or a bath. The communal washing facilities meant stripping to the waist. This would uncover the scars on his torso. No doubt attracting unwanted attention.

Instead, he contented himself with a change of shirt and a shave. He'd tried shaving on the train to the clicky clack music. The sudden jerks of the train held too much jeopardy when wielding a cutthroat razor close to his jugular.

He lingered over his ablutions for far too long, reluctant to get on another train, but he must.

"I'm coming!" Mary called as she hurried through the main room. Another knock on her front door. This time more urgent.

She threw the door open, out of breath and hair in disarray. Susan squirmed in her arms.

The telegraph runner hurriedly removed his cap. "Sorry to disturb ya, Ms. Crane. There's a telegram for Joseph, I mean Mr. Crane." He held out the envelope.

"Thank you, Jimmy."

"Mr. Clarkson said I was t'wait. In case of a reply."

Mary frowned. Joseph left three days ago. He would be in Chicago soon. Yet it sounded like Mr. Clarkson thought the telegram urgent and would need an immediate response.

The boy blinked in surprise when Mary thrust Susan into his arms. "Ma'am, I'm not paid to—"

With a deep breath, Mary opened the envelope and read:

To Joseph Crane, Summer Cottage, Bronze Canyon, Wyoming. Friend missing. In deep trouble. Come if you can. Caroline Fairfield.

Joseph already knew his friend was hurt. Now missing too. What was going on? Sam must be in a bad way. Joseph needed to know about this urgently.

"Thank you, Jimmy. I would like to send a reply. Please wait. I will be as quick as I can." She started to shut the door.

"Ma'am!" The boy's anguished cry caught her attention. He struggled to hold out a kicking and screaming Susan. "Yes of course," she murmured, taking Susan back.

"No problem, Ms. Crane. I can sit out here an' wait," the boy grinned, pointing at the bench outside.

Mary shut the door and dumped Susan unceremoniously on a sofa. She sat at Joseph's desk. He was busy writing. The desk, strewn with pages of his scribbling and reference books on all manner of subjects. *Half of Bronze Canyon's new lending library must be here.* She carefully shuffled things to one side to make space. Found pencil and paper, before settling to compose her messages.

To Caroline she wrote,

Caroline Fairfield, Ardmaddy Place, Waltham, Boston. Joseph already on way. Expect him in two days. Mary Crane.

To Fooks she wrote a quick telegram telling him about Caroline's message. She sent it to the Wells Street Depot in Chicago, where his train would terminate. They'd agreed before he left Mary would telegram there if she had more news about Swan.

CHAPTER FIVE

The conductor had already shouted "All aboard", and Fooks ran to catch the Chicago train, jumping on as the engine jerked to a start. By the time he'd found his seat, the change of shirt was rendered superfluous, the new one quickly soaked with perspiration.

Fooks soon struck up a conversation with a young family. They farmed in southern Dakota, and were on their way to Chicago to visit their boy's grandparents.

"Bet you're looking forward to seeing your grandparents huh?" Fooks asked.

"Suppose," the boy said, sadly. "Have to wear these stupid clothes though."

"Now Davy, you want to look nice for Granny and Grandpa, don't you?" said his mother, fussing at the boy's clothes.

The expression the boy gave his mother spoke volumes. Fooks suppressed the laugh threatening to burst out of him. *Better get used to it Fooks. Susan will be the same in a few short months when she starts to talk.* His daughter already had a disapproving look. One which told her parents in no uncertain terms how she felt. The thought of his daughter brought a lump to his throat. *Missing her already.*

When his parents became worn out with playing with him, Fooks amused Davy by teaching him Snap. Until it was time to settle him for the night. Fooks spent the next hour staring out of the window before settling himself. Tomorrow he would be crossing the Mississippi for the first time in his life.

The train pulled into Clinton shortly before nine the next morning. Once underway again, the Mississippi River Bridge came into view. All stone pillars and metal box girders. Over a mile long, the bridge spanned an island in the middle of the river. Once across in uncharted territory, he had a moment of apprehension. *Had Tobias felt like this?*

Before Fooks knew it, the train rattled through the suburbs of Chicago. He gazed in wonder as the buildings became wider and taller. He'd never experienced anything like this before. San Francisco, the closest he'd seen to this level of metropolitan life. *Not sure I like it.*

Fooks hoped he would make his connection in time. Already running an hour late, he had no idea how far away the depot for Boston was. Or by what means he would make his way across a vast and intimidating city. Late or not, first he went to the telegraph office, intent on sending a telegram back to Mary, finding one from her waiting for him. It read:

> *Message from CF. Friend missing. In deep*
> *trouble. People searching.*

Fooks gathered from the cryptic message police were searching for Tobias. What did that mean? What had happened? With his anxiety increasing, answers would have to wait until he arrived in Boston, still a long way off. He went in search of help with renewed urgency.

"Sure," said the concierge, "ask Parmelee outside. They'll be able to guide you."

"Parmelee?" Fooks bit his tongue. The man thought him an idiot. "I'm new to the city."

"The Parmelee Transfer Company. They run horsecars between all the city's railroad depots."

"Thanks." With a tip of his hat, Fooks walked away, nervously anticipating his first view of an Eastern city.

Fooks glanced back as he stepped out of the terminus, at the magnificent exterior of the Wells Street Depot, red brick with Ohio sandstone. The immense walls reminding Fooks of medieval castles. They stood five stories in places, and a central clock tower rose high above street level. Fooks felt dwarfed.

Outside, all was hustle and bustle. Throngs of people arriving and departing, loading and unloading of baggage. Shouts and cries, horses clip-clopping, jangle and rattle of the horsecars. Whistles from trains. Blasts from steam ships on the Chicago River and, further away, Lake Michigan. Assailed by noise, smells, and the frenetic activity of Eastern life. *Not what I'm used to.*

He found the Parmelee agent and explained where he headed. By all accounts, less than a mile. He could walk but the second stop on the number six horsecar would take him. Fooks opted to take the horsecar, not wanting to lose his way.

A chill wind blew through him, straight off the distant Lake Michigan, as he waited in line for the number six. He dropped his bag onto the ground, pulled up the collar of his Mackinaw jacket and thrust his hands deep into the pockets.

The queue was long, and several number sixes came and went before Fooks reached the head of the line. By then the biting wind had almost cut him in two. Glad to cram onto the horsecar and enjoy the shared warmth of human bodies.

His brief tour of Chicago didn't get very far. The bridge over the Chicago River swung out of the way to allow for ships to pass. The horsecar stopped for ages.

Fooks fretted about time. His next train, wasn't due to leave until 5 o'clock, but he was already later than he'd planned. He tucked his pocket watch away with difficulty in the cramped conditions. He sighed. Money getting tight. He couldn't afford a hotel. He simply must catch the next train.

Finally, across the bridge, the horsecar traveled along Fifth Avenue, Chicago's financial district and its canyons of commerce. *Closed in here. Can't even see the sky. Have they ever heard of grass or trees?* The horsecar trotted along at a fair clip, passing the headquarters of banks, law firms, newspapers, insurance and shipping companies. His concern about missing his train began to recede.

His concerns came to the fore again at the first stop, outside the Dearborn Station, the depot he wanted. The entrance for the Chicago and Northwestern railroad lay around the corner on the south side. Should he walk from here or wait? By the time he'd decided, they were moving again.

Fooks squeezed himself out of the cramped horsecar, and glanced up at this new depot. Built the year before, its twelve-story clock tower was made of red pressed brick. The external walls of the three-story building were constructed of pink granite, topped by many steeply pitched roofs. Another modern castle.

Inside, he opened his pocket watch. Too much to do. Telegram Mary that he'd seen hers, buy his ticket and snatch something to eat from the legendary Fred Harvey restaurant. Did he have time?

The train to Boston left at 5:06. By five o'clock Fooks sat on what he hoped would be his last train for a while. Another two nights to contemplate, and he already regretted not paying the extra for the sleeping car.

On this railroad, second-class seating was cane. This would prove to be uncomfortable after a while. On the plus side, the gaslight, brilliant Pintsch, a new invention, much used in Europe. According to the brochure, one could read a book or newspaper with the same ease and pleasure as at home. Perhaps without the interruptions of a small child. *Bonus.*

He still had a long way to go, and he was nervous. His jaunt around Chicago reinforced how far from home he'd traveled and how unsettled he felt by not knowing how things worked. Not a feeling he liked. *Only two more days until Boston.*

CHAPTER SIX

The train meandered its way across the states of Indiana, Ohio, and Pennsylvania. Places Fooks knew about only from books. For a man who had been traveling for days, the landscape was of no appeal. He just wanted the journey to end.

The exception being the Hoosac Tunnel. He'd read about this, the longest tunnel in North America. First large-scale commercial use of nitro- glycerin. He'd used small quantities in his heists, and couldn't conceive how much was needed for construction on this scale. If you didn't handle it right... *boom.*

Finally, the journey ended. Here in Boston at last. Ready to find out about Tobias. The first thing he did was send a telegram to Mary, and once again a message awaited him. It read:

CF sending man called Williams to meet you. Worry not. Mary.

Fooks smiled. Mary had reasoned correctly that he'd be alarm him if someone he didn't know waited for him. He stuffed the telegram into his pocket. *Okay, let's go find this Williams.* In truth he was glad he didn't have to do anymore thinking about traveling and finding where to go all the time. Hopefully Williams would take care of all that for him.

As he walked across the head house to the exit, a man approached. A middle-aged man, of stout appearance. He removed his bowler, revealing slick back hair. "Mr. Crane, Joseph Crane?"

"Yes."

"I'm Williams, sir. Madam dispatched me to meet you."

Fooks blinked in query. "Madam?"

To Fooks' surprise, Williams glanced around and dropped his voice. "You know her as Miss Caroline Fairfield, sir. I trust you're aware of whom I speak?"

"Oh. Yes, of course."

"Do you have any baggage, sir?"

"Just this bag."

"Allow me sir."

Fooks relinquished his bag. Should he need them, his gun and money were in his jacket pockets.

"The carriage is waiting outside. This way, sir."

Outside, mayhem ensued. Pedestrians, horsecars on their rails, private carriages and even one of those newfangled bicycles, jostled for position. To his amazement, a steam train forced its way across the street. Fooks shuddered at the congestion, the ear shattering noise, and the smells. *Eewh.*

"Is it always this busy?" he asked.

"Yes," Williams confirmed.

Fooks followed Williams, not before glancing back at the building. The Fitchburg Railroad Depot stood austere with its undressed granite walls. Modest in comparison with those in Chicago. The four round towers with their crenelations tried to add some grandeur to the façade.

They didn't entirely succeed. *Stop it Fooks. Architectural critique is not why you're here.*

Williams led them the length of the depot with its many windows. They stopped at a carriage of expensive design. The driver sat perched outside, protected somewhat from the elements by a roof. Inside the carriage, the roof lining was blue satin and the seat, deeply buttoned leather. Fooks settled back in comfort. Quite the finest vehicle he'd ever traveled in.

The carriage jerked forward. The driver of the carriage showed his skill when they turned across traffic. "Where are we going?" Fooks asked.

They quickly ground to a halt, before crossing the mayhem of Causeway Street. Fooks caught sight of two further railroad depots when he glanced down the thoroughfare. Both of substantial construction, one with an Italianate clock tower and the other a dome. *Sheesh, how many railroad depots does a place need?*

"Madam is at Fairfield House. She requested I bring you there."

"Fairfield House, not somewhere called Ardmaddy?"

"Yes sir. Fairfield House is Madam's Boston residence. Ardmaddy is Madam's country estate."

Fooks made an O with his lips. The more he heard of Madam, the less he was liking her.

Not knowing what to make of that piece of information, he stared out of the window. *All life is here.*

The carriage took an oblique right onto a busier thoroughfare. They traveled along this for a short way before entering an open space. An off-center round railinged enclosure, with a fountain and lamp post on top, stood in front of yet another railroad depot, this one of neo-classical appearance. The intention: traffic should use the enclosure to negotiate around, but not every vehicle did. Instead, there appeared to be no logic to the direction of travel. It was a free for all.

"What is this place?" Fooks asked, planning to avoid it in future.

"Haymarket Square," Williams replied. "Is this your first time in Boston, sir?"

"First time this side of the Mississippi." Fooks swallowed hard. A horsecar came unnecessarily close to his side of the carriage. "Do folks have any idea where they are going in this town?" he snapped.

"No sir but the horses do." Williams focused straight ahead.

Thankfully now on a long, wide, straight street, able to trot along at a brisk clip. The carriage jolted over the cobbles. Fooks suspected his teeth were shaking loose. Having survived near certain death in Haymarket Square, this was a small price to pay.

"Is it much further?"

"About half a mile sir."

Several more turns until a right took them onto a major road, leading across the bridge over the Charles River.

"Are we going over the river?" Fooks asked, having assumed "Madam" lived on the mainland of Boston. "Never mind," he added, when the carriage immediately turned left.

Now the roads became appreciably quieter and leafier. The buildings older, with an air of money and refinement. This was more like he'd expected Boston to be. He wasn't at all surprised when the carriage entered a genteel square. Townhouses stood on both sides with a laid-out garden in the center, fenced by iron railings. Most of the terraced houses on the square were bow-fronted red brick, favoring the Greek Revival style from earlier times. Some with black iron balconies. All with classical decorations and steep steps leading to the front doors.

CHAPTER SEVEN

They pulled up outside one house about halfway along the square. Fooks stepped out of the carriage in trepidation. This was Boston. Massachusetts. A world away from what he knew. *Oh well, here goes.*

After climbing the steps, Fooks entered a spacious hall. A man dressed in a uniform of some sort, with tails, took his hat and jacket. Who knows where his bag had gone? He supposed he'd see it again later. A sweeping staircase dominated one wall. Williams led him onto a landing and into an elegant drawing room.

Fooks walked to the bay window and stood gazing out, hands on hips. Despite the lace curtains, he had a good view over the square. Now up higher with a better view, the garden in the middle was in fact oval. The corners of his eyes crinkled as he watched two children running and shrieking around on the lawn, nanny in attendance.

He turned and took in the room. No heavy oak wood here. Everything light and airy. The huge mirror above the mantle reflecting light back into the room. The high ceiling helped with the feeling of space. The central chandelier glittered where the rays of sunlight struck the crystals. The colors of the curtains and soft furnishings, muted and, if he wasn't mistaken, of Chinese design. Two sofas facing each other dominated the room, separated by a low table.

A room of taste and refinement, but also homely. Family photographs, house plants and books scattered haphazardly on every flat surface.

"Good afternoon, Mr. Crane."

Fooks spun around. A beautiful, elegantly dressed, immaculately coiffured blond lady entered the room. Yet there was no disguising how tired and drawn she looked. Fooks swallowed. He suddenly felt very nervous. This must be the wrong address. All he could do was nod.

She came forward, holding her hand out. She repeated her greeting, her speech precise and her voice refined.

Fooks shook her hand.

"Please sit." She indicated a sofa, and herself sat herself gracefully on the one across from it.

"Ma'am, I don't think—"

"I understand you are wishing to see Samuel Martin."

Irritation swept through Fooks at the interruption. He recovered quickly and tried his best smile. "Ma'am, I'm real sorry to bother you. There must be some mistake."

She raised her eyebrows in surprise. "You are not Joseph Crane from Bronze Canyon, Wyoming?"

"Well yes ma'am, I am but—"

"Then what is the mistake?" Her imperious face demanded an explanation.

"Um." Fooks sat on the other sofa with a bump. "I..." He waved a hand, unsure of what to say.

"Your Samuel Martin is here." She laced her fingers together on her lap. "Or rather, he was, until very recently."

For a moment, Fooks didn't register what she had said. "My Samuel Martin?"

Caroline frowned. "You appear confused. I asked you to come because Samuel is in trouble. I thought you might be of some help."

"Ma'am?"

Caroline straightened her skirts. "Now before we go on, I must ask you some questions. To satisfy myself you are indeed the Joseph Crane of whom Samuel has spoken."

Fooks stared. "Questions?"

"Yes," she confirmed, and went on as if nothing was unusual in asking questions. "How are you acquainted with Samuel Martin?"

Fooks moved uncomfortably. He wasn't willing to reveal too much until he'd learnt more. "I've known Sam for a long time. He and I worked together for a lot of years."

"Would you mind telling me how he comes to have a scar on his left thigh?" She paused. "A bullet wound; I believe." She gazed intently at her guest.

Fooks blinked at the bizarre direction the conversation had taken. He hesitated, not understanding why he should have to answer such a personal question. And it was personal. So personal only he and Tobias had the answer, and not one he took pride in. Yet now was not the time to dig in his heels. She obviously knew about the scar on Tobias' thigh. How did she know? He wasn't going to get an answer unless he co-operated. So, this was a test, but a test for what?

"Please answer the question. It's important."

"I don't remember," he said quietly.

"You don't? Or you can't?" The question demanded a precise answer.

Fooks licked his lips. The incident she referred to had occurred during one of his Florian Fooks episodes. The black rage that descended on him from time to time. As usual, he didn't remember precisely what happened. He took a deep, stilted breath. "I can't," he admitted. "I only know what Sam told me." He shook himself. "Look, why is this important? I need to find my friend quickly. He's hurt," he blurted out, patience snapping.

"Yes, Mr. Crane, two men shot him, and now he is missing," Caroline snapped back. "Someone is trying to frame him for murder."

Fooks stared open mouthed.

Caroline continued. "The police have this house and my estate at Waltham under surveillance. If he returns, the police will arrest him."

Fooks paled at the mention of police.

Opposite, Caroline composed herself. "I hope you understand I needed to verify who you say you are. I had to ask a question to confirm your identity. Samuel tells me very few are aware how he came by the scar."

"Did I pass?" Fooks scowled.

"Yes, Samuel said you wouldn't remember. He told me *you* were responsible, Mr. Fooks."

At the mention of his real name, his head snapped up. He frowned. He was missing something here. He didn't like that. Yet there didn't seem to be any point in denying who he was. "You know w-who I am." The slight stutter testified to his inner turmoil.

"Of course," Caroline said, with almost a smirk, before she bit her bottom lip. "I knew exactly who you were when I first came into the room. Samuel described you very well."

"Oh." He put his head down, embarrassed. Swallowing, he said, "I appreciate your caution. I don't understand what's going on here. Do the police...do they..." Fooks' thoughts came hard and fast. He could barely keep up.

Caroline took a deep breath. "Someone murdered my uncle, Robert Kinsey."

"I'm sorry," Fooks murmured.

"Thank you. Samuel—" she swallowed hard, "went to call on him three nights ago. It appears he was the last person to see him before..." She touched a handkerchief to her eyes and took another deep breath. "Before he died."

Fooks' spine turned to ice. "Ma'am, how did your uncle die?"

"Shot, Mr. Fooks."

Fooks rubbed his cheek, and rose. Unconsciously, he paced away from her. He raised his face to the ceiling, eyes involuntarily watering. "And you've no idea where Sam is now?"

"No."

He spun on his heel and gaped at her. He groped for the sofa and he took his place opposite her once more.

Caroline finished her explanation. "He hasn't been anywhere I can think of, and he hasn't been in touch. I don't know where he is."

"I don't understand." Fooks shook his head. "You don't know where he is? He was hurt. How can he just disappear?" He leaned back into the sofa.

Caroline gave Fooks an icy stare. "Fortunately, Samuel's injury wasn't serious. He remained convinced Uncle Robert was behind the shooting. He told me he had his reasons but wouldn't tell me what they were. I believe he went to confront him." She shook her head. "I don't know what happened exactly. Events appear confused. Uncle Robert was in his study, the door locked and the key missing. Two of the household staff broke the door down and found Robert. Dead."

Fooks rose again and paced. This time he ran a hand through his hair, the other went to his hip. He hadn't expected this. Could Tobias have done it? Would Tobias have done it? The man was stubborn, and if wronged would exact revenge, but killing? *No, no, no. There's more to this. Must be.*

He came to a halt in front of the window, both hands on his hips, considering. Movement behind him startled him out of his thoughts.

Caroline had moved to the wall beside the fireplace and pulled the bell cord. A light tinkling followed.

"I think you'd better tell me exactly what happened, ma'am."

"First some tea. Or would you prefer coffee?"

"I don't want tea!" he spat, stalking back to the center of the room. "I want answers."

Caroline pulled her shoulders back and raised her chin defiantly. She bit back. "This is not about you. I require refreshment. Now," she licked her lips, "would you prefer tea or coffee?"

Fooks accepted her rebuke. "I'm sorry ma'am. Yes, of course. Coffee. Please."

Caroline retook her seat. She sat stiffly; her hands clasped in her lap. Fooks returned to the opposite sofa. He leaned forward, elbows on his legs, rubbing his thumbs impatiently.

They sat in silence until Williams entered. "Would you serve tea, Williams. Mr. Crane will take coffee."

"Of course, Madam."

When the door closed, Caroline spoke again. "Perhaps if Samuel learns you are here, he will come home. Or at least get in touch."

Fooks swallowed the lump in his throat. "Home?"

Caroline appeared surprised at his question. "Yes. This is his home now." She shook her head in disgust at herself. "Perhaps I'm assuming too much."

"Will you start at the beginning ma'am? I've a lot to catch up on."

"Yes of course." She took a deep breath. "Although it is difficult to determine exactly where the beginning is." She glanced away for a moment. "I'm forgetting my manners. You must be tired from your long journey. Perhaps you would like to go to your room and freshen up first?"

"I'd like to hear arnhat happened more."

"There isn't much more to tell you. Samuel was leaving the golf club. Two men came up to him. They asked him if he was Samuel Martin. When he said yes, they," Caroline bit her lip, "they shot him."

"Did he know who they were?"

"No. He said he had never met them before." Caroline took a deep breath. "He fell, of course."

"Did he lose consciousness? Where was he shot? Did they get away?" Fooks rose to his feet, rattling out his questions.

Caroline gave him a disapproving glare. "Mr. Fooks, if you allow me to finish, I will answer all your questions in good time." She gestured meaningfully at the sofa.

He sat contritely. "Yes, ma'am." *Why does this feel like being in front of teacher?* "Please go on."

"Thank you." Caroline composed herself again. "No, he didn't lose consciousness. The bullet grazed the top of his hip. There was a lot of blood but luckily the bullet didn't lodge inside him. Despite the crowds that came to help, the men ran away." She paused. "The club summoned a doctor and made one of their hotel rooms available.

"Their doctor treated Samuel and he spent the night at the club. In the morning, the doctor allowed him to return home. We went out to Ardmaddy to allow him to recuperate for a few weeks. However, Samuel was anxious to come back to Boston, but he wouldn't tell me why. I didn't think he was ready."

"Sounds like him, ma'am."

"He went out but he didn't tell me where he was going, which isn't like him. The next morning the police arrived in force. They told me he'd been to my uncle's house the previous evening." Caroline paused. "Later, staff found my uncle dead."

Fooks rolled his jaw. He wanted to ask more. A lot more. Before he could, Williams interrupted them, bringing refreshments. On the plus side, the interruption allowed him to organize his thoughts. Shuffling them into a coherent stream, rather than blurting out random questions. *Learnt not to do that again.*

"Was Sam sure your uncle was behind his shooting?" Fooks asked, when they were alone again.

"It's possible. He and Uncle Robert had reason to dislike each other."

Fooks stirred his coffee thoughtfully. "Why?"

"It's a dispute of long standing. We met in Bronze Canyon when my uncle was forcing me to go back to Boston with him. I didn't want to go." Caroline smiled at the memory. "Samuel stopped him. They have disliked each other ever since."

Fooks narrowed his eyes. Much more behind what she'd said, but for now he chose not to enquire.

He sipped his coffee and grimaced. *Sheesh, that's weak.* "You haven't seen Sam since?"

Caroline shook her head. "No. He hasn't been in touch. No word at all. The police can't find him."

"He's gone to ground," Fooks murmured. He rubbed his cheek. Where on earth would he start searching for him in a place he didn't know?

CHAPTER EIGHT

Taking Caroline up on her offer to freshen up, he followed a footman upstairs and to the room given over for his use. She said a gong would sound for dinner, but not at what time. When he entered he saw his suit hanging over the closet door and then his bag open on a chair. He turned to question the footman, but the door already closing.

"Good afternoon, sir."

Fooks head snapped around. A smiling young man came out of an inner door. He was about his height and dark haired. In fact, he bore a striking similarity to himself. *This is disconcerting.*

"Huh? Who are you?" Fooks demanded.

"I'm Cowdry sir."

"So?"

"I'm Mr. Martin's valet."

Fooks stared open mouthed. "Mr. Martin's valet!" The last word, a high-pitched squeak, and Fooks cleared his throat in irritation.

"Yes sir. As Mr. Martin is away right now, madam thought I might be of assistance to you."

"D-did she now? What exactly do you do for, er, Mr. Martin? I mean as his valet." Fooks swallowed hard.

"I attend to Mr. Martin's clothes and personal possessions. I dress him, sir."

"You dress him!"

"Well not literally sir. I make sure his clothes are laundered and in good order and ready when he wants them. I have to anticipate Mr. Martin's requirements."

"I see." Fooks swallowed a lump. "You've er seen to my bag."

"Yes sir. I've hung your suit jacket here to allow the creases to drop. I'll take it with me to be pressed downstairs. Your shirts are in the closet. Underwear in the drawers and your washing accoutrements are in the bathroom. Through here, sir." He indicated the room from where he had come.

Fooks took it all in. He still couldn't decide whether to be grateful or annoyed. He did feel mildly violated. His bag was private. Finally, he decided he was too tired to worry about it. Nothing very personal in there anyway.

"Thank you," he murmured.

"If you would like, I can run you a bath, sir?"

"Er." Now he thought about it, that would be nice. "Yes, thank you."

Cowdry went off to do that, and when he came back, took the suit jacket and folded it carefully over his arm. "I'll leave you to freshen up sir," he said. "Unless there is anything else?"

"No." Fooks shook his head. "No thank you." He waved dismissively.

"Very good sir. I will be back at seven o'clock to help you dress."

"Huh?"

"For dinner, sir. It's always promptly at seven thirty."

Frowning, Fooks scratched his head. "Yes, yes of course. Um..."

Cowdry paused in the open doorway. "Yes sir?"

"There's a gong...apparently."

"The dinner gong sir. It's struck at 7:32, but guests are expected downstairs sometime before."

Fooks gave a loud groan after Cowdry left. Tobias Swan, legendary fast draw and feared gunman, had a valet. *Sheesh.* Nothing about this situation was simple. He sank onto the bed, putting his head in his hands.

"Where does the name Fooks come from?" Caroline asked.

Dining at Fairfield House was an elegant affair. Caroline dressed for dinner in a blue satin evening dress. Her jewelry sparkled. Fooks usually considered wearing a suit, smart attire. Tonight, facing this immaculately turned-out woman, he felt like the poor relation. *Ah, suppose I am.*

They had spoken little over dinner so far. The suddenness of her question jerked Fooks out of his thoughts. He gave a curious frown, unsure why she was asking. "My Pa."

The eye roll Caroline affected reminded Fooks of his partner. *Tobias really must have impacted hard on this woman.* "I meant what part of the world does the name come from."

Fooks flashed a quick grin when he understood. "Oh, yes of course." He swallowed hard and cleared his throat. He wasn't used to talking about his family, and found it hard, even with Mary. While he thought how to reply, he focused on his dinner. *Nice, but too rich for me.* "England. The south coast. Dorsetshire," he said, in a mumble, before reaching for his glass. He took a deep glug of wine. *Finest claret.*

"And is that where your father came from?"

"Yes, ma'am."

"Your mother too?"

"Yes. Well, no." Fooks winced. "Not exactly." Caroline expected more. "My grandparents were German, but the family lived in England during Ma's childhood." He hesitated. "My parents met on the boat coming over to America."

"How romantic."

"Hardly." Fooks winced. "They married out of necessity." Caroline raised an eyebrow in interest and Fooks winced again. "I was...on my way." He didn't meet her eye. Today the circumstances of his birth embarrassed him. *Never done so afore. Why now?*

Caroline's lips made an O. "Florian is a German name?"

"Yes ma'am."

"Samuel tells me you prefer to be called Fooks. Don't you like Florian?"

"No ma'am."

"Why not? Seems a perfectly acceptable name to me." Caroline concentrated on buttering her roll, and didn't see the flick of irritation crossing Fooks' face.

"Yes ma'am, I suppose." Fooks studied his dinner, keeping his head down. He hoped if he didn't answer she would move onto something else.

"Do you have any brothers and sisters?" she asked instead, before clamping her white teeth on the roll.

This time Fooks failed to keep the irritation from his voice. "No. Do you?" He raised his wine glass to his lips and drank deeply.

"I'm sorry if I'm making you uncomfortable. My husband has talked about you at considerable length. You obviously mean a lot to him and I'm trying—"

Fooks snorted violently, spraying wine over his face and hand. "Your what?" He coughed, swallowed and cleared his throat. "Sorry, wrong way. Your what?" Fooks' eyes popped.

Caroline watched as Fooks wiped his face and hand.

"My husband. Samuel Martin, or Tobias Swan, as you know him."

"You and Tobias are married?" Fooks' voice rose several octaves above his usual baritone.

Caroline frowned in surprise. "Well yes, of course. I thought Samuel told you. He said he'd written."

"He did." Fooks spluttered. He took up his wine glass and drank deeply. "If you call a three-line note, telling me he's okay and doing good and not to worry. He drained the glass. He held the stem between his thumb and forefinger, and twirled the glass, as he contemplated Caroline. "Now I'm worried."

"Why? Samuel has made a new life here in Boston. With me. We have a good marriage. He's started a business, which is doing very well. We have a wide social circle. We go to the theater, the opera, the ballet. What is there to worry about Mr. Fooks?"

"You!" Fooks threw his napkin down. He'd lost all interest in eating. "I don't mean to be rude, Ma'am, but I don't know you. I don't trust you."

"You don't trust me?"

"I rarely trust anyone I just met, especially if they know who we really are." He glared at her hard, wanting more of an explanation.

Caroline's lips parted. "Of course, I know who he is. Do you think so little of your friend? Would he enter into something so binding as a marriage without apprising me of all the facts beforehand?"

Fooks licked his lips, accepting the rebuke. He rubbed his forehead. Not before noticing Caroline's glare. He hurriedly removed his elbow from the table.

"No ma'am," he mumbled. He put his hands over his eyes and shook his head. "You'll have to excuse me. I've had a long journey and there's a lot to take in. Perhaps." He paused, wanting to be polite. "Perhaps we should leave talking about this until the morning." He slowly pushed back his chair. "Right now, I'm beyond tired."

Caroline glanced at his half-eaten dinner. "Well, of course. If you think that's best."

"I'll be able to tell you what action we should take in the morning."

"Can you get me access to the room where your uncle was murdered?"

Fooks joined Caroline for breakfast. He'd apologized for his behavior the previous evening, which she accepted with a gracious incline of her head. Caroline watched him attacking his breakfast with relish, although he did wrinkle his nose at the devilled kidneys.

They ate in silence, Fooks deep in thought. She remembered Samuel telling her Fooks liked to be left alone when thinking. After all, she had asked him here to help. The least she could do was give him room to formulate a plan.

She was stirring her tea idly when his sudden question startled her. She looked up to find him staring intently at her.

"Yes, of course." She set aside the teaspoon. "I should visit my aunt and cousin anyway." She paused. "Why is it helpful?"

"If I can view the set up. See how and where your uncle died, I'll be able to tell you if Tobias did it or not."

"You think he did?" Caroline gasped.

"No. No, not in cold blood, no." He leaned on the table and shook his head. "Tobias wouldn't kill him. There mighta been some provocation, but I need to view the scene."

"How will you be able to tell?"

"When Tobias left here, what was he wearing?"

Caroline bit back a tut of exasperation. *Why wasn't he answering her question first?* "Gray suit, white shirt and his gray overcoat."

"What did he say before he left? About where he was going?"

"He told me he had something to discuss with Robert and he'd be back later. He asked if I would delay dinner until eight."

Fooks sat back with a nod of satisfaction. "There you are. If Tobias went with the intention of killing him, he wouldn't be thinking about food." Fooks rose and paced to the window.

Caroline turned in her seat and watched him, staring out of the window. She turned back to drink her tea. *Samuel said he was infuriating. He was right.*

After several minutes, Fooks returned to the table. "I need to be able to ask questions."

For a moment, Caroline hesitated. "You can," she said, cautiously.

"I mean officially. The police will have their investigation, of course, but I want to ask my own questions. I'll need your help, ma'am."

"Yes of course. I hoped you would. What do you require?"

Fooks licked his lips. "You're familiar with this town. I dare say the mention of your name will open doors."

Caroline raised her chin. "I would like to think so."

"Then engage me as your private detective, and we're in business."

"A private detective?"

"Yes. Look, Tobias didn't kill your uncle, but from what you tell me the police already think he's their man. We have to prove otherwise before the police find him. It's the only way, Caroline."

He called me Caroline. How familiar.

"Won't you need identification?"

Fooks rummaged in his pocket. "Good job I brought this with me. Isn't it?" He held a metal shield, with a rounded bottom and cinched in waist. His eyes sparkled.

Caroline gasped. "That's a Pinkerton Detective's shield."

"Yep."

"But it can't be yours. Where did you obtain it?"

Fooks chuckled. "Caroline, you're forgetting. I'm an outlaw. I've had it for a long time. A former associate knew someone in the Agency. *Acquired* it, shall we say, for my use. Come in handy a time or two. Just be grateful I have it. Now. Will you help me?"

CHAPTER NINE

Fooks and Caroline glanced at each other when they walked into the hall of the Kinsey townhouse. Although wide, the dark wood paneling necessitated lit lamps in the middle of the day. The only natural light came from a small window by the side of the front door. A darkened corridor lay off to their right. To the left a sweeping staircase. A Turkish design rug covered the floor, helped to offset the room's oppressive feel. There were two doors, by the side of one stood a long case clock, ticking loudly.

A uniformed police patrolman sat beside the other, whose surround showed signs of damage. Caroline lifted her chin in question at the butler, who opened the front door to them.

"I'm afraid the police haven't finished with the room yet, madam." The butler cast an eye in the patrolman's direction. "A parade of young men appear to make sure no one enters. Most inconvenient."

Overwhelmed by the fumes from furniture polish and gas lamps, Fooks cleared his throat.

"Very well, Grieveson. Leave it with me. I will see what I can do." Caroline turned to Fooks. "Come along, Crane."

Fooks blinked at the commanding voice. Meekly he settled into her slipstream. Caroline swept across the hall to the tune of the clock loudly striking the hour.

The policeman stood when they approached. With a pull of his tunic, the young man prepared to square up to the determined woman bearing down on him.

Fooks hid a grin. *Not often I feel sorry for the law.* "Good morning, officer."

"Ma'am"

"I'm Caroline Martin, Mr. Kinsey's niece. I would like to see for myself where my late uncle was murdered. You will let me in, please."

The officer swallowed hard. "No ma'am, I'm afraid I can't do that. My orders are not to let anyone in. Not without my captain's permission."

"Very well. What is your name?"

"Pearson, ma'am."

"Very well. I doubt you are aware of all the intricacies of this case, but it's my husband who is the main suspect. Of course, that is a ridiculous notion and as such I have engaged a detective at my own expense." She gestured to Fooks. "This is Mr. Crane. I would like him to view the scene of the crime as part of his investigation. I expect nothing less."

Pearson's eyes flicked from one to the other. "Ma'am, I still can't let you in. I'm sorry. I have my orders."

"Yes of course." Caroline turned to Fooks. "What will you do? Will you give Uncle Allan a full report?"

"Of course, Mrs. Martin. Pinkerton's usual procedure, and I'll be sure to include the officer's name. Pearson, wasn't it?"

Fooks turned away to study the door and its surround. Signs of where the rescuers battered the door to get in evident in the ruined woodwork. Fooks ran his thumb over the splintered architrave.

Pearson pulled at his collar and swallowed. "Pinkerton's?"

Caroline raised an eyebrow in surprise. "Yes, the Pinkerton Detective Agency. Surely you've heard of it?"

"Y-Yes ma'am, of course."

"Mr. Crane reports directly to Allan Pinkerton, a very dear friend of my late father."

Fooks winced slightly. *Don't overdo it, Caroline. Best keep lies simple.*

Pearson blanched. "Oh." He appealed to Fooks with wide eyes.

Fooks took pity on him and reached into his pocket. "Does this help?" In the palm of his hand, he held the Pinkerton's detective shield.

"Um..."

"When is your captain due to return?" Fooks asked, determined to take control over the charade. Before Caroline committed them to anything else.

"Later this morning, sir."

Fooks pocketed the shield. "I'm sure I'll still be here when he arrives. We can sort out the courtesies then. Now." Fooks' hand closed over the door handle. Pearson gave a strangled groan. Fooks' smile became broader, as he pushed open the door. "I'll be sure to include in my report how exemplary you were in co-operating, Officer Pearson."

He disappeared over the threshold into a study decorated in browns and reds. A meager light filtered in through the sash window, necessitating the use of side lamps. A large mahogany desk stood in the center of the room; a leather chair behind. A rich blue and red rug covered most of the floor, only revealing the parquet below at the walls. The left wall, covered entirely with books, broken by hints of pillars. To the right, a fireplace, lamp tables and occasional chairs.

Caroline acknowledged Pearson and followed. Fooks shut the door after her. She remained a few steps inside the room, her eyes gluing themselves to the rug in front of the bookshelves. The outline of a fallen body chalked into the fibers.

"Where will you begin?" she asked, her voice faltering.

Fooks put a hand to his forehead, the other to his hip as he walked fully into the room. He too studied the chalk outline.

"Hard to tell from this which way round he fell," he murmured. Kinsey may have fallen on his left side, left arm outstretched, back to the bookshelves. Or, he might have fallen facing the shelves, with his right arm outstretched. The angle of the legs, depicted by the chalk outline wasn't conclusive either way.

"Why does it matter?"

"It matters if he knew his murderer." Fooks frowned. "A strange place to be though. Unless..." He broke off and pressed his lips together, thoughtfully.

"Unless what, Mr. Fooks?"

Fooks glanced at her. "Mr. Crane." He inclined his head at the door. "Just in case."

"Of course."

Fooks turned back to the shelves, put his hands on his hips. "Can't be sure this room is exactly..." He shook his head. "Dunno if the police touched anything. And if so, what." Apparently deciding something, he strolled across the room and threw open the door. "Pearson, would you come in for a second, please?"

"Oh, I dunno sir. My orders—"

"Yes, I know. Stop anyone coming in." *That worked out well.* "Bet your captain would like to know what I'm doing in here. Come in and you can keep an eye on me." Fooks beckoned to the policeman.

With a hand on Pearson's shoulder, Fooks propelled him over to the chalk outline. "Now Kinsey was found slumped against these bookshelves, facing the door."

"Yes sir."

Fooks slapped Pearson on the shoulder for confirming his suspicions. "A 0.45 in the chest will do that to you." Fooks chewed his bottom lip.

"It wasn't a 0.45 sir."

"It wasn't?" Fooks gave an incredulous stare. "My information—"

"A 0.22 sir."

Fooks grunted, sniffed and shook his head. "The office must be slipping to get something like that so wrong." He nodded to Caroline. "I'll mention this to Allan when I return. Heads will roll."

"It's not common knowledge sir," Pearson said, quickly.

"No. No, of course not." Fooks walked forward and examined the shelves above the outline. Nothing obvious stood out, as he stood hands on hips. He wiggled his jaw from side to side, thinking. "Is Martin your only suspect?"

Pearson shrugged. "Can't think of any others. Staff confirmed Martin visited here that night—"

"Thank you. I'll be sure to mention you in my report, Officer Pearson. You'd better go back to your post in case your captain arrives and finds you missing. Don't want a blot on what I can tell will be an outstanding career."

Pearson beamed. "Thank you, sir."

As the door closed, Caroline walked over to Fooks. "I didn't believe Samuel when he said how persuasive you can be."

Fooks shrugged. "Pearson told me what I wanted to know," he said, innocently. "And while we're on the subject, was Allan Pinkerton a dear friend of your father's?"

"Not a *dear* friend exactly." Caroline winced a guilty expression. "In fact, not even a friend. More of an acquaintance."

"Ah." Fooks gave a short laugh. Now who was the persuasive one.

"Have you seen enough now?"

Fooks folded his arms and studied the shelves. "No," he murmured. "Quite like to poke around some more. While I've got the chance."

"Very well. I will leave you to your inspection. I must visit my aunt and cousin to see how they are holding up."

Fooks waited until the door had closed before striding to the shelves. Now he was alone, still nothing obvious. Yet he had a hunch something was here all the same. "Hmmm. Wonder how tall Kinsey was?"

He stepped back and gazed at the chalk outline. Tilted his head to one side, he frowned. "Why were you here in this particular spot?" He studied the shelves again. "Perhaps something here?"

He took another step back and stood hands on hips again, taking in the expanse of books before him. A slight smirk appeared on his lips. "Of course." A moment later he'd crossed the distance, his dimples widening. He ran his fingers down the bookcase side of a tall book filling the entire space between shelves. "Ha." *Hinges. Why should there be hinges here?*

He explored the other side until his sensitive fingers found a slight depression. He pressed; a click, and the spine of the book flipped open, revealing a hollow inside. Now he could pull aside a fixed section of books acting as a false front. Behind he found a safe, inserted in the wall.

He chuckled to himself and had his hand on the dial when raised voices sounded outside. Quickly closing the fake front, he crossed to the desk. When the door thrust open, he was nonchalantly examining a letter.

"So, you're Mrs. Martin's private detective, are you?"

A thickset middle-aged man with gray streaked hair and a bulbous nose asked the question. Between his lips, he held an unlit half-finished cigar. Although dressed in plain clothes, by the way Pearson hopped behind him, it was clear he was the police captain in charge.

"Yes, Joseph Crane." Fooks held out his hand, subsequently ignored.

"I'm Captain Loomis and I'm in charge here. Pinkerton should have informed me they were sending someone. Got any identification?"

Fooks brought out the Pinkerton shield. He handed this over and the captain inspected it carefully.

"This all you've got? Don't you have any other identification?" he barked.

Fooks glared at him. Sighing as if it was all too much bother, he reached into his inside jacket pocket. From his wallet, he offered an identity card. The captain was keen to inspect and study the card. The photograph was indistinct. He glanced at Fooks several times, before thrusting it back with an impatient growl.

"This is out of date," he said, spitting the word *date* in disgust.

Fooks' mouth fell open in mock horror. "Oh no, is it?" He snatched back the card. "Ah. Meant to get a new identity card last week when I was in the office. As you can read, I'm based in Chicago, and I had to rush to catch a train on Mr. Pinkerton's orders. Musta clean forgot. Thanks for pointing this out." He shook his head as a rebuke to himself. "Only a little out of date. I'll see to it next chance I get." Fooks tucked the card away and ended with a pleasant, tight-lipped smile.

The captain glared at him. "Get outta my crime scene." The low tone left Fooks in no uncertainty that he'd pushed his luck far enough.

CHAPTER TEN

Wonder what they've got to say for themselves.
Fooks went in search of Caroline, her aunt and cousin.
Caroline told him later the room where he found them was
a salon. Looked like an ordinary drawing room to Fooks
when he entered. Caroline made the introductions to meet
her aunt and cousin.

Anne Kinsey, middle aged, dressed in deepest
mourning black. Everything else about her was gray. Her
hair, her skin, her eyes.

Brook Kinsey was not a handsome man. His hook-
like nose and his jowls already beginning to loosen
prevented even a generous interpretation of the
description.

Fooks politely acknowledged Robert Kinsey's wife and
son before sitting. He declined the tea offered.

"What did you discover, Mr. Crane?" Caroline asked,
stirring her tea.

Fooks hesitated. He wanted to keep some thoughts to
himself for now.

"I found Pearson the police patrolman extremely helpful." He glanced at Mrs. Kinsey. He didn't want to upset her. *Be neutral, Fooks.* "He told me, the firearm used was a 0.22—"

"How is that relevant?" Brook snapped. "My father is still murdered!" He rose to his feet.

Fooks bit his tongue. "It's very relevant. A 0.22 is not the usual caliber for a gunman. A 0.38 or 0.45 is more their choice. It suggests to me," he went on, raising his voice to stop Brook interrupting, "the weapon used is for self-defense, rather than intimidation."

Brook flopped back into his chair and lounged untidily.

"How is this helpful?" Caroline asked, clasping her aunt's hand.

"It tells me this wasn't an organized crime assassination." Fooks took out a notepad and pencil. "May I ask a few questions, please?"

"Yes of course," Mrs. Kinsey said graciously.

"Did Mr. Kinsey have any enemies?"

Brook grunted. "No good businessman goes through life without making enemies. The police are patrolling the grounds as a precaution."

Fooks swallowed. *So, he thinks there was. Interesting. The police patrols are a complication I could do without.* "Very wise," he said, contradicting his thoughts. "Do you have concerns about anyone in particular?"

Brook slumped back, sullen. "I'm not aware of any. Ephraim may know more."

"Ephraim?"

"Ephraim Smith. He is Father's business partner."

"Ah, yes I'll certainly want to speak to him." Fooks made a note of the name, before turning back to Brook. "Did your father have an office?"

"No. He conducted most of his business from the study downstairs."

"What about people who worked for him? Can you give me any names?"

Brook rolled his bottom jaw from side to side. "No, but Gray will probably help you there."

"Gray?" Fooks turned first to Caroline. She raised her chin towards Brook.

"Albinus Gray does all the paperwork for Father. Drawing up contracts and such like."

"Are you familiar with your father's business activities, Mr. Kinsey?"

"Some. I assisted with a few matters."

Fooks made a note. "And where might I find Albinus Gray?"

"Downstairs. There's a room he uses. There's also a girl sometimes. Don't know her name."

"Are they here now?"

Brook rubbed his forehead. "No, I suggested they take a few days off. Until things settle."

"When are you expecting them back?"

"On Thursday," Brook said, irritably, and sat forward. "What has this to do with my father's murder?"

"That's what I mean to find out. Were they present on the night?"

Brook shook his head. "I don't know. Gray and the girl were here during the day, but I don't know what time they left."

Fooks licked his lips and glanced at Caroline. "Do you believe Samuel Martin is responsible?"

Brook scowled. "No. Cousin Caroline is quite persuasive on that point," he said, with a growl. He gave the impression he wasn't convinced.

Caroline rolled her eyes.

Hmm, things to find out here.

"On the night he died—"

"Murdered, Mr. Crane." Mrs. Kinsey spoke with a force which surprised Fooks.

He acknowledged the correction. "On that night, apart from Samuel Martin, did Mr. Kinsey have any other visitors?"

"I wouldn't know." Mrs. Kinsey shook her head and looked at her son, who was frowning.

"I wouldn't know either. Perhaps the servants." He broke off with a faraway gleam in his eye.

"I've already asked Grieveson," Caroline said. "He says not."

"Where were you at the time, Mr. Kinsey?"

"Out." Brook cocked a leg over the arm of the chair.

"Where?"

"At my club, if you must know," Brook said, in a bored voice.

"Are there witnesses to prove that?"

"Of course. The club was full, and I don't like your tone sir!" Now he sat up and leaned towards Fooks. His hands clasped the arms of the chair, threatening to push up.

"Brook, Mr. Crane has to ask these questions. It's nothing personal," Caroline said, quickly.

Brook scowled.

Fooks turned to Mrs. Kinsey. "And you ma'am?"

"In bed. I retire early." She paused. "You can ask my maid. She helped me get ready for the night."

"Thank you, ma'am. You didn't hear a shot, Mrs. Kinsey. Or any noise?"

"I sleep very soundly. Mr. Kinsey likes to stay up late, and we haven't shared a bed in years. He doesn't...didn't wish to disturb me."

Fooks studied his notes for a moment. "Do you have any knowledge of what is in Mr. Kinsey's will? I'm presuming he had a will."

"Yes, Robert had a will," Mrs. Kinsey said. "As far as I'm aware, he left the house to me and a trust fund to provide for my expenses. The house will become Brook's on my death. I'm not fully conversant with Robert's other financial arrangements. They changed frequently. However, the last time we spoke about such matters, he had left a considerable amount to Caroline."

"What?" Brook jumped to his feet. "I don't believe it"

Caroline appeared equally stunned. "Neither do I."

"It was some time ago Brook. Your father changed his mind often."

Caroline swallowed hard. Fooks narrowed his eyes. *Family politics here?*

"I think you should leave now," Brook said, in a growl. "Mother needs to rest."

Caroline gathered her skirts and stood. "Yes of course. This is necessary Brook. Despite all Robert's provocations, my husband did not kill him. Mr. Crane will determine who the real murderer is. Then perhaps we can put this all behind us." She turned to Fooks. "Is there anything more to do here today?"

Caroline hailed the butler when they met in the hall. "Ah, Grieveson, Mr. Crane would like to ask you some questions. About the night of the murder."

"Of course, ma'am, if it will be of help."

"Shall we go through into the receiving room? We'll be more comfortable." Caroline swept away, leaving Fooks and Grieveson to follow.

"Sit, Grieveson."

Grieveson hesitated. For a servant to sit in company was unusual. He perched uncomfortably on the edge of a chair. Fooks took out his notepad and pencil, flicked over several pages to find a clear sheet. Pencil poised; he gave his attention to Grieveson. "Will you tell me exactly what you saw and heard? Start with the arrival of Samuel Martin."

"I answered the knock on the door. A rather impatient knock if I may say so. Mr. Martin pushed passed me, demanding to see Mr. Kinsey. I tried to stop him, but he wasn't listening."

Fooks pursed his lips. *Yep, that's my partner, all right.*

"What time did Mr. Martin arrive?"

"A little after seven."

"What happened, Grieveson?" Caroline asked, glancing at Fooks.

"Mr. Kinsey opened the study door when Mr. Martin arrived. No doubt alerted by the shouting."

"No doubt," Fooks agreed, in a murmur. He motioned for Grieveson to carry on.

"They went into the study and the door closed. I couldn't make out what they were saying. The conversation became heated rather quickly. I lingered in the hall. Just in case Mr. Kinsey might need my assistance. Until I was called away. It was sometime before I returned. By then all was quiet."

"You didn't check on Mr. Kinsey?"

"No. Mr. Kinsey doesn't like to be disturbed when he's in the study."

"But surely under the circumstances," Caroline cried.

Grieveson cleared his throat. "I'm sorry Madam, I didn't."

"You didn't hear a shot?" Fooks asked. "Or any other strange noise?"

"No sir."

"Any other members of staff present in the hall at the time?"

"No. All the staff were at dinner, sir."

"Ah. So, is that why you left the hall?" Fooks seized on the excuse.

"No. Mrs. Warner, the housekeeper, and I dine separately from the others. We had already eaten."

"Why were you called away?" Caroline asked, impatiently.

"For an incident in the office."

Fooks leaned forward in anticipation of hearing something interesting. "What sorta incident?"

Grieveson scratched his head, winced and rubbed his chin.

"Grieveson, whatever it is may be crucial. Only Mr. Crane can determine the importance, with all his years of experience in these matters."

Fooks winced. *Oh, she was good.*

"Mr. Kinsey kept a small staff connected with his business affairs. There's an office for their use in the back corridor." Grieveson sniffed. "I regret to inform you, madam, Miss Miller alerted me to the possibility of a mouse." He spoke quickly.

Fooks snorted a laugh aloud.

Caroline gave him a sigh of irritation. "A mouse?"

"Yes madam," Grieveson confirmed in a murmur.

Caroline sat back, fixing Fooks with an icy stare. "Behave," she mouthed, and turned to Grieveson once more. "And was there such a creature?"

"I alerted several of the staff and we searched. We found no trace of a mouse or any such animal."

Fooks shook his head. *Get a grip, Fooks.* "When did you discover something was wrong?"

"When I closed up the house for the night. I knocked discreetly on the study door. I received no answer, so I tried the door. It was locked."

"Was Mr. Kinsey in the habit of locking the study door?"

"Rarely, if at all. I thought it strange, so I knocked louder." Grieveson hesitated. "It was late. Nearly midnight, and it did occur to me Mr. Kinsey might have fallen asleep."

"When you didn't get an answer, what did you do?"

"I alerted Mr. Carter and Mr. Foster."

"And who are they?"

"Mr. Kinsey and Mr. Brook's valets. They are both of a muscular nature. Mr. Foster tried to effect entry outside via the window, but to no avail. So, they had no choice but to break the door down. When they did..." He came to a shuddering halt.

Caroline blanched. To spare her, Fooks cut across Grieveson. "You alerted the police of course."

"Yes sir, immediately."

"Has the key to the door been found since?"

"No sir. Its whereabouts remains a mystery."

"Hmmm, thank you. I think I have enough for now." Fooks put his notepad and pencil away.

Caroline inclined her head. "You may go, Grieveson. Thank you."

Grieveson jumped like he'd been scalded. "Thank you, madam, sir." He had begun to beat a hasty retreat when Fooks called him back.

Fooks walked over to him, rubbing his forehead and frowning. "What happened to the girl from the office? Miss Miller?"

Grieveson blanked. "I'm not sure, sir. I suppose in all the confusion, she went home."

"Thank you." He closed the door on Grieveson and turned to Caroline gravely. "I'll need to speak to Miss Miller as soon as possible."

"Brook said she and Mr. Gray will not be back here until Thursday. I doubt Brook knows where either of them live."

Fooks stood hands on hips, chewing his bottom lip. Finally, he growled in frustration. "Then they'll have to wait until then. I hate not being able to get on." He puffed and waved a hand dismissively. "Let's go back and let me think."

CHAPTER ELEVEN

"Mr. Fooks, can't you think without moving?" Caroline asked.

Fooks and Caroline returned to Fairfield House. He currently paced in the drawing room, thinking hard, Caroline trying to concentrate on her embroidery. In the end, she carelessly cast it aside.

Fooks continued on his way towards the window, where he paused. He gazed out at the square. He didn't see the beautifully landscaped garden in the middle. Hands behind his back, he started on his return journey into the center of the room.

"Mr. Fooks!"

He started. "Huh?"

Caroline rolled her eyes. "Finally," she said, under her breath. "I asked if you had to move whilst thinking."

Fooks scowled. "Yes," he snapped. "I do." He sniffed. *Perhaps I've gone too far.* Throwing himself into a chair, he said, "There's a lot to think about."

"I realize that. Have you come to any conclusions?"

Fooks still scowled. He disliked being interrogated while he was thinking. "Not especially. Too many people still to see. Too many questions. Too many *unanswered* questions. Period." He stared across at her. "This isn't straightforward."

"Will you get there?"

Fooks levered himself up and stalked to the window. "Oh yes. Eventually."

Caroline fumbled with her embroidery before setting it aside again. "Perhaps it will help to talk about what you've learned," she said. "Two heads are better than one," she added, brightly.

Fooks gave her a sour look, before pacing again. "I'm used to figuring everything all out and talking with Tobias. I'm not sure." He regarded her doubtfully. "I'm not sure it will work with someone else."

"Because I'm a woman?"

"No," he denied, too quickly. And he knew it. He lowered his eyes and stared at the rug, tracing the intricate pattern. Aware Caroline watched him, until finally, he growled and threw himself back into the chair he'd come from. "At the moment we don't know very much. Tobias didn't kill your uncle; I can promise you that."

"Why are you so sure?"

"Because the murderer used a 0.22. Not Tobias' gun. He's a 0.45 man. A Colt 0.45 man. Colt do make a 0.22, but he wouldn't use one. He complains about my Schofield, and it's just as good as his 0.45. In my opinion. But he doesn't think so." He shook his head. "There's no way Tobias would use a 0.22. Neither would he kill a man in cold blood."

She swallowed hard. "How do we prove it?"

"Yep, that's the problem all right." Fooks wriggled his jaw from side to side. "And what I'm working on." He paused. "I think I need to take a look in the safe I found."

"Why? What are you expecting to find?"

He shook his head. "I dunno, but in my experience, men who have safes hidden in their walls usually have something to hide. Whatever it is, might prove to be crucial in understanding why Kinsey was killed."

"We'll have to find out who knows the combination."

Fooks shook his head. "No need."

"What do you have in mind?" she asked, doubtfully.

Fooks grinned. "A little night time poking around."

Fooks peered around the corner of Kinsey House. Neither seeing nor hearing any police patrols. He turned up the collar of his jacket against the biting wind before creeping along the side of the building until he reached the study window. Simple enough catch. Scanning around again, he went to his inside pocket for his tools. He selected the appropriate tool and about to set to work when a noise startled him. He stepped back quickly, intent on hiding in the bushes.

Someone crept along from the other side of the house. Couldn't be a patrol. He hadn't met a lawman yet, who was any good at sneaking. This person was.

Fooks crouched and waited. All was dark. He'd timed his own venture here for when the moon went behind a cloud. This person had clearly done the same.

No sound. Fooks strained his ears, hearing the distant noise of traffic and natural night sounds. *They can't have gone away. I'da heard them.*

Heart thumping in his chest, he rose slowly, and then *whoosh....*

CHAPTER TWELVE

"Sheesh. Flo, I nearly took ya head off!"

The branch hit the ground with a thud.

Fooks stared, his mouth opening and closing.

"Tobe! Wha'?"

The shadow which became Tobias Swan clasped Fooks by the upper arms. "Boy, am I glad to see you."

"Then why were you gonna hit me with a...a...a tree?"

"I thought you were the police."

"Oh great. That would really work out well for you right now," Fooks grumbled.

He squawked suddenly when Swan clamped a hand over his mouth and pulled him into the shadows. The sound of footsteps curtailed their reunion. Fooks shook off his surprise, recognizing the danger of the situation instantly. Swan pushed Fooks roughly against the wall, hand still clamped over his mouth. The press of his body told him how uneasy Swan was.

The shadow of a man appeared in the now hazy moonlight, scanning both ways. Swan and Fooks became one with the wall. When the man passed, Swan ventured a glance out, only to retreat swiftly when another shadow appeared.

"Thought I heard something," the second shadow called. "Gonna take a look."

"Okay. Watch yourself."

Fooks slipped Swan his Schofield.

As the second man took a step towards them, Swan poised, gun in hand. The crunch of his footsteps on the gravel path masked Swan cocking the gun. The pair remained still and silent. Fooks' heart hammered in his chest, discovery something neither wanted to contemplate.

"Awh, must have been a cat or something," the second muttered. His footsteps tramped away.

Swan eased back the hammer. Fooks puffed out his cheeks, letting out a sigh of relief.

The two men stood studying each other in the dim light. Fooks strained his ears for sounds of the receding guards. Swan's sharper hearing had become an invaluable asset in their previous profession. Fooks waited for Swan to indicate all clear.

Swan regarded the Schofield in his hand, and shook his head. He tutted disapprovingly.

Fooks pulled it from Swan's grasp. "What are you doing here?"

"Can ask you the same thing," Swan said, in a hiss.

Fooks jabbed a finger at the darkened window behind them. "I'm trying to get in there."

"Me too. Figured there might be clue or something."

"There is. A whole safe full if we're lucky."

"I'll keep watch while you do ya thing." Swan waved a hand at the window. "An' give me that," he added, wrestling the gun back from Fooks, before slipping away. Despite being apart for over two years, they'd quickly slipped back into their previous comfortable relationship.

Fooks studied the window. From inside his jacket pocket, he brought out his tools. With another glance at the objective, he selected the appropriate instrument, then set to work teasing down the locking catch. A moment later he winced. The click of success sounded all too loudly in the still night air. He froze when the bushes behind him shook, then relaxed; Swan returning.

Together they pushed at the window. Slowly. Trying not to make a sound. Except it wasn't moving. At one time, someone had painted the window shut. Fooks reversed the tool he'd used earlier and scored the side of the window casement, breaking the paint seal. He handed the tool to Swan to do the same on the other side. Only then could they manage to raise the window to its fullest.

Fooks ducked in first and stood between the window and the drapes, waiting for Swan to clamber in behind him. Only then did Fooks cautiously part the drapes and step into the room proper. Fooks lit a candle retrieved from his pocket. He located a brandy glass, upended it, and dribbled melted wax on the base before sticking the candle down.

Swan followed into the room and closed the drapes behind him, leaving the window open behind. He joined Fooks to stand in front of the chalk outline. "This where he fell, huh?"

"Yep." Fooks nodded. "Good to see you again, partner."

"You too, Fooks. I'd hoped ya'd come when ya read in the papers 'bout me being shot."

Fooks raised an eyebrow. "Oh, you were so sure I'd come, were you?"

Swan twitched his head. "Moderately."

Fooks eyed him. "Seen you looking better." He took in the unwashed curly light brown hair and days of stubble on his face. His clothes, disheveled, but expensive. Yet the blue eyes were bright, albeit tired.

"Yeah, well I've been in hiding since I heard 'bout the shooting." He gestured at the room in general. "What are you looking for?"

"Here earlier, and I found a hidden safe. Figured I'd take a peep inside."

Swan grunted. "Ya were here earlier?"

"Yes." Fooks glared at him hard. "With your wife!"

Swan winced. "Ah, yeah 'bout that—"

"Tell me later. We've other concerns right now. Before we get to the safe, what d'you think about the position of the body?"

They studied the chalk outline.

"Well." Swan let out a puff. "I'd say he came over here to get a book to read."

Fooks raised his head slowly to glare at his partner. "Big reader, was he?"

"Phht. Doubt it. Not that kinda man." He waved his hand at the expanse of books before them. "These are all jus' for show."

"You came to see him the night he died. How did you leave him?"

"You have to ask?" Swan gasped. "Alive. I left him alive," he added, firmly. "Sitting right there behind the desk."

"Anyone see you leave?"

"Nah. I was so angry I let myself out. Mighta heard me though. Made enough noise."

Fooks grunted and chewed his bottom lip. "Police tell me he was shot with a 0.22." He stepped forward and positioned himself carefully by the chalk outline. "How tall was he?"

"'Bout our height."

"Hit him in the chest and he fell here, facing the door."

"He musta known his murderer. Ya have to get close to kill someone using a 0.22."

"Yeah, that's what I thought." Fooks scanned around the room. "Any other way into this room, other than the door?"

"Not that I know of. The fire was alight." Swan cast a critical eye around the room. "Secret door perhaps?"

Fooks twitched his head doubtfully. "If we go around tapping on the walls, someone'll come investigating. Was he the type?"

"Nah." Swan shook his head. "Wouldn't occur to him."

"He hid his safe," Fooks reminded him.

"Most folks do when there are folks like you about." Fooks false smiled.

"Where is this safe anyway?" Swan asked.

Fooks grinned and repeated his actions from earlier, throwing back the fake door.

"Well, I'll be. I never knew that was there." Swan whistled.

"What you're supposed to think."

Fooks stood hands on hips, licking his lips, contemplating the safe.

"What d'ya think?" Swan asked, when Fooks made no comment.

"Willis and Carter 1882. Latest model."

Swan pursed his lips. "Sooo can ya crack it?" He waited expectantly for his partner.

Fooks took a deep breath, folded his arms and his tongue explored his mouth. "Hardened lumps of mashed potato," he murmured. The thought of his daughter momentarily made him question why he was here.

"Huh?"

"In my store. I have a catalog for this manufacturer." Fooks waved a hand in the direction of the safe. "Can get a fifteen percent discount if I sell one."

Swan harrumphed. "But can you crack it?" he asked again.

"Dunno, never tried." Fooks stepped forward. "Five number combination, almost silent tumbler." He pulled a face. "Technology has moved on since our day, Tobe."

"But you can crack anything. Ya said there wasn't a safe alive ya couldn't crack."

"I said that five years ago when it was true." Fooks winced. "And breaking into safes without the owner's permission isn't exactly law abiding y'know."

"Neither is breaking into someone's private residence, but here we are. So are ya saying ya can't do it?"

"I didn't say that," Fooks said quickly. "I jus' need to work up to it. Go and poke around in the desk and try not to make any noise." He waved Swan away.

Fooks pulled up a chair, put his ear to the safe and his fingers around the ridged tumbler. At one point he got up and retrieved a glass. With this upturned and pressed against the safe, he did better. For the next ten minutes, he frowned, listened hard and moved the tumbler slowly right and left.

"How ya doing?"

Fooks slumped in his chair. "I've got two I think."

Swan exhaled noisily through pursed lips. He continued rifling through the contents of the drawer.

Fooks spun the tumbler several times and settled back. *This isn't going too well. Think I've lost my touch.* He pressed on, gradually relaxing into the familiar routine. How many times had he sat in front of a safe doing exactly this? Too many, and he'd hoped he'd never have to do this again, unless for a legitimate reason.

"Ah."

A flicker of irritation creased Fooks' brow. "What part of 'try not to make any noise' don't you understand?" he snapped at Swan.

Swan smoothed out a crumpled paper. He'd found it wedged in the back of the top drawer. He smiled knowingly. "Will this help?"

Fooks snatched it from him. With a heavy sigh, he read the paper. Then he grunted and Swan chuckled. He'd handed Fooks the safe's original combination from the manufacture.

"Might. Unless he changed it." *Most folks don't, so I might get lucky.*

Fooks huffed and spun the tumbler several times. With the paper in one hand, he moved the tumbler to the required numbers with the other. A glance at Swan, nodding encouragement, Fooks gave the handle a push. They swapped grins at the opening click.

Fooks swung the door of the safe open. Inside were three shelves. On the top one, a tray of jewelry boxes. Beside these, another smaller tray containing an ink pad and a selection of rubber stamps. The partners quickly dismissed these, their attention going instead to the middle shelf. On top of a cash box lay a few documents. Fooks settled them on his lap. He scanned them quickly, before dismissing them as unimportant.

His attention fell onto the cash box. He checked whether it was locked, grunted when it was, and found the canvas sack from his inside pocket, containing his lock picks. He selected the appropriate one and inserted the tip into the lock. A wince and some finagling had the lid open. Inside, instead of cash, more documents. These proved more interesting, and Fooks quickly absorbed himself in reading.

Swan watched for a few minutes. He soon became bored, and his eyes strayed back to the interior of the safe and he whistled.

Fooks glanced up. Swan reached for a sizable stack of bank notes.

"Must be ten thousand dollars here." Swan flicked them, breathing out a gasp. "All in small bills too."

"Put 'em back Tobe. We don't do that anymore remember?"

Swan tutted. "You're no fun since we went straight."

Fooks smacked his lips and carried on reading.

With a puff, Swan put the bank notes back and explored the bottom shelf. He grunted at a number of silver items.

"Why do people keep things like this in a safe?" he asked, holding one of a pair of candlesticks.

"Valuable I guess," Fooks murmured. He frowned. "Hmm."

Swan returned the candlestick with a chink. "Ya got something?"

"Hmm, mebbe." Fooks' frown deepened.

"What ya got?"

Fooks took on a thoughtful expression.

"Fooks?"

Fooks sniffed, his forehead still creased into a frown. He regarded the document again.

Swan took a deep breath.

"Flo!"

Fooks' head snapped up. "What?"

"What have ya got?" Swan dropped his eyes meaningfully at the paper Fooks held.

"Oh," Fooks frowned again. "Think it's a tontine."

"Huh?"

"A tontine."

"What's one of them?"

"In this case it's an investment scheme."

"So?"

Fooks grunted at the document. "It's—"

Swan held up his hand. Fooks froze. Swan heard something. Fooks didn't. Yet he knew from bitter experience to trust his partner's superior hearing. He sat and waited. Then it filtered through to him and he gaped. Someone was descending the stairs.

With practiced ease, the pair swung into action. Swan returned the discarded documents to the safe. Fooks swept the interested-in pile to the poacher's pocket of his jacket and swung the safe door closed. He spun the tumbler. Swan stood ready to close the fake bookshelves. The chair Fooks sat on to open the safe already put back.

The footsteps outside now reached the hall and sounded even louder. The partners shared a concerned glance. Swan blew out the candle, squeezing the top with moistened fingers to diffuse the trail of smoke. He bolted for the window. An unseen hand pushed the door handle as Swan dived headfirst through the open window. Fooks followed, a fraction of a second later, just as the door began to open. Banging his ankle on the window ledge, incapacitated his leg. The drapes fell together behind him, leaving a crack in the middle.

"Sheesh." Fooks let out a gasp of pain.

With Fooks' leg numb, Swan struggled to clear the limb from the ledge and close the window. The shadow of a man entered the room. He held a lit oil lamp. The feeble glow allowed enough light to see where he was going but not enough for an investigation. Swan watched the man light another, more powerful lamp, capable of bathing the whole room in a soft yellow glow.

Fooks lay gasping in the flowerbed under the window. Swan, keeping to one side, watched the man approach the window. Brook Kinsey. Swan's hand lay warningly on his partner's shoulder. Fooks swallowed and tried to silence his breathing.

Swan shrank back when Brook threw aside the drapes.

CHAPTER THIRTEEN

As they held their breath, Brook Kinsey checked the window latch. Finding it unlocked, he frowned and secured the catch. He pulled the drapes firmly across the window, plunging Swan and Fooks into darkness. Swan put his ear closer to the window. At the same time his fingers dug painfully into Fooks' shoulder, holding him in place. Police patrols still in the grounds remained a likelihood and might have seen the light from the study window.

Swan and Fooks left via the rear of Kinsey House, Fooks limping where pain still stabbed his ankle. They climbed over the wall into Acorn Street, the quiet road both had used to enter. Swan helped Fooks to roll stiffly over the top of the wall. The jump down generated an explosive hiss from Fooks. The front of Kinsey House sat on Mount Vernon Street, one of Boston's more affluent thoroughfares, a short walk, or limp, away. Once there, Swan hailed one of the cabs that plied their trade on this busy route into the city.

To Fooks' surprise, Swan's destination was the Boston and Maine Railroad Depot.

"Why are we going there?" Fooks asked, once they were underway.

"Thought we'd ride up the hill. Show ya some sights."

"It's dark," Fooks reminded him.

Swan shrugged. "First place I thought of in the opposite direction to where we wanna go." He grinned. "Thought it would give ya time to figure a way to get me into Fairfield House. You say the police are watching?"

"So Caroline said." Fooks ran his tongue over his top teeth. "I didn't see anyone when I left."

"How did ya leave?"

"By the front door."

"Wearing that jacket?" Swan referred to Fooks' distinctive Mackinaw jacket.

"Yes. It's cold out."

"Thought ya'd got rid of the thing by now."

"The jacket's warm and I like the poacher's pockets. I can carry all sorts of things with me." He fixed him with a dark look. "You were with me when I bought it."

"Give away who ya are though."

Fooks peered out at the cityscape trundling by. "Yeah, I know."

"There's the State House." Swan pointed at the edifice on their right, with its gilded dome. Built on the highest hill in the city, stone steps led from the street to a hall on the ground floor. "Huge ain't it? Bigger'n Denver. You can go up to the dome. See the whole city laid out in front of ya like a map."

Fooks craned his neck. "Yep." He settled back into the seat.

Swan bit his lip. "I thought ya'd be more enthusiastic being in a big Eastern city for the first time."

Fooks mastered his patience with difficulty. "It's the middle of the night. It's dark. It's cold and you're in no position to play tour guide. Where have you been for three days? Caroline is out of her mind with worry."

"I've been, awh, perhaps best I don't tell ya. Don't want folks getting into trouble 'cos of me. I went an' got drunk in a free an' easy where folks don't ask too many questions. Saw the newspaper headline the next morning. Thought I'd better lay low for a while, so I couldn't let Caroline know I was all right. I've been around though. Watching."

"What do you mean?"

"Exactly what I say. Kinsey's dead. Someone killed him. And not me. Two men working for him held me up. One shot me. Ya hear about that?" Fooks nodded. "The police think I killed Kinsey. If they reckon so, you can betcha so do those men. I laid low 'cos I didn't want 'em coming after me and endangering Caroline. But now you're here, time to go home. Undercover." He tapped Fooks' arm next to him. "Ya said ya left through the front door?"

"Yes. Like a proper person."

"What time did ya say ya'd be back?"

"I didn't. Cowdry said he'd wait up. Showed me the back door."

Swan rummaged in his pocket and held up a key. "I've got this an' a plan."

Fooks' face fell and he let out a low groan. Swan glowered. "This is part of my plan." Swan waved the key.

"Oh, yeah, I'd forgotten about your plan." Fooks rolled his eyes.

"You haven't even heard it yet," Swan said, indignant.

"Go on." Fooks waved a hand for Swan to get on with outlining his plan.

"We swap coats. You take this." He thrust the key at Fooks. "With this here overcoat over ya arm and using the key, anyone watching will see you and not me. While I go in the back way, wearing that jacket of yours, like ya planned. When Cowdry sees me, he'll let me in." Swan grinned triumphantly. "What d'ya think? Will it work?"

Fooks spent several agonizing minutes inspecting the key before he spoke. He and Swan stood the same height, but Swan stockier. This hadn't changed during his time in Boston. Now a lot stockier, compared to Fooks' slender and wiry build. When he next spoke, it was begrudgingly. "Has merit."

"What d'ya mean?" Swan demanded. "Best I can do on the spur of the moment. Can you come up with anything better?"

"No, I guess I can't," Fooks said, reluctantly. "Okay, we'll give it a whirl."

Even in the dead of night, Fooks recognized Haymarket Square. Still resembling a free for all. The Boston and Maine Depot stood before the square, and the cab lurched across the traffic to pull up on the left side of the building. Fooks shakily climbed out to peer at the classical architecture.

"We'll wait for this one to go and then we'll find another to take us back," Swan said, turning away from paying the fare. He'd pulled a scarf from somewhere, covering his mouth and nose. "C'mon, I'll buy you a cup of coffee."

Fooks gaped. "At this time of night?"

"First passenger service outta here is at seven, but freight runs all night. Porters have to take a break now and then."

The coffee was barely palatable, but Fooks and Swan drank it anyway. They had taken a seat at a rickety table well away from a group of working men, who were laughing and talking loudly.

Fooks glanced across at the group and dropped his voice. "Well, are you gonna tell me?" Fooks asked.

"'Bout what?"

Fooks widened his eyes. "Your wife. What d'you think I meant?"

Swan grunted. "Yeah, you're right. I *do* owe you an explanation. Did Wash tell ya 'bout the train wreck which happened while you were away?"

"Yes. He filled me in on that *part*." Impatience made Fooks snap and he dropped his gaze in silent apology.

"Caroline was in trouble. Her uncle, Robert Kinsey—y'know, the dead man? —pursued her all the way to San Francisco. She thought she'd lost him but she hadn't. He'd made his presence known to her on the return train before it wrecked. They got separated in the confusion."

"Why was he after her?"

"Awh, he wanted her to marry someone of his choosing. She was a recent heiress. Under the terms of her father's will, she had complete control over her financial and business affairs. Kinsey was a misogynist. He didn't like it. He felt he should'a been appointed her guardian." Swan paused, staring into his mug, swirling the dregs. "She had to get away, and she came wanting to buy a horse." He drained the mug, grimacing at the bitter end. "Pulled the late shift in the livery that night."

"Ah." Fooks raised his head in understanding.

"Yep. Could easily been ole Walt." Swan reached forward and put aside the mug. "But it weren't. It was me." He settled back in his chair and fidgeted with his fingers resting on the table. "Once she told me her story, I had to help."

"'Course you did."

Swan gave Fooks a glare and chose to ignore the remark. "I took her back to our cabin, and she hid there while Kinsey an' his men searched the town. They left the next day when the train got back on its tracks."

Swan traced a pool of wetness across the table. "Caroline asked me to marry her an' I thought about it an' said yes." He didn't meet Fooks' eyes.

Fooks wasn't very often lost for words but right now he was. He stared at Swan in disbelief. *This explanation had better be good.*

A muscle in Swan's cheek twitched as he considered his next words. "Started out as a marriage of convenience. Convenient for her to be married, convenient for me to get away from Wyoming."

"And me," Fooks said, bitterly.

"No." Swan's denial was firm. "Just an opportunity, Flo. One I felt I couldn't pass up. Worked for both of us." He pursed his lips. "Didn't stay a marriage of convenience for long though." He didn't meet Fooks' eye. "Caroline is my wife in every sense of the word."

Fooks' eyes popped. "You didn't—"

"No." Swan shook his head. "Kinda mutual."

Fooks had his doubts, but motioned for Swan to carry on.

"So here I am, husband to Caroline Fairfield, one of the richest women in Boston right now."

Fooks took a sip of his coffee. Too bitter, even for him, and he slid it away. He considered what Swan had told him. "Not what you're used to Tobe." He spoke quietly. "Caroline knows you're really Tobias Swan. Is the marriage legal?"

Swan scowled. "'Course its legal. I told Caroline who I really was beforehand. Y'know, give her a chance to back out, but she was determined to go ahead. So, we went to the only person I knew who would marry us using my real name. Judge Heyford. He arranged it with a reverend. Drew up the pre-nup thingy as well."

"Pre-nup thingy?"

"Yeah, Caroline wanted me to sign this piece of paper. Anything we each had before the marriage would remain our own. She didn't want me to have control of her fortune. Can't blame her. I didn't want her having control of my thirteen dollars and twenty-five cents neither." He twitched his bottom lip. "All I had in the world, and I worked hard for it."

Fooks closed his eyes and bit his lip.

"I shoulda asked sooner. How are you an' Mary?"

"Life with Mary is great." His mouth curved into a scimitar. "Took me a while to settle into married life but I reckon I'm there now." He took a photograph from his wallet and held it out.

"What's this?" Swan studied the photograph. "Cute kid." When he looked across at Fooks for an explanation, the other dimpled. Swan bent his head to the photograph again. This time, more closely. Another glance at Fooks and realization dawned. He whooped. "Yours?"

"Yep. My daughter Susan."

Swan laughed. "'Course she is. Know those dimples anywhere. You name her for ya Ma?"

"Yes." He reached to take the photograph back and glanced fondly at it. "She's about eight months here. I need to be back by the end of May, Tobe. It's her first birthday then. I wasn't there for her birth, and I daren't miss it."

Swan chuckled. "You didn't waste much time," he crowed.

Fooks felt his cheeks burning. "Yeah, well…"

"How come ya missed her birth?"

Fooks groaned and rubbed his eyes. "Brad and Sid paid me a visit. Got themselves framed for murder."

"Brad and Sid? Murder?" Swan laughed. "No, don't believe it."

"Neither did I. So, I went to Angelworth and investigated."

"Did ya sort it?"

Fooks smiled faintly. "What do you think? Anyway, Mary was almost due, and by the time I got back, Susan had arrived."

"Sounds like a long story." Swan glanced around when the group of working men scraped back their chairs. "Look, we oughta get back. An' you've gotta read those documents. Sounds like they might be very interesting."

The working men departed laughing and slapping each other on the back, leaving Swan and Fooks as the last two customers. It wasn't long before they too left.

CHAPTER FOURTEEN

"Hold it right there, Martin."

Fooks feigned surprise to see two police patrolmen with guns drawn and pointed at him. More ran to join them.

"Can I help you, officers?" he asked, politely. He turned on the top step of Fairfield House.

"You're not Samuel Martin," the first said, more senior than the others.

"No. Did you want me to be?" Fooks didn't expect an answer and wasn't disappointed when he didn't receive one.

"Who are you?"

He was about to answer, when the door opened. "Mr. Crane, good evening, sir," Cowdry said.

"Yes, thank you. Very good." He swept off his homburg and handed it over, glancing back at the scowling patrolmen.

"Come away, men. We'd mighta known it wouldn't be that easy."

Inside, with the door shut, Fooks chuckled. "Is he in?" he asked, knowing Cowdry would guess who he meant.

"Yes sir." Cowdry took Swan's overcoat from Fooks. "He went up the back stairs to his rooms."

"We should tell Mrs. Martin."

"I expect he'll do that himself sir."

In Swan's rooms, Fooks found himself surplus to requirements. Swan and Caroline embraced enthusiastically.

Cowdry came in behind him. As he peeled away to the bathroom, the couple finally broke apart. Fooks stiffened. He'd never seen this look on his partner's face before. A dalliance brought a genuine affection, but this was something different. *Sheesh, he's really in love with her.* Judging by the shine in Caroline's eyes, the feeling is mutual. Fooks swallowed a lump in his throat. This was all so sudden and unexpected. What should he feel? Betrayal? Hurt? Pleased? Excluded?

While Swan bathed and ate a light supper, Fooks amused himself by reading the document he'd glanced at in Kinsey's study. Swan joined him later. Comfortably ensconced in an armchair, a warm robe and a glass of whiskey completing his homecoming. Fooks accepted the offered drink.

"Gonna tell me what happened with Kinsey?" Fooks asked.

"Dunno where to start really. It's late an' I..." Swan broke off, eying the connecting door which led to Caroline's bedroom, "I kinda have other plans y'know."

"The potted version then."

Swan sighed. "His men shot me an' I wanted to know why. Have it out with him once and for all."

"Caroline isn't sure why you think that."

"Well, who else, Fooks? The man tried to force Caroline to marry someone he could control, an' I spoiled his little plan. With me outta the way he could get back to his previous scheme."

"What made you think he was behind it?"

"The bullet nicked me in the side, but what to do? I had no gun on me. I couldna shot back. I went down pretending, hoping if I made it look good, they'd think they'd done their job and leave. Missed my vocation, Fooks, worked. I saw 'em run off and climb into a double Brougham. It's pretty distinctive, even here. An' the only man I know who owns one, who'd want to hurt me, is Robert Kinsey.

"I needed time to heal up while I thought what to do about it. When I was ready, I went to confront him. D'ya know what he said to me? He offered me money to divorce Caroline and leave Boston. I wasn't doing it an' I told him straight." Swan shook his head. "Man was desperate to get his hands on Caroline's money. He said I'd better watch out for myself in future in case I had another accident. I took that for a threat, an' rather than stay in case I did something I would really regret, I left."

"The door to the study was locked. Rescuers had to break in," Fooks said.

Swan reddened. "Oh, yeah. As I stormed out, my hand caught on the key to the study in the lock. Stupid of me, I know, but I locked the door."

"What did you do with the key?"

Swan shook his head. "I tossed it away before I left the house. Dunno where it went."

"Did anyone see you leave?"

"I don't remember anyone in the hall." He pulled a face. "I wasn't really looking Fooks."

Fooks stared into the distance, rubbing his thumb and forefinger together. "Lots of places in the hall to hide. Someone coulda seen you. Seen what happened to the key. Went in after you and shot him."

"Suppose."

"What do you know about him? Did he have any enemies, who might want him dead?"

Swan pursed his lips. "Dunno much 'bout his business affairs but I heard he sailed close to the wind. Employed some hard cases." He rolled his eyes. "As I found out."

"These two men who shot you, have you ever seen them before?"

Swan shook his head. "Gave the police their descriptions. A tall, skinny fella with yellow blond hair. Mebbe early thirties, and a short stocky fella with dark hair and a broken nose. Mid-forties, I guess. Can't see them shooting Kinsey. He was their meal ticket."

Fooks brought out the document he'd read earlier. He unfolded it carefully. "This might be a motive for murder though," he said, slowly.

Swan frowned. "What is it? The document ya found in the safe?"

"One of them. Haven't read them all yet. But this one, as I suspected, is a tontine—"

"As I asked earlier, what's a tontine?"

"A tontine is a financial contract between a group of people. In this case a group of investors took shares in the building of the Hayes Theater in Boston."

"I've been to that theater. It's on Washington Street."

"That's right." Fooks glanced at the document. "In 1875—"

"About ten years ago."

"The term is for twenty."

"So, just about halfway through."

Fooks glared at him. "Yes," he said, through gritted teeth. He returned to the document. "There were 1600 shares of $100 each."

"So that's ..." Swan's left index finger flicked back and forth. "One—"

"One hundred and sixty thousand dollars, yes."

Swan whistled. "A lot of money."

"Enough to build a theater." Fooks put his head down, ignoring the daggers coming his way. "Kinsey had three hundred shares, so his initial investment was $30,000. Dividends amounted to 5% per annum. In Kinsey's case, $1,500. At least initially."

Swan whistled. "Sheesh. Why didn't we know about this afore? Man can make himself some easy money.

Better'n robbing banks and trains. An' all for doing nothin'."

Fooks turned the document over, read for a moment, and his eyes widened. "Hey get this." Fooks grinned. "Kinsey's nominee was Charles Fairfield. D'you suppose that's Charles Fairfield, the railroad magnate?"

"Yeah, reckon so. He's Caroline's father. So, it fits."

"What?" Fooks' eyes popped. "Caroline's father was *Charles* Fairfield?"

Swan smiled ruefully at Fooks' reaction. "Yep. When I told her who I was, she said we'd cost her father an awful lot of money over the years."

Fooks grunted. "Putting it mildly." He shifted uncomfortably. "No wonder she seems pretty hostile."

Swan waved a hand dismissively. "Aw, we're past that."

"You maybe, but I was the ideas man, remember? It's 'cos of my schemes we robbed all those trains so successfully. *His* trains."

"Forget it, Fooks. We've cleaned up our act since." Swan raised his head and frowned. "What's a nominee?"

"Each investor has to nominate someone. The dividend payout each year depended on their nominee still being alive."

Swan pulled a face. "Don't sound right to me. Like betting on someone's life." He shook his head. "Society folks huh?" His head jerked. "But it do make sense. Charles Fairfield died four years ago. So, I guess Kinsey hasn't received any dividend since then?"

Fooks twitched his head. "I presume."

"Can't be a motive for murder then."

"Guess not." Fooks bent his head over the document again.

Swan sipped at his coffee and waited.

A moment later, Fooks raised his head and then his hand. Infuriatingly, Fooks dropped the document to his lap and stared off into the distance. "It could be a motive for murder, y'know," he muttered.

"But if the nominee is dead." Swan noted Fooks' smug face. "What?"

"It goes on to say," Fooks said, slowly, "only the shareholder and the administrators of the scheme know the name of the nominee." His grin became broader. "Kinsey's heirs wouldn't realize this thing is no longer valid."

Swan pulled a doubtful face. "He coulda told 'em when Fairfield died."

"Suppose, but why would he? The thing's invalid. No, I'm wondering," Fooks stared into the distance again, thoughtful. "How did Fairfield die?"

"Pneumonia."

Fooks grunted. *Nothing suspicious.*

"C'mon, ya had another thought."

"Yes. I'm wondering how many shareholders are still in this. Y'know, whose nominees *are* still alive. 'Cos according to this agreement, when it gets to the last two, the tontine is wound up. The last two shareholders split the 5% dividend. Which," he broke off and grinned at Swan, "to save you the bother of calculating, is $4,000 per year each."

Swan false smiled. "I got that, thanks."

Fooks folded the document and tapped Swan on the arm with it. "This could be a motive for murder."

Swan gaped. "Y'mean one of the other shareholders coulda...not knowing Kinsey's nominee is dead?"

"It's a possibility. There's nothing in here about revealing names to the others when a shareholder's interest lapses. I suspect not if the nominee is secret. They find out someone has died when they receive more money one year than they were expecting."

Swan glanced at the connecting door again. "Look, er, we done for now?"

"Sure. I'm tired too." Fooks smirked and levered up. "Looks like I've got places to go and people to see in the morning."

Caroline reluctantly accompanied Fooks to the tontine scheme administrators on Tremont Street. Although she'd wanted to stay with Swan, he'd persuaded her Fooks would find out more if she went along.

Templeton, Taylor and Lee arrayed themselves on the far side of an oak desk. All three elderly gentlemen were dressed in somber ill-fitting clothes. Fooks presumed they were standing in order of their firm's title. The taller of the three, on the extreme left, gestured to the two straight-backed chairs for their guests. "I'm Templeton."

"Taylor."

"Lee."

After the curt introductions, each sat. Fooks made sure Caroline was seated correctly before he took his own seat by her side.

"Good morning gentlemen, thank you for seeing us on such short notice," Caroline said. Lee blatantly took out his pocket watch, and sniffed, before returning it to his pocket. "I'm Mrs. Caroline Martin, and this is Mr. Crane of Pinkerton's Detective Agency."

A disagreeable rumble issued from the other side of the desk.

Caroline licked her lips and pressed on. "I understand my late uncle, Robert Kinsey had an interest in a tontine administered by your firm. Mr. Crane has a suspicion this may have something to do with Uncle Robert's recent murder. Of which I'm sure you've heard."

"Yes, Mrs. Martin, we are aware of Robert Kinsey's sad demise. Your late uncle's interest in the tontine to which you refer became moot some years ago." Taylor spoke after glancing at his partners.

"Can you tell us who the other shareholders are or were?"

"We cannot," said Templeton.

"I don't understand why," Caroline burst out. "Surely—"

"Mrs. Martin, Templeton, Taylor and Lee are a long-standing and highly respected law firm. We did not get this reputation from being carefree with our client's information."

"I quite understand, but surely in the circumstances—"

"Are you able to speak to us in general terms, gentlemen? Rather than specific," Fooks cut into Caroline and suffered her irritated glare.

The partners huddled and Caroline and Fooks waited for the hushed voices to stop. When they broke apart, Templeton spoke, "We're not at liberty to divulge the names of the shareholders. We are prepared to tell you this. Originally the tontine had six shareholders. Including Mr. Kinsey."

"You said originally. Does this imply one or more of the shareholders is no longer a participant in the tontine?"

"Yes," said Lee.

"However, it is possible to transfer or bequeath a shareholding," Taylor added.

"I suppose by giving me this information you are telling me that at least one of the shareholders is not the original?"

"I believe you are the detective, Mr. Crane," Taylor said.

Caroline sucked in a deep breath. Fooks looked askance at her. *Just like Tobias. Perhaps those two are more well-matched than I thought.*

"Very well, I'll try a different tack. Does the change of shareholder effect the nominee?"

"No. The shareholder can change, but not the nominee."

"Ah. And are all the nominees still alive?"

"No." It was Lee who spoke. *Did he only ever speak one word at a time?*

"And I don't suppose you can tell me about the nominees?"

"Your supposition is correct, Mr. Crane," said Templeton.

Lee took his pocket watch out again. This time he tapped it. "Gentlemen, it's time," he said, shattering Fooks' theory of how many words the man spoke at any one time.

"One more question and we'll go." Fooks didn't wait for agreement. "Has anyone else asked you about the tontine recently?"

The partners exchanged looks. An unspoken conversation went on between them. Finally, Templeton spoke. "Beneficiaries of the deceased shareholders."

"As is their right," added Taylor.

"And now, Mrs. Martin, Mr. Crane, we really must draw this meeting to a close." In emphasis, Lee jumped to his feet. His partners did likewise.

Fooks and Caroline found themselves all but pushed out of the door and on to the street.

"How rude," she said. "A complete waste of time." Caroline summoned her carriage from further along the street.

"Not necessarily."

"What do you mean?" she asked, sharply.

Fooks bit his lip. When the carriage drew up, he opened the door and helped Caroline in. Before he followed her, he called up to the driver, "The Hayes Theater please."

Caroline waited until he settled in before asking, "Why are we going there?"

"'Cos the Hayes Theater is what the tontine is all about. I'd like to find out what the manager knows." He widened his eyes at her. "He might be able to tell us more than Templeton, Taylor and Lee. Especially as you're with me. Do that gracious lady thing you pulled with the poor police patrolman. We'll have no trouble finding out."

Caroline raised her nose. "I've no idea what you mean, Mr. Fooks."

CHAPTER FIFTEEN

The carriage started off, and Fooks had a sudden thought. "We won't have to go via Haymarket Square, will we?" he asked. Negotiating through the traffic chaos again filled him with dread. Twice the previous night should be enough for anyone.

"No. Rest assured we will go nowhere near Haymarket Square." Caroline patted his arm. "Unless of course you want to?" she asked, innocently.

He scowled at her. "No need to put yourself out," he replied. "Ma'am."

The Hayes Theater was situated on Washington Street, heart of the theater district, with several other theaters and music halls in the vicinity. *Must be hell along here, come show time.*

Once inside, they gave their names and asked for the manager.

A rotund little man in a light green tweed suit came out to meet them. He sported a handkerchief, resembling a large purple flower, in his top pocket.

"Ah, Mrs. Martin, how wonderful of you to grace this humble establishment with your presence." Caroline smiled sickly at the greeting of the theater's manager, Henry Downton. He raised the back of Caroline's hand to his lips.

Fooks winced at the greeting. *Suppose Caroline is used to this.* He clearly heard Caroline suck in a breath of displeasure. Downton was too overawed to notice. He led her across the foyer into a room marked private, holding on to her hand firmly.

"Please, my dear lady, settle yourself in this chair and tell me what brings you here today." He indicated the chair on which he expected her to sit and only when she was firmly ensconced did he let go of her hand. Fooks smirked when relief crossed her face.

She soon rallied to state the reason for her visit. "Mr. Downton, I understand my late uncle, Robert Kinsey, was a shareholder in the Hayes Theater."

"Indeed, he was. One of the original investors."

"No doubt you have heard of his passing?"

"Yes, yes, sad business. I do hope the police catch the person responsible soon."

Caroline shifted in her seat. "The police are currently of the opinion my husband is responsible."

Now Downton moved uncomfortably. He mopped his brow with the purple handkerchief.

"However, this is of course ridiculous, so I have engaged my own investigator. Mr. Crane is one of Mr. Pinkerton's finest operatives."

For the first time, Downton acknowledged the presence of Fooks. He swept his hand theatrically to another chair. Fooks sank onto it, trying to keep a smirk from his face, but failing. The glare from Caroline sobered him immediately.

"Mr. Downton, we've reason to believe my uncle's investment in your business was somewhat unusual."

"In what way, dear lady?" Downton gave his brow another mop, before stuffing the handkerchief away and sitting behind a cluttered desk.

"The nature of his interest, Mr. Downton. Are you aware of what I speak?"

"You mean the tontine? Yes of course."

"Mr. Crane's investigation into my uncle's murder has uncovered some disturbing queries regarding his interest in your theater."

Downton blanched. "Disturbing queries? Pray, what can they be? My establishment is run entirely above board. I resent any—" The handkerchief was out and mopping again.

"Please calm yourself, Mr. Downton. The queries have nothing to do with your running of the theater. More to do with the capital structure at its inception. We merely wish to understand the details of the investment."

Downton seemed relieved. He cleared his throat. "I'm not sure I can tell you much. I'm not party to an individual investor's financial arrangements, you understand. The lawyers Templeton, Taylor and Lee are the tontine's administrators."

"Yes, I'm aware, but as is the way of such men, they were less than helpful to me. A mere woman." She paused for effect. "I hoped I might prevail upon someone like yourself, a man of a more enlightened disposition, to answer my questions." A century before, Caroline might have fluttered a fan at this point.

Downton swelled before their eyes. "If I know, I will gladly answer."

"Thank you. Perhaps Mr. Crane should ask the questions."

Fooks wasted no time. "What do you know about the initial investment, Mr. Downton?"

Downton cleared his throat. "All the original investors have boxes as part of the arrangement."

"Can you tell me their names?"

"Yes of course. There's no secret. One moment, I will find the names for you." He rummaged around on his desk. Fooks and Caroline swapped glances. Downton found a thick ledger. "Now let me see. They hold the best six boxes in the house. C belonged initially to Mr. Herbert Bagley, but since his death it's used for paying customers. D to Mr. Montgomery Whitlock. E to Mr. Robert Kinsey. F to Mr. Chester Miller, although his box passed to his children on his demise. G to Mr. Eugene Camden; and H to Mr. Harvey Slocomb."

Fooks scribbled furiously in a bid to keep up. When he finished, he puffed. "So let me get this straight: three of the original investors are deceased?"

"Now that Robert Kinsey is, er, yes."

"Do you happen to know their addresses?"

Downton hesitated. "I shouldn't divulge such information."

Fooks flicked a glance at Caroline. She shook her head in disgust, before plastering on a smile in Downton's direction.

"Mr. Downton, Mr. Crane is investigating a brutal murder. He should speak to everyone associated with my uncle. Any little clue, no matter how insignificant, may prove crucial in the apprehension of his killer."

"Yes of course, dear lady, I completely understand. Very well. Given the circumstances, I will have my girl furnish Mr. Crane with the details," Downton said, begrudgingly. "I trust, sir, you will keep such information confidential?"

"Of course." Fooks studied his notes. "Now. You said Mr. Miller's box passed to his children. What are their names?"

Downton considered. "I'm not aware of their names. Mr. Miller junior and Miss Miller were their father's heirs."

Fooks glanced at the list he'd written. "This syndicate had six investors. Can you tell me the extent of each shareholder's interest?"

"I'm afraid not. Need to know basis, and I didn't need to know. This is a private arrangement between influential businessmen. Those types of men are notorious for wanting to keep their dealings out of the public domain. Including mine."

"Quite so, quite so," Fooks murmured, contemplating his next question. "Has anyone asked you about the tontine before?"

"The heirs of Mr. Bagley and Mr. Miller. I couldn't tell them very much other than to refer them to Templeton, Taylor and Lee."

"Did any of the shareholders take an active part in the running of the theater?"

Downton stiffened. "Mr. Kinsey poked his nose in from time to time."

Fooks and Caroline swapped glances.

"What do you mean, Mr. Downton?" Caroline asked. "Poked his nose where exactly?"

Downton focused on mopping his brow. "It is of no account now as Mr. Kinsey is—"

"Come now, Mr. Downton. Anything you tell us about my late uncle's business affairs can only help in finding his killer. Surely you wouldn't argue with my wish to exonerate my husband and levy blame on the real murderer?"

"No. Of course not, Mrs. Martin. My reticence to say is because I've no wish to speak ill of the dead."

"Very admirable, but in this case perhaps I might prevail upon you—"

"He seemed determined to involve himself in the creative direction of the theater." Downton licked his lips. "Unfortunately, he had no real understanding of our audience. Or of my artistic fellows. Several long-serving and much-loved members of the ensemble quit because of his meddling. I'm afraid to say his interference become insufferable. To the point revenue fell and audience numbers declined."

"And what did the other shareholders think of his actions?" Fooks asked.

"I'm sure I don't know. I only ever see them when they avail themselves of their boxes. Which for some is very irregular. None discuss theater business with me."

Fooks stood. Unlikely Downton had any more useful information.

Caroline took his hint and rose. She reluctantly held out her hand. "Thank you, Mr. Downton. You have been most helpful. We won't take up any more of your valuable time." She suffered Downton's caresses again before sweeping out.

In the carriage outside, Caroline pulled off her gloves and threw them to the floor. "Ugh! Odious man."

Fooks' eyes sparkled in amusement. "But helpful." He waved the list of addresses triumphantly. "He's also added himself to my list of suspects."

"Do you think—"

"There's still a long way to go. Hopefully I'll get to speak to Gray and Miss Miller tomorrow when they're back at Kinsey House." He folded his legs and arms, satisfaction on his face.

Late that night, unable to sleep, Fooks sat in his room at Fairfield House, feet on a pouffe, reading the other documents from the safe. Most concerned Kinsey's business affairs, but one was more sinister. A typewritten note, unsigned. It read:

> *Know what you are. Men are on notice and will drop everything to do what's necessary. Back off.*

Fooks frowned. "Hmm."

A light knock on the door and Fooks slid his eyes over to the clock on the nightstand. The hands showed ten after two. In the morning. *Bound to be Swan.*

"Yes?"

The door opened and Swan's head appeared, grinning. "Thought ya'd be up." He silently entered the room.

"Come in, why don't you?" Fooks tried to keep the irritation from his voice while he gathered the papers. He hated being thought of as predictable, but this interruption shouldn't surprise him. Swan was all too familiar with his late-night habit.

"Ya don't change do you Fooks?" Swan said, with a chuckle. He took a seat by Fooks, ignoring the rhetorical question.

"Of course, I'm up. I'm a Pinkerton." Fooks beamed, broadly. "We never sleep." He quoted their motto and sobered. "I sleep better these days usually. Believe me, after months of being kept awake by a crying baby you learn to grab sleep when you can."

"Being a father suiting ya?"

Fooks smiled slowly. "Yeah, its real good. We're over the worst of the teething now." He rolled his eyes. "I think."

"What ya got there?"

"Oh, the other papers we found in Kinsey's safe."

Swan raised his eyebrows. "Anything interesting?"

"Mainly business, but what do you think to this?" Fooks passed over the note.

Swan studied it for a moment before handing it back. "Short and to the point."

"Looks like blackmail to me."

"Wouldn't surprise me. Kinsey wasn't exactly pure as the driven snow."

"So you keep saying. D'you have any proof?"

Swan pursed his lips for a moment and shook his head. "Nope. He was too clever for that. He had folks who worked for him though." He shrugged. "Maybe ask them?"

"Who d'you suggest? Brook became evasive when I asked him."

"'Cos he don't know. He likes to act all big and knowledgeable because he lives in the same house, but in reality, he knows very little. Kinsey has an office manager. Dunno his name, an' I think there's a girl who does things."

"I think Brook said his name is Albinus Gray. Did Kinsey have a separate office?"

Swan shook his head. "Not that I'm aware. Thought he ran his business affairs from the study ya saw." He raised his head. "Still using the Pinkerton shield and identification Sticky got hold of for ya?"

"Yep." Fooks said. "The identity card is out of date though. A Captain Loomis who is in charge of the investigation pointed it out."

Swan grunted. "Came in useful," he murmured. "Gonna get a new one?"

"Tobe, I'm a law-abiding storekeeper remember?"

"Who carries fake identification, breaks into folks' houses and burgles their safes."

Fooks glared at him. "Shut up," he said, with a growl. "What are you doing up at this hour anyway? You like your sleep too much. Ah." Suddenly he realized and put his head down to hide the smirk on his lips.

Swan had the good grace to redden. "Never mind that. What else did ya find out in those documents?"

"Like I said, mainly business but, er," he turned behind him to the nightstand, "this one is interesting."

He passed it over. Waited. And waited some more.

Swan frowned, rubbed his chin and pursed his lips. Finally, he sniffed and handed it back.

"Lot of numbers. Looks like a set of accounts to me. You'd know better'n me."

Fooks nodded. "Yeah, what I figured. 'Cept, I think something's wrong."

"Like what?"

"Don't add up for one thing."

Swan held out his hand and received the document back. He studied it again. "Ya right, it don't." He caught Fooks' frown. "What?"

"I haven't studied it properly yet, but I reckon someone had their fingers in the pie."

"Who?"

Fooks shrugged. "Can't tell from this. Need to get a sight of the main accounts. Figure I'd go and speak to Albinus Gray tomorrow." He picked up the short note again. "Y'know Tobe, this could be a blackmail note to you."

"Kinsey never sent me anything."

Fooks hesitated. "How about *to* him?"

Swan stiffened. "What are you saying?" When Fooks didn't speak, he added, "D'ya think I sent the note?"

"No," Fooks denied emphatically. "But it's a little hard to prove who did."

"Maybe Kinsey planned to send it to whoever cooked the books?"

Fooks pursed his lips. "Awh, could mean a lot of things. I tell you what, we won't solve anything here tonight. Go back to your room and let me sleep on it. I'll see what Albinus Gray has to say tomorrow."

CHAPTER SIXTEEN

The next morning, Fooks went alone to Kinsey House. When the carriage stopped outside, a movement caught the corner of his eye.

Two men hid at the junction, one looking his way. When Fooks regarded them fully, one ducked away and the watcher turned his eyes to the ground. Neither bearing suggested police. *Hmm, if I didn't know better, I'd say they were watching me.* He sighed. *Something else to deal with. Later.*

Inside Kinsey House, Fooks found the office. The manager, Albinus Gray, was a small, middle-aged man with a stooped posture.

"Yes, Mr. Brook informed me you would call," Gray said, when Fooks introduced himself.

"Is now a good time?"

"As any." Gray indicated Fooks should take a seat at the desk with the typewriter on it.

"The girl who types not here?" Fooks asked, stating the obvious.

He received a barely veiled look of disgust. "Miss Miller? No, she left to attend to a personal matter."

Fooks' eyes narrowed. Miller. He'd heard that name before. "No doubt I will catch her another time." He took out his notepad. "How long have you worked for Mr. Kinsey?"

"I would say about ten years."

"Are you privy to all Mr. Kinsey's business affairs?"

"Most of them."

Ah, so that's the way it's gonna be, is it? Fooks crossed his legs and stared at Gray hard. "What was Mr. Kinsey's business?"

"If you want me to pigeonhole his affairs, I will say, he conducted investments."

"What sort of investments?"

"His interests were many and various."

Fooks could tell by Gray's demeanor **that** he wasn't going to say precisely. Fooks scribbled that down, ending with a deliberate period. "Did Mr. Kinsey have any business associates?"

"Yes, with varying degrees of closeness. Mr. Ephraim Smith is his main business associate."

"Does Mr. Smith work from here?"

"No. He has his own office on the other side of Boston."

"What is the nature of their business partnership?"

Gray hesitated. "It's not for me to divulge the nature of the arrangement."

"No, quite." Fooks chewed his bottom lip, thoughtfully. "I will speak to Mr. Smith in due course. Do you have much contact with him?"

"He and Mr. Kinsey meet here regularly. I pay his expenses."

"How often are they paid?"

"Once a month. After I checked the details naturally."

"Naturally. Was everything usually in order?"

Gray nodded.

Not getting anywhere with this line of questioning. Perhaps I'll circle back later. Let's try a slightly different avenue. "Can I see the accounts?"

Gray hesitated. "Is that strictly necessary?"

"Strictly? Yes, please."

"The accounts are confidential, Mr. Crane. I should check first."

"Who can you check with? Mr. Kinsey—"

"I will check with Mrs. Kinsey or Mr. Brook." Gray stood.

Let the man go through his procedures.

After Gray's footsteps receded, Fooks inspected the bookshelf behind where Gray had sat. As Fooks suspected, this year's account ledger was there. He cast a wary eye at the open door, before heaving the heavy, leather-bound ledger onto the desk. He understood enough of accounts from The Hardware Store books.

Fooks quickly took out the pages of accounts he'd brought with him. He found the relevant page in the ledger and compared. A quick glance told him there were differences. If what he'd found was correct, the ledger should be understated. Yet no way of knowing for sure without seeing the original documents, invoices and expenses and such like. He turned several more pages, inspecting the entries carefully. He couldn't find any further discrepancies from such a cursory glance.

He closed the ledger with a thud and tucked away the alternative accounts. He rested his hands on top of the ledger, thinking. "Hmmm." Then when footsteps sounded in the corridor, he quickly returned the ledger to the shelf. He was once again in his seat when Gray reappeared.

"I spoke to Mrs. Kinsey. She has agreed to you seeing the accounts."

"Excellent," Fooks said, with a smile when the ledger he'd so recently inspected was presented to him.

"These are the accounts for this year. Previous years are audited and kept elsewhere."

Fooks drew the ledger towards him.   From his pocket, he brought out a glasses case, making a great show of polishing the lenses with the cloth provided. Finally blemish free to his satisfaction, he put on the wire-rimmed glasses and opened the ledger at a random page.

Several long minutes of grunts, sniffs and hmmms followed as Fooks ran his eye and his finger down the columns of figures.

"Is there a problem, Mr. Crane?" Gray asked, after a while.

Fooks started. "What? Oh no. Everything appears in order, Mr. Gray." He closed the ledger and slid it across the desk towards Gray.

Gray's look seemed to say 'naturally' and he put the ledger away. Afterwards he stood, expecting the interview to end there. He grunted in disappointment when Fooks gestured to the chair once more.

"Did Mr. Kinsey make any enemies?" Fooks asked, when Gray settled.

"I'm not aware," Gray paused, thoughtfully, "of any at the moment."

Fooks narrowed his eyes. *Odd choice of words.* "You worked for him for ten years. How did you like working for him?"

Gray sat still and silent for a moment. "He could be challenging."

"In what way?"

Gray face took on a pained expression. "His instructions were not always well thought out. There were often discrepancies between what he said and what he did."

"Can you give me an example?"

"No." Gray added, "I can't think of a specific one right now." Fooks stared at him, intently. "Perhaps one will come to me as we talk further."

"Perhaps," Fooks murmured, and glanced at his notes. "Did you get on well with Mr. Kinsey?"

Gray picked up a pencil and played with it. "We were not overly friendly. Mr. Kinsey was not given to showering praise on his employees."

"I see. Would you say Mr. Kinsey treated you badly?"

Gray frowned. "What exactly do you mean?"

"Was he ever violent?"

"He liked things done in a certain way. I accommodated him to the best of my ability."

"He was exacting in what he expected of you and you worked for Mr. Kinsey for ten years without complaint. Long time. Did Mr. Kinsey recognize your devotion to him?"

"He paid a good salary, which I am happy with."

"Not quite what I asked you, Mr. Gray."

"It's the only answer I have."

Fooks licked his lips. "Were you looking for alternative employment?"

"I suspect I am now."

Fooks swallowed. "So, before this happened, was your intention to leave?"

Gray winced. "Yes, but not of my choosing. Mr. Kinsey told me he intended to give Mr. Brook this job."

"What did you think to that notion?" *This'll be interesting. I doubt Brook's wild on the idea.*

"Mr. Kinsey could do as he pleased."

"Yes, but you musta been somewhat peeved, given the length of time you'd worked for Mr. Kinsey and all his challenging demands. Now he was about to give your job to his son. How did you feel?"

Gray raised his chin. "I'm sure Mr. Brook will manage."

Fooks pressed his lips into a thin line. *Hmmm, here is a man trying to keep a brave face, knowing he was being slighted.* Fooks discerned Gray's discomfort with this line of questioning. He decided not to prolong it any further. He had all the information he wanted on the subject.

Fooks chewed his bottom lip. "Very well, I'll leave this for now. When did you last see Mr. Kinsey?"

"In the afternoon. At five. I asked to leave early."

"What is your usual finishing time?"

"Six o'clock, but sometimes I work later."

"Why did you want to leave early?"

"I wished to attend my daughter's school play that evening."

"Did you leave Miss Miller alone in the office?"

"She had some typing to finish and she usually leaves around six. I asked Grieveson to look in on her to make sure she was all right."

"Thoughtful of you."

Gray inclined his head in acknowledgment.

Fooks went on. "So, you were at your daughter's school play at the time of the murder?"

"I believe so, yes."

"Do you know about the tontine Mr. Kinsey had invested in the Hayes Theater?"

"Yes, but the yearly dividend stopped about four years ago."

"Why did it stop?"

Gray shrugged. "I presume Mr. Kinsey's nominee died. Templeton, Taylor and Lee are responsible for the dividend payments. Perhaps you should try them."

Fooks pulled a face. "I've already done so. Do you know who his nominee was?"

"No."

"But you do understand this form of investment is secured on the life of another person?"

"I do."

"Do you own a gun, Mr. Gray?"

Gray cleared his throat at the abruptness of the question. "I do not."

"Ever used one?"

"Mr. Crane! Never in my life," he said, with a gasp.

"It is alleged Mr. Kinsey sent the two men who shot Mr. Martin? Were you aware of this?"

"No."

"Did Mr. Kinsey have men who, er," Fooks paused, "he called on for more forceful persuasion?"

"I've no idea."

"Do you think it likely Mr. Kinsey had such men he could call upon if needed?"

"I've really no idea."

Fooks took a deep breath and folded his notepad. He was getting nowhere here. Either Gray wouldn't say, or Gray truly didn't know. He patted the notepad resting on his crossed knee. "You said Mr. Smith has his own office. Where exactly?"

"On the corner of Milk Street and Congress. He has someone there who manages his correspondence and his diary. Name of Pritchard. I would suggest telephoning for an appointment. Mr. Smith is invariably out of the office."

Fooks blanched at the mention of the telephone.

CHAPTER SEVENTEEN

Really must get to grips with this new technology, but not in front of strangers. "Perhaps I could ask you to do that?" Fooks asked and swallowed. *Say yes. Say yes.*

Gray produced a small book from his desk drawer. He leafed through until he found the correct page, before going to the telephone apparatus on the wall.

Fooks watched in fascination as Gray lifted the earpiece on the left of the box and cranked the handle on the other side several times. Seconds ticked by before anything else happened, then Gray spoke into the central mouthpiece. "3-7-8 please."

Further time elapsed before, "Ah, Pritchard, Gray here. I have a Mr. Crane in my office. He's a Pinkerton detective. Yes. Yes, concerning Mr. Kinsey's passing. He'd like to see Mr. Smith. When would be convenient? Yes, I'll hold."

"Soon as possible, Mr. Gray, given the circumstances," Fooks said.

A moment later, Gray held up a finger, listening.

"Nothing sooner?" he asked, into the mouthpiece. "Very well, I'll communicate this to Mr. Crane. Thank you. Goodbye."

Gray hung up the earpiece and gave the handle one last turn. "Not until Friday morning of next week."

Fooks opened his mouth. "That's over a week away!"

Gray sat, shrugging. "I'm sorry Mr. Crane. Pritchard is aware of the reason, but Mr. Smith is simply not available before."

Fooks growled. He thought briefly about going along anyway, perhaps waylaying said gentleman outside in the street. Instead, he stood. "Oh well, I suppose that'll have to do. Will he be at the funeral on Saturday?"

"I expect so." Gray opened his mouth, horrified. "Really Mr. Crane, it would hardly be appropriate—"

"No of course not. Thank you, Mr. Gray. I think that'll be all for now." He was about to leave when he noticed a safe in the corner. In truth, he'd noticed it when he first walked into the room, but now was the perfect opportunity to ask about it.

"Who knows the combination to this safe?"

"Mr. Kinsey and I."

"Not Miss Miller?"

"Absolutely not." Gray's answer was emphatic. "Miss Miller is employed to type. Nothing more."

"How long has Miss Miller worked here?" Fooks retrieved his notepad.

"Six months, I would say."

"And before Miss Miller?"

"The previous typewriter operator went off to marry."

Fooks made as if to go when he stopped again. "I forgot to ask. How was the school play?"

"A middle schooler production, Mr. Crane. Hardly up to Globe Theater standards." Gray actually grinned. "But I wouldn't have missed it for the world."

Fooks smiled and gave a cheery wave goodbye. He twitched his head as he walked along the corridor, deep in thought. He almost collided with Captain Loomis coming the other way.

"Crane, I heard you were here again. What are you up to this time?" Loomis snarled around his lit cigar.

Fooks recovered from his surprise quickly and looked delighted to see him. "Captain Loomis, how nice to see you again," he said, greeting the police captain like a long-lost friend. "Are you well?"

"Never mind that. What are you doing here? You've been asking questions again, haven't you?"

Fooks shrugged. "Of course. It's what Mrs. Martin is paying me for. We both want to find Kinsey's murderer, don't we? Y'know Captain, the Pinkertons and the police have a long history of co-operation. Why don't we pool resources? What are your clues? Is Martin your only suspect?"

"Don't give me that Crane. I'm gonna check you out. If the Pinkerton's Chicago office doesn't have a detective called Joseph Crane—"

Fooks blinked in surprise. "Oh, did I say Chicago? I meant New York. Recently transferred and, well, force of habit y'know—"

"Now listen here Crane." The hand holding the cigar jabbed its forefinger into Fooks' shoulder. Smoke trailed into Fooks' nose but he resisted the urge to cough. "I don't know who the heck you are but I'm warning you. Stay outta my investigation. Or I'll be forced to arrest you for interfering with police business. Got it?" A further jab reinforced his message.

"Yeah, sure, I promise to stay outta your investigation. Don't mind if I conduct my own though, do you? Got a couple of leads I wanna run down."

Loomis stuffed the cigar back in his mouth. "Stay outta my way." He stalked off along the corridor.

Fooks watched him go, pursing his lips thoughtfully. Loomis might be a problem. *Don't I have enough to deal with?*

"You again?" came the annoyed greeting, when Fooks met Brook Kinsey in the hall on his way out. The younger man dressed smartly. An overpowering smell of cologne lingered about him.

Fooks glanced down at himself. "I appear to be, yes." He ignored the hostility. "I'm glad I ran into you. I have a few more questions."

"Can't they wait? I'm on my way out." Brook continued towards the front door.

"Oh, they won't take long," Fooks said. He ignored the hint of refusal and purposefully stepped in front of Brook.

Brook, pulling up short, tossed his head.

Fooks took this as permission to begin. With a quick grin, he pulled out his notepad and leafed through it. "I've been speaking to Gray. He tells me your father expected you to take over from him. Were you aware of this?"

"Yeah, Father mentioned it."

"And how did you feel about it? After all, I understand Gray worked with your father for some years. He knew the ropes."

Brook shrugged. "It's what Father wanted."

"You don't sound very enthusiastic."

"Why should I be?"

Fooks pursed his lips. "I dunno. Chance to work with your father. Learn his business. Maybe take over in due course."

"Too many other things to do right now."

"Like what?"

"My business, Crane. Now if—" He made for the door again.

Fooks touched Brook's arm. "Not necessarily. If it's relevant to your father's murder—" His voice became colder.

"It isn't," Brook said, through gritted teeth. His scowl intensified when Fooks made a notation in his pad.

"Your mother mentioned that, in one iteration of your father's will, he left the remainder of the estate to Mrs. Martin. You seemed upset. Why?"

"Wouldn't you be if your father left his money to a cousin who has more than enough already?"

Fooks pulled a face, considering. "Perhaps, but you aren't sure yet. When is the reading of the will?"

"After the funeral. On Saturday afternoon."

Fooks bit his lip and grunted. *Two days away.* "I guess you'll find out then. By the way, can you tell me the combination of the safe?"

"The one in the office? No."

"I meant the one in your father's study."

"There isn't a safe in Father's study."

"Hidden behind the bookcase." Fooks raised his eyebrows in surprise. "You mean you didn't know about it?"

Brook grunted. "If it's hidden, how did you find it?"

"Got a nose for these things." Fooks smiled enigmatically and tapped his nose. "When you've been in this business as long as I have, you can sniff 'em out." He glanced at the ruined study door. "Speaking of the study, have the police found the key yet?"

"Not to my knowledge. Now is that all, Crane?"

"No, not quite. Do you own a gun, Mr. Kinsey?"

Brook stared at him. "How dare you?"

"Simple enough question. Why can't you answer?" Fooks' voice took on a noticeably harder tone.

"I choose not to. Now if you'll excuse me." He pushed roughly past.

Fooks watched with a smirk as Brook stalked to the door. *Yep, definitely rattled.* Time to find out more about Mr. Brook Kinsey. Perhaps Swan could help.

CHAPTER EIGHTEEN

As Fooks walked into Swan's suite at Fairfield House, Swan bounded to his feet eagerly. "Ah, 'bout time ya got back. What have ya found out?"

Fooks flopped into the nearest chair. Swan crossed to the decanter and poured two glasses of whiskey.

"Here." Swan held out a glass to his partner. "Ya look as though you can use this."

"Yes." Fooks took a long pull and rested his head back, letting the warmth sink slowly down inside him. "Been a helluva day."

"Found out anything?"

"Too much." Fooks took another sip.

Swan frowned at him. "What's that supposed to mean?"

Fooks sat up. "It means I'm not sure I can keep all this straight." He shook his head. "There's lots of different avenues to explore. I'm getting more questions than answers right now." He shook his head again.

"This may help." Swan put down his glass and yelled, "Cowdry!"

Fooks blinked in surprise. *Thought we were alone.*

Cowdry appeared from the dressing room. "Yes sir," he said, and more quietly, "You bellowed."

Fooks heard the last remark and hid his smile. He was beginning to like this young man, who always happened to be in the right place at the right time. Swan had found an unlikely ally here in this strange new world he'd chosen.

"Cowdry, Stephen Lesley out at Ardmaddy has a blackboard he uses occasionally. Tomorrow, would you arrange for it to be set up in my rooms there? We'll be going down on Sunday."

"A blackboard sir?"

"Yeah, it's for writing things on. It'll help Mr. Crane keep track of his investigation."

Swan flopped back into his chair as Cowdry returned to the dressing room.

"You..." Fooks began, but Swan held up a hand. He appeared to be listening. Swan nodded in satisfaction at the faint click of a door. He gestured for Fooks to continue.

Fooks grinned. "I was gonna say, how natural you are ordering folks about."

"Don't come natural but I guess I'm used to it now. Cowdry and me have an understanding, you might say. Reminds me of you sometimes."

"Perhaps. Who's Stephen Lesley?"

"He's the estate manager out at Ardmaddy. Been working closely with him the last few months."

Yep, Tobe has sure settled in well here. "Why are we going to Ardmaddy? Out at Waltham, isn't it?"

"Easier for me to hide out there. Ya'll like Ardmaddy. Lots of room and open country." He paused. "Getting the feeling ya not enjoying Boston, Fooks."

"Not too much. Isn't moving you risky?"

Swan twitched his head. "Risky staying here, but lots more places to hide out there. I'll be safer."

Fooks pondered for a moment, before giving his attention back to the matter in hand. "What d'you know about Brook Kinsey?"

Swan twitched his head. "Typical son of a powerful man. Rich, lazy, never done a day's work in his life, hangs out with others like him."

"What does the death of his father mean to him?"

Swan grunted. "End of the gravy chain."

"Working as his father's assistant in place of Albinus Gray wouldn't sit very well, would it?"

Swan laughed. "I couldn't see it happening."

"Well apparently it's what Robert Kinsey had in mind."

Swan laughed again. "Always figured he was muddled in the head."

Fooks licked his lips. "I ran into Brook as I was leaving Kinsey House earlier. Asked him if he owned a gun. He wouldn't answer."

"Awh, don't read too much into it. He owns nothing. Not even the clothes on his back. Pa paid for everything." Swan paused. "I seen Brook at the Club. He's a wild gambler—"

"A gambler? Has he got debts?"

"'Xpect so. No doubt Pa bailed him out regular."

Fooks considered. "Kinsey might have wanted Brook to take over from Gray in the hope Brook would learn the value of money—"

"Can't see it myself."

Fooks rose slowly, thinking. "Unless Kinsey threatened to cut him off." He began to pace. "How's this? Kinsey gets fed up with bailing Kinsey Junior out, so he suggests he comes work for him in place of Gray. If he doesn't clean up his act, he'll cut him out of his will. But Kinsey hadn't thought up a scheme to get rid of Gray before he's murdered."

Swan chewed his lips. "Possible I suppose."

Fooks turned on his heel and frowned at Swan. "What club? Brook mentioned a club to me."

"The Stratton Country Club." Swan beamed with a twinkle in his eye. "It's a gentleman's club a ways outta Boston. I'm a member."

Fooks sank back into his chair and swallowed. "You're a member of a rich man's club?" His eyes popped.

"Sure I am. I'm a rich man these days. It's a good club. Although I go mainly for the golf. Got a real low handicap. Picked it up real quick."

Fooks shook his head. "Golf!"

"Yeah, if we get this thing sorted, I'll take ya for a round." Swan raised his eyebrows. "Mary might appreciate you having a hobby."

Fooks twitched his bottom lip at the mention of his wife. "I need to get this sorted soon. I miss her and Susan."

Swan gave him a sympathetic look. "Wish I could help ya more—"

"I know. I'm getting there." Fooks nodded, determined. "Just gotta do this methodically. Can't be rushed."

"What are your plans for tomorrow?"

"I wanted to see Kinsey's business partner, but he can't fit me in until next week." Fooks widened his eyes. "You'd think he would find space for me, wouldn't you?" He took out his notepad and flicked through his notes. "Can't waste time, so might as well track down some of the other tontine holders." He pursed his lips. "Perhaps start with Eugene Camden."

The next morning Fooks took a cab to visit Eugene Camden. The driver asked if he was sure when Fooks gave him the address. Scanning around when they stopped, Fooks conceded he might be right.

He'd arrived near to the port, and this didn't strike him as the address of a wealthy businessman. The street was tenement housing. Working men loitered on the corners smoking, and ragged children played in the street.

The stares coming his way made the hairs on the back of his neck prick up.

He checked the address again. Yep, definitely it. He shrugged. Might as well inquire within, as they say.

He climbed the steep steps and knocked. No answer. He knocked again, louder.

A first-floor window pushed up and a tousled male head appeared. "Who's that tick-tocking on my Rory?" yelled the head.

Fooks stepped back and almost fell down the steps, grabbing the handrail just in time. "Sorry to disturb you. My name's Joseph Crane. I'm looking for a Eugene Camden. Is that you?"

"No mate. No Eugene Camden round here."

"Given this address. Perhaps he lived here a while ago?"

"I've lived here donkey's ears mate. I ain't never heard of no Eugene Camden."

A window of the house next door raised and another head appeared. "What's the box of toys all about? I'm trying to get my bo-peep."

"Geezer's here looking for a Eugene Camden. Do yer know him?"

The second head shook. "I never heards of him. I'll ask Peg." The head disappeared. "Peg, you ever heard of a geezer called Eugene Camden?" he yelled inside.

"Why d'yer wanna know Eddie?" came back a female voice belonging to Peg.

"Geezer out here at next door's Rory."

"Geezer? What geezer?" A female head appeared next to Eddie.

Fooks tipped his hat.

"Oh, I say." She patted her blond curls and adjusted her gown over her ample bosom. "Don't often get gents like you round here during the day. What's yer name, dearie?"

"Ma'am, my name is Joseph Crane, and I'm looking for Eugene Camden."

"What d'yer want him for?" asked the first head.

"You mind your nose, Harold Stanton," Peg called.

"He knocked on my bleedin' Rory, Peg Carter. I gets to ask the questions."

Fooks flicked his eyes from one to the other.

"Well go on Harold Stanton, ask the questions."

"I already told him. I don't know no Eugene Camden."

"That's 'cos yer don't remember names."

"I remember yours," Harold roared back before peering down at Fooks. "What's his boat race like?"

Fooks gaped. "Boat race?"

"Yeah." Harold waved a hand over his face. "What's he look like?"

Fooks shrugged. "I don't know."

"What's he say?" called Peg.

"He says he doesn't know."

"How can he look for someone if he don't know what he looks like?"

"I don't know. You ask him."

It was at this point that Fooks decided it'd be wise to make his escape. He turned, tipped his hat and called a thank you. Unfortunately, he hadn't realized how close to the edge of the steps he was. The next thing he knew he was whirling in space.

CHAPTER NINETEEN

"Yeow!"

Years of hard living cushioned Fooks for the impact. He'd learnt how to fall and limit the damage to his body. Yet he still grunted. Pain crashed through his body as he bounced down the steps. *Out of practice. Ow. Ow. Ow.*

"Now look what yer done," said Eddie. "Geezer's fallen down the apples and pears."

Fooks sprawled in an untidy and painful heap on the sidewalk. He staggered to his feet slowly and brushed himself down. *Just about all-in-one piece.*

"He's got himself in a right old two and eight now," said Eddie. "What d'yer wanna go and do that for Peg?"

"Well, I didn't push him, did I? You all right, dearie?"

Fooks straightened his hat. "Yes, thank you."

He walked away, pinching the bridge of his nose. He was getting a headache; he was sure of it. Not to mention hip, arm, shoulder and leg ache.

Before he'd walked much further, a young woman stopped him. "Overheard yer asking for Eugene Camden."

"Yes ma'am. Do you have any idea where I can find him?"

The woman pulled her shawl around her and sniffed. "No, but the heap of coke who lived there ages ago went abroad, I hear."

Fooks pointed back to the lethal steps. "Back there? Number thirteen?" Only now did he recognize the irony of the number.

"Yeah. You the police?" Her eyes popped. "Has he gorn and murdered someone?"

"No ma'am." He tipped his hat. "Much obliged ma'am." He hurried away, more than willing to dismiss Eugene Camden from his list of suspects.

Fooks had to walk some distance to a more affluent district before he could hail a cab again. By then he was aching all over and just wanted to sit down. The first cab he hailed sailed by, the driver giving him a black look, and a second did the same.

He viewed himself in the plate glass of a shop window. The fall on the steps had done nothing for his appearance.

Fooks straightened his clothes and brushed away some of the dust. Only then did he start off in the direction of Fairfield House, hoping he wouldn't have to walk all the way. As he figured out where he was, he saw them. *Ha, a tall skinny fella with yellow, blond hair and a short stocky fella with a broken nose. Reckon you're the two who shot Swan.*

He glanced quickly about. He'd been around hard cases for long enough to be fully acquainted with their method. His current surroundings presented a prime opportunity for them to waylay him. *Great. Not sure I feel up to it, but I suppose now's as good time as any.*

As he walked past an entrance to an alley, he wasn't disappointed. He was ready when they ushered him firmly into the alley. Walls rose high on either side. No windows looked out. Only wide enough for two men to walk abreast. A short way inside, a meager light permeated.

Stocky tried to get behind him. Fooks went to stop him. He found himself shoved against the wall. Stocky leaned against him, trapping his right shoulder in place.

Fooks kept his back to the wall. *Let's face 'em head on.* Stocky held a knife against his throat. Skinny stood back watching.

"What d'you want?" Fooks asked. His eyes flicked from one to the other. In his left pocket, his fingers closed around the reassuring presence of his Schofield.

"Heard you've been asking questions," the stocky fella said, his voice low and gravelly in Fooks' ear.

Fooks pursed his lips. "Can you be more specific?" Fooks winced when the point of the knife nicked him. Hot blood trickled down his neck.

Stocky looked to Skinny for an answer.

"'Bout the Kinsey murder." Skinny kept his gaze locked on Fooks. "The cops are after the fella who did it, so why are *you* asking questions?"

Fooks struggled. Stocky held him tightly. The knife nicked him again. He stopped struggling. "Okay. Okay. What d'you wanna know?"

"Who hired you?"

"Mrs. Martin. She's convinced her husband didn't kill Kinsey. So, I'm looking in a different direction."

Stocky growled. "We don't want ya looking in another direction." His words were slow and deliberate.

His breath smelt acrid. *Cheap cheroots. Ugh.* Fooks grunted. "I have to go where my investigation takes me."

"Your investigation is wrong," Stocky snarled.

Skinny took a step closer to Fooks. "Martin is as good as hanged. Why rock the boat?"

"Simple." Fooks paused and grinned slowly. "'Cos he didn't do it."

Skinny narrowed his eyes. "You got proof?"

"Not yet, but I'm working on it." Fooks willed Skinny to accept his word.

Skinny laughed briefly. "So now here's the thing. We don't want anyone else but Martin in the sights for Kinsey's murder."

"Oh?" Fooks feigned surprise. *Did these two men kill Kinsey? Doubt if they're gonna admit it to me. Perhaps there's another reason.* "Why?"

"Our business," Stocky growled in Fooks' ear and tightened his hold.

"Yeah. Yeah, I get that. Now," Fooks swallowed, "you look like a reasonable fella." He addressed his remark to Skinny, having concluded he was the more intelligent of the two. "Why does it matter to you who killed him?" Fooks paused, and hoped he was doing the right thing by pushing it. "Unless of course you know who did. Someone," he deliberately looked askance at Stocky, "closer to home." He finished slowly, letting his words and their meaning wash over them both.

"Hush your mouth," Stocky hissed. He raised the knife before Fooks' eyes.

Fooks tightened his fingers on his Schofield, irritated that it was in his left pocket, but it would have to do. He hoped there was enough light in the alley for what he had in mind.

He turned his head towards Stocky, enduring the man's halitosis. "Cut me again and your friend dies," he said, coolly and calmly.

Stocky laughed. In his pocket, Fooks pointed the Schofield at Skinny. He thanked a deity he wasn't sure existed, for his suit probably already ruined beyond repair. If he fired they'd be a nice hole in his pocket. *Shame, but hey ho, needs must.*

"You're bluffing," said Skinny. He eyed Fooks warily.

"I never bluff." Fooks said it quietly. The click of the hammer sounded loud in the close alley. The hammer rested above an empty chamber, but they didn't know that.

"Okay. Okay." Skinny held up his hands. "Let him go."

Stocky growled, noting the extended pocket pointing in Skinny's direction. When he met Fooks' eyes, Fooks twitched his head and jabbed the gun more forcefully.

"Let him go!" Skinny screamed.

Stocky moved away slowly to stand beside Skinny. Fooks brought the gun out and transferred it to his right hand, where it belonged. He released the trigger. "Now, gentlemen, let's start this conversation again."

In full outlaw leader mode now, Fooks had done playing. He motioned for them to raise their hands.

"Now I have a few questions of my own. Why do you want Martin to take the fall for Kinsey's murder? Is it because you know someone else did it?" He glanced from one to the other. "Or is it 'cos you don't want the police looking for you two?"

Stocky made a lunge. Fooks caught the huge flying fist in his left hand, flipped the palm up, twisted and forced it towards the ground. Stocky yelled.

Fooks leveled the gun at him and cocked it. His finger curled around the trigger. Skinny tugged Stocky back into line. Disgruntled, Stocky rubbed his wrist and glowered at Fooks.

Satisfied they would behave, Fooks released the trigger again. "Let's finish our discussion," he said, reasonably. "The police have a good description of the two men wanted for shooting Martin. I'd say it matches you two perfectly."

Skinny shifted uncomfortably. "Who are you?" he growled.

"Joseph Crane," Fooks said. *No reason not to tell them.*

Skinny shook his head. "No, you ain't. You're something else."

"Perhaps this is what you mean." Fooks awkwardly crossed his body for his right pocket. The two stiffened. "Calm yourselves. I meant this." He held up the Pinkerton's shield.

Skinny sucked in a deep breath and let it out slowly. Stocky took a step back.

"Now," Fooks was all business, "we have a better understanding of the situation; I'll give you two boys a piece of advice." He paused, gauging their reaction. "I'm looking into Kinsey's murder, but it isn't taking me in Martin's direction. Which means I won't be considering Martin's earlier shooting. So, you can take it from me, you two boys are safe."

Then he marshaled the authoritative voice he'd used to keep the Guardian Wall Gang in line. Dropping the tone low and slow, he added, "Unless you get in my way."

Don't think those two will bother me again. Fooks watched the two men turn and run. He put a hand to his neck and his nose wrinkled at the blood he came away with. He waited until they had gone before following slowly. Out on the street, he looked both ways. No sign of them. *Good.*

It was early evening by the time Fooks returned to Fairfield House. He eased his aching body into a warm foamy bath with pleasure. A relief to finally be still and silent. He closed his eyes and allowed himself to drift off.

Only to jerk upright with a splash a moment later when the bathroom door crashed back against the wall.

"Ya back. Thanks for coming to see me."

Swan closed the door and tipped Fooks' clothes from the chair. He made himself comfortable.

Fooks leaned his head back. "You can see that I'm in the bath?" He stated the obvious in an icy tone.

Swan appeared innocence personified. "So? I've seen ya in the bath afore. You me for that matter."

Fooks scowled. "I've had a long day. I wanted to have a nice soak before I came to you."

"I'm here now. What did ya find out?"

"Some things."

Swan tsk'd.

"What's that supposed to mean? I've been all over Boston in the past few days. Some parts I never wanna go to again, I might add."

Swan looked put out. "Don't ya like our fair city? More civilized than New York. Less windy than Chicago. More culture than San Francisco. What's not to like?"

Fooks ignored him. "I haven't been to those places, so I can't compare," he said, when Swan expected an answer.

"Ya been to San Francisco. I've been with ya."

Fooks stared at the ceiling and licked his lips, biting down his irritation. "Leave me alone, Swan."

"Oooh, he called me Swan." He stood, feigning surprise. "I'd better do as he says."

"Yes, you'd better. I'll come and find you when I'm finished."

Fooks rested his head back and tried to find the relaxed state he'd been in before his rude interruption. No matter how hard he tried, it wasn't coming back. In the end he gave up and attended to his ablutions.

Half an hour later he emerged from the bathroom, tying the robe belt. To find Cowdry pottering about in the main room.

"Nice bath, sir?"

"The bath was fine; it was the company that wasn't."

"Pardon me, sir?"

Fooks waved a hand for Cowdry to forget it. Instead, he crossed to the tallboy and took up a comb. "Cowdry, you're English, aren't you?" he asked, suddenly, turning to face the valet.

"I like to think of myself as American now, sir."

"Yes, but you originally came from England. Didn't you?"

"Yes sir."

"I met some people today, who sounded English. They used words I understood but not in the context I understood. What's a Rory?"

"Sounds like cockney rhyming slang. I'm not *that* familiar with it. I hail from the Home Counties myself." Cowdry touched his lips in thought. "Was your encounter near the docks sir?"

"Yes."

"That would fit then sir. I understand there's an enclave of Cockneys working as dockers."

"But do you know what it means?"

"I believe it means a door sir."

"Ah. And boat race?"

"Face sir."

"Heap of coke?"

Cowdry frowned. "I'm not sure, sir. In what context was it said?"

"The heap of coke who lived there."

Cowdry thought some more. "If they are Cockneys, it might mean the bloke, I suppose. The man perhaps?"

Fooks raised an eyebrow. "Geezer, maybe?"

Cowdry smiled. "Yes sir, they might have meant the geezer."

Fooks shook his head, thinking back to apples and pears and bo-peeps. Then there was Rory. Different language. He shrugged. Must make sense to someone. Nothing he should concern himself with. Well, he'd spoken to some notable characters in the past few days, some who might well have an interest in killing Kinsey.

He eased his shoulders back. He'd better go see what Swan wanted. Tomorrow brought the funeral. *Suppose I'll have to go. The murderer might be there.*

CHAPTER TWENTY

The next day, Fooks accompanied Caroline to Robert Kinsey's funeral, way out to Forest Hills Cemetery at West Roxbury, one of the newer burial grounds serving Boston.

Rather than join Caroline and the Kinseys, Fooks sat in the back row of the chapel, watching the mourners pass by. Most he hadn't met before. He recognized Henry Downton, and the Kinsey butler. Albinus Gray nodded. He joined a girl, presumably Kitty Miller, already seated, in a row nearer the front. *Ah, catch you later miss.* Fooks scanned around the other mourners. Mrs. Kinsey, wearing a veil, sobbed into a handkerchief. Brook supported her. *Under sufferance, by the looks of it.*

With the service about to start, Captain Loomis arrived. Unlit cigar clamped between his teeth, he climbed into the pew on the other side of the aisle to Fooks. He glared at Fooks.

Great. No doubt he'll collar me afterwards.

Fooks was correct. After the internment, Loomis inclined his head to Fooks, inviting him to walk back to the church with him. *Drat, I wanted to catch Kitty.*

"Captain Loomis, good of you to make the time—" Fooks greeted brightly.

To his surprise, Loomis yanked him behind a tree. Fooks waited patiently for Loomis to light his cigar.

Loomis took a deep inhale and, cigar clamped between his teeth, said, "Stay outta my way. You're hampering my investigation."

Fooks blinked innocently. "How am I doing that? Just asking questions is all."

"Yeah, and I'm following you all around town. Folks don't want to speak to me 'cos they've already spoken to you! They're under the misapprehension we're on the same side."

"Aren't we?"

"Naw, we're not. I've been checking into you. Neither Pinkerton's in Chicago nor New York have ever heard of a detective by the name of Crane. Now who the devil are you?"

Fooks swallowed. "I'm simply someone hired by Mrs. Martin to investigate the murder of her uncle and clear her husband."

"Don't be cute, Crane. I think you're a crook. Which crook I don't yet know, but I'm working on it."

Fooks pursed his lips. "Brown hair, brown eyes, average build." He shrugged. "The description could match a lot of crooks." He beamed. "I hope I won't have to sue for wrongful arrest."

Judging by the color Loomis went, Fooks thought he would explode. *Hmm, might have overstepped the mark here.*

"Now you see that right there?" Loomis shook his cigar furiously in Fooks' direction.

Fooks blinked in surprise. "What right where?"

"The smart mouth of yours. That'll narrow it down some."

Yeah, it will. Fooks straightened his face.

"You're asking too many questions and upsetting a lot of people. I'm telling you again to stay away from my investigation."

"I am, Captain. I can't help it if your investigation leads you in the same direction as mine." *A step or two behind, by the sounds of it.* "Have you another suspect other than Martin? Like I suggested before, why don't we pool our resources?"

"Because you don't have any authority. Now I'm warning you again. Stay outta my way or I will arrest you. And it won't be wrongful either."

Loomis stalked away. Fooks watched him go, thoughtfully. *Hmmm, Loomis is smarter than I first thought. Better tread carefully from now on.*

He scanned around. *Now where's Kitty?*

He spotted her, offering her condolences to Mrs. Kinsey. He hovered nearby until she walked away.

"Miss Miller?" He stopped her in her tracks.

"Yes?"

"Joseph Crane. I'm the detective looking into Mr. Kinsey's murder. I'd like to ask you some questions."

Kitty's mouth opened. Before she could speak, Albinus Gray caught her arm from behind. He propelled her away.

"Come along, Miss Miller. We have a lot of work to do. No time for gossiping."

Fooks stood staring after them, hands on hips. *Interesting. Why should Gray stop me talking to her?*

Fooks hung about watching the other mourners leave. Not one gave him cause to wonder about them. The requisite people appeared upset. No one unnecessarily angry. He itched to go. Graveyards were not his most favorite of places. It was a relief when Caroline bade goodbye to her aunt.

"Yes Aunt Anne, of course I'll come to the reading of the will. Should Uncle Robert leave anything to me, I will make arrangements beneficial to you and Brook."

"Thank you my dear." Anne patted her hand. "Thoughtful of you. Will you travel with Brook and I?"

"I'm not on my own, Aunt. Mr. Crane is with me." With this she gestured to Fooks.

Anne Kinsey flashed him a look of disapproval. She lowered her voice to speak to Caroline. Fooks couldn't hear what they were saying. By the way Caroline squeezed her aunt's hand, he presumed it wasn't complimentary to him. *You're not fitting in here are you Fooks?*

Brook Kinsey jumped to his feet when Caroline and Fooks walked into the drawing room of Kinsey House. "What's he doing here?" Brook demanded, tossing his head towards Fooks.

Caroline squared up to her cousin as he marched forward.

"In the absence of my husband, I've asked Mr. Crane to accompany me."

"This is private, Caroline," Brook said, in a growl.

Apart from Anne Kinsey and Brook, there were two other men present. Fooks figured both for lawyers, but only one held a document in his hands. Fooks shrugged. *Guess rich folks need more'n one legal eye.*

"I'll go Caroline," Fooks said, turning.

"No, I desire you to stay, Mr. Crane." Fooks stopped and Caroline turned back to Brook. "Mr. Crane will sit quietly and take no part in the proceedings, Brook. You won't know he's here." She waved Fooks to a distant chair and swept to sit beside her aunt. Once seated, Caroline took her aunt's hand.

Fooks sidled to the indicated chair, aware of Brook's eyes on him. Once seated, he tried to keep the smugness he felt from reaching his face.

The lawyer with the document cleared his throat and pushed on half glasses. He peered over the top of them at

Brook. "This won't take long, but you might be more comfortable seated, young man." His voice was firm.

Brook grunted in frustration and slumped into the nearest chair.

"Please start, Mr. Hadley," said Anne Kinsey, leveling an eye at her son.

Hadley cleared his throat again and studied the papers he held for a moment before beginning to speak. "Good afternoon, ladies and gentleman. I'm John Hadley, personal lawyer to the late Robert Kinsey. Allow me to introduce Mr. Gideon Morgan, commercial lawyer to Mr. Kinsey. I shall now begin reading the will."

Hadley cleared his throat again. "In the name of God, Amen, I Robert Kinsey of Kinsey House, Mount Vernon Street, Boston in the County of Suffolk and Commonwealth of Massachusetts do make, ordain and declare this instrument to be my last will and testament, revoking all others.

"First, all funeral charges and expenses shall be paid by my executor hereafter named and come before the following bequeaths are discharged.

"To my wife, Anne Kinsey, I leave the property known as Kinsey House, Mount Vernon Street, Boston, for her use and enjoyment for the remainder of her years. A yearly income of $2,000 is to be paid to her for the expenses of running said property. Thereafter, Kinsey House shall become the property of our son, Brook Kinsey."

Yeah, this much we know.

"My business partnership with Mr. Ephraim Smith shall be wound up and all proceeds attributing to my share be added to my estate.

"As to the residue of my estate and property, and which shall not be required for the payment of my debts, funeral charges and expenses in and about the executor of this my will, and the administration of my estate, I bequeath to my niece, Caroline Fairfield."

Brook leaped to his feet. "Why would he do that?" he shouted, at Hadley. "She's already rich beyond the dreams of avarice."

Anne Kinsey, clearly embarrassed, said, "Brook please sit and let Mr. Hadley finish."

"No Mother, this needs to be sorted out here and now."

Caroline sighed. "Brook, I've already said, I—"

"I don't want to hear from you," Brook screamed.

Fooks sat on the edge of his seat, watching, ready to step in if Brook became violent towards Caroline.

"Stop being so rude and sit down," Anne said.

"No Mother—"

"Brook! I shan't tell you again. Sit down, child."

"Mother, I am *not* a child."

Anne Kinsey rose to her feet. She wasn't a tall woman by any means, but in the moment, she seemed to tower over her son. "Then stop acting like one."

Brook stomped to the door, where he turned. "This isn't finished. I'll contest the will." He wrenched the door open, allowing it to bang against the neighboring table, and stalked out.

Fooks pursed his lips. *Sheesh, what a dope.* He made eye contact with Caroline, who twitched her head towards the open door. He gaped. *Surely she doesn't want me to go after him?*

Caroline frowned, shook her head slightly. "Please close the door, Mr. Crane." She turned back quickly to comfort her aunt. Anne Kinsey had already returned to her seat and quietly snuffled into a handkerchief.

By the time Fooks returned and sat down again, Anne Kinsey appeared composed. She waved a hand, handkerchief clutched firmly, at Hadley.

"I apologize for my son. Please continue." Her voice shook.

Poor woman, what a cross to bear.

"There isn't much to add." Hadley cleared his throat and attended to the document once more. "Lastly, it is my desire that Mr. Gideon Morgan," here he nodded at the other lawyer, who inclined his head, "of Beacon Street, Boston be my sole executor of this my last will and testament.

"In witness of all and everything mentioned above, I set my hand this day twenty-third day of March in the year of our Lord, one thousand eight hundred and eighty-two.

"Signed Robert Kinsey.

"In the presence of Mr. John Hadley, Mr. Ephraim Smith and Mr. Gideon Morgan." Hadley rested the document on the arm of chair. "Are there any questions?"

Caroline turned to Anne, who shook her head.

"It seems all straightforward," Caroline said.

"Not exactly." Gideon Morgan withdrew a white sheet of paper from his top pocket, which he handed across to Hadley.

"What's this?" Hadley unfolded the sheet, and read. A flicker of surprise creased his brow.

Fooks sat up. Caroline leaned forward. "What is it, Mr. Hadley?"

"It's a codicil."

Fooks frowned. He wasn't familiar with the word.

Right on cue, Hadley went on to explain. "It's an addition to a will, making an amendment to a specific bequest. In this case—"

"Before you go on, Hadley," said Morgan, "perhaps I should explain who I am and my relationship to Mr. Kinsey."

Hadley waved a hand, inviting him to do so.

"My name is Gideon Morgan. Like Hadley I am a lawyer. While he deals with personal and family law, my specialty is commercial. I advised Mr. Kinsey on the legality of his business dealings. At our last meeting a month ago, he confided in me his concerns about his son, Brook." He pointed at the document Hadley held. "The codicil requires me to act for Brook Kinsey should I deem him to be incapable of succeeding his father in his partnership with Mr. Ephraim Smith. Mr. Robert Kinsey has laid down strict guidelines for me to determine Brook's capacity. Proceed, Hadley."

With a glance at Morgan, Hadley began to read:

"I Robert Kinsey, resident of Boston, Suffolk County, Commonwealth of Massachusetts, declare this is a codicil to my last will and testament, dated twenty-third day of March in the year of our Lord, one thousand eight hundred and eighty-two. I amend this will in the following manner.

"First, the partnership I have enjoyed with Mr. Ephraim Smith should be held in trust for my son, Brook Kinsey, until such time he is able to take control of his share.

"Second, the trust shall be administered by Gideon Morgan and he shall determine Brook's fitness to take control. To aid him in this determination, Gideon Morgan should apply the following criteria:

"Brook should no longer frequent gambling establishments or other places where gambling is conducted.

"Brook should restrict his alcohol consumption to a minimum and be verifiably sober for a year.

"Brook should curtail his friendship with the following who have such a pernicious influence on him that his conduct shames his mother and me."

Hadley looked up. "Mr. Kinsey lists three names, who I won't name in this *public* setting." His eyes went directly to Fooks on the word public.

Fooks shrugged. *No skin off my nose.*

Hadley turned back to the document. "The fourth and final criteria is Brook should work with Albinus Gray and Ephraim Smith, if they are agreeable, to learn and understand the business.

"When all these criteria are met to the satisfaction of Gideon Morgan, all business activity shall be transferred to Brook.

"In the event, Ephraim Smith is not amenable to the partnership continuing with Brook, then I ask Gideon

Morgan to commence winding up procedures. All residue to be placed in trust for Brook and only released into his control when the above conditions are met.

"In all other aspects my will and testament shall remain. I, Robert Kinsey, the testator, sign my name to this instrument this thirty-first day of March, in the year of our Lord, one thousand eight hundred and eighty-six.

"Signed Robert Kinsey.

"In the presence of Mr. Gideon Morgan, Mr. Ephraim Smith and Mr. Alan Pritchard." Hadley set the document aside. "That adds a level of complexity to Mr. Kinsey's affairs I didn't expect."

"It's not my area of expertise and I drafted it as we spoke. However, I believe everything is in order," Morgan said.

"Indeed Mr. Morgan. Quite in order." Hadley looked up with a rueful grin. "Who gets to tell Brook?"

CHAPTER TWENTY-ONE

"He's not going to like it," Swan said, when Caroline told him the gist of Kinsey's will.

Fooks stood by the door of Swan's suite with a grin, ready to go to dinner.

"No. Poor Aunt Anne. I don't envy her having to tell him."

Swan held Caroline's upper arms and looked at her in sympathy. "Then to spare your aunt, you must."

Caroline looked up in horror. "I don't—"

The dinner gang interrupted. Fooks opened the door and looked back. Caroline gave Swan a quick kiss. "Not sure that's a good idea, Sam. We'll speak later."

Caroline and Fooks realized they couldn't keep eating in Swan's rooms, as it was beginning to look suspicious. Tonight, they opted to dine together downstairs. They ate in near silence. Afterwards they adjourned to the drawing room, where Caroline attended to her embroidery. Fooks had helped himself to the library and a stack of books lay at his elbow. His nose was buried in another. Neither spoke until a commotion outside came to their attention.

"I wonder who it is?" Caroline asked.

A flicker of irritation crossed Fooks' face at the question. *How do I know?* He closed the book and uncrossed his legs, ready for action.

Brook Kinsey crashed through the door. He could barely stand up. "He left everything to you. Haven't you got enough?"

"Brook—" Caroline started, getting to her feet, Fooks a second behind her.

"I'm sorry madam. He pushed passed me," Williams said, in apology, a pained expression on his face.

"It's all right, Williams. Please close the door."

As Williams closed the door, Caroline drew herself up, preparing to deal with her intoxicated cousin.

"With all this." Brook waved a hand around the room, the momentum nearly knocking him off his feet. He swayed alarmingly. Caroline went to steady him, but he shook her off. "Dontcha touch me."

Fooks rolled his eyes.

Caroline stood with her hands clasped in front of her. "Brook, please sit down."

"Don't wanna sit. You're gonna pay. Dearest cousin. You're gonna pay."

"I said I would settle—"

"Nah. Not in a while. Now!"

He wrestled with his clothing for a moment, before bending over. "Ah ha!" He wrenched a gun free of his pocket. He held it loosely as he swayed.

"Brook!" Caroline took a deep breath.

"Ya see this?" He brought the gun up nearly to his face, squinting at it. He frowned in deep concentration, tongue at the corner of his mouth. With both thumbs, he forced the hammer down, missed, and tried again.

Fooks moved across the room in a flash. He forced Brook's arms above his head, meeting no real resistance.

The drunk man was almost floppy. Fooks squeezed the gun from Brook's grasp.

Brook yelled. "Gimme. Gimme that back." He made a lunge for Fooks.

The swaying man came on. Fooks shot out a hand, caught Brook in the chest and pushed.

Brook fell into a chair, panting. "Whatcha do?" He grasped the arms of the chair and struggled; feet flailed about underneath him. "Let me up."

Fooks checked the gun wasn't cocked and slammed it onto a sideboard. "Stay there, Brook." His voice was commanding.

Brook scrambled his feet under him and pushed up.

"I said, stay there." Fooks raised his voice. The lightest of touches sent Brook sprawling into the chair again.

Fooks stood over him, fingertips in the pockets of his vest. "Now listen to me, Brook Kinsey, you're drunk. You need to sober up, and pronto." Over his shoulder, he said, "Ring for some coffee. Black."

He turned back to Brook. Behind him Caroline's dress rustled as she moved to the bell cord. Fooks leaned over, his face hard. Brook cowered in the chair.

"Now you listen to me. Enough. D'you hear?"

Brook's face screwed up. "Don't hurt me." His voice became a whimper. "Please." He cried, tears rolling down his cheeks. "I didn't mean it. Please don't hurt me."

Fooks' tongue explored his mouth and he stood back. Brook curled into the fetal position and sobbed.

Fooks growled. *Sheesh, do I wanna hit you.* He waved a hand dismissively. "Pathetic," he murmured. Caroline stood some way off, looking anxious. He pressed his lips into a thin line. "Are you okay?"

Caroline nodded.

With a glance back at Brook, Fooks said, "Sober him up and send him home."

Caroline looked doubtful. "You don't know my cousin. Perhaps we should take him to Ardmaddy with us tomorrow. Let him calm down. I don't want him upsetting my aunt."

Fooks shook his head, his fingertips finding the pockets of his vest. "Not a good idea." *Has she forgotten about Swan?* He was the main reason they were going to Ardmaddy. "We've things to do at Ardmaddy and no time to babysit." He waved towards the now sleeping figure. Fooks shook his head again in disgust and growled. "Take him home in the morning and explain about the codicil. Give him something else to rail against."

"Brook, where have you been?" Anne Kinsey cried, when her son entered the hall of Kinsey House the next morning. She looked him up and down in horror at his disheveled and stained clothes.

As he traipsed upstairs, she waited anxiously at the head of the stairs. When he made to continue on up to the bedrooms, she caught his arm. "I've been so worried. Where have you been?"

"I've the mother of all hangovers. I want my bed."

"Not so fast, young man. You owe me an explanation. And an apology."

"Not now, Mother."

Anne barred his way when he attempted to push past her.

"Yes, now." She pointed firmly to the drawing room.

Shoulders slumped; he turned in her direction. Anne acknowledged Caroline with a grateful smile before she followed Brook in a flurry of skirts. Caroline reached the top of the stairs, stripping off her gloves. She entered the drawing room. Behind her, Fooks climbed the stairs reluctantly. *Great. We're not just dropping him off then.*

Delaying their departure to Ardmaddy, Swan insisted Fooks accompany Caroline and Brook to Kinsey House.

Fooks resented having to act the unpaid bodyguard, but Swan's argument proved persuasive. He wasn't letting Caroline go alone with Brook. Not after the gun incident.

"Does he *have* to be here?" Brook said, with a snarl, when Fooks crossed the threshold. Brook slumped in a chair, rubbing his forehead.

Fooks stood just inside the door, hands clasped in front him. He cast a look sideways as the door shut behind him. *Believe me I don't wanna be here anymore than you want me here.*

"Mr. Crane is here for my benefit. Not yours," Caroline said, spreading her skirts and sitting. "As I told you on the way here, Uncle Robert's will contains additions that you missed when you stormed out."

"The sooner I tell you what they are, Brook, the sooner you can go to bed," Anne said. "I want you to listen carefully. They are important."

Brook chewed his bottom lip and sighed deeply. "Get on with it then." He waved a hand dismissively. He swallowed hard. His face took on a green tinge and Fooks scanned the room for a receptacle. Just in case.

Anne began. Brook listened in silence, growing more and more angry at each condition. He sat straighter, fingers curling into fists. His face contorted. When Anne finished, he levered up and made for the door.

"Aren't you going to say anything?" Anne demanded.

Brook deliberately elbowed Fooks aside in his haste. Fooks stepped back, glancing at Caroline.

"Brook—" Caroline was on her feet.

Brook opened the door and turned. "I hope they catch your husband soon, Mrs. Martin." He spat the last two words. "I for one will be there to see him hang." He shook. "It's about time he got his just desserts." Brook leveled his gaze at Fooks. "Maybe the police'll do for you too while they're at it. Whoever *you* are."

He turned and left Fooks puzzling over Brook's last comment. *Could he know? Did he know?*

CHAPTER TWENTY-TWO

Fooks frantically slapped the roof of the carriage, urgently commanding the driver to stop. "Whoa, there." Fooks stuck his head out of the window and yelled up when they jerked to a halt.

"Sorry, I forgot something."

He smiled at Cowdry. "Stopped just in the right place."

Cowdry nodded. "Yes sir. Most fortuitous."

With a wink, Fooks scrambled out before the driver could get down to undo the door. Cowdry prepared to follow him.

"Just be a few minutes," Fooks called over his shoulder, hurrying back to the open front door of Fairfield House.

Mid-morning and the Martin household prepared to leave Fairfield House for Ardmaddy. Two carriages lined up outside. Servants busy with loading baggage into one and milling around on the sidewalk. Fooks and Cowdry set off in one carriage, coming to a stop within a few yards. Caroline and her maid had already gone to church. They would return later and travel in convoy with the baggage vehicle to Ardmaddy.

When Fooks returned he allowed himself a smug grin. Swan had joined them, wearing Fooks' distinctive Mackinaw jacket. They exercised the reverse subterfuge from a few nights ago.

"Glad you could join us," Fooks said, once they'd set off once again.

Swan grinned. "Worked like a dream, thanks to Cowdry."

Cowdry flushed. "It was nothing sir."

"He's showing a real talent for sneaking. Think I'm gonna have to watch him."

Ardmaddy stood eleven miles outside Boston, on the outskirts of the town of Waltham. Having left late, night was falling as they arrived, turning into a drive and stopping in front of massive wrought iron gates, with a crest in the center of each. Swan shrank back when a man came out of the gatehouse. He didn't want to be seen. A brief conversation took place between their driver and the man, before the latter hauled aside the gates.

"Nearly there now," Swan said, shifting upright. "What's the matter, Joe? Ya look like ya sucking a lemon." Swan noted Fooks' scowling face.

Aware of Cowdry, Fooks glared at Swan and shook his head, before turning away to stare out at the passing grassland. He expected to see a house straight away, but another five minutes passed before signs of habitation came into view between trees. First the odd brick building, then an enormous stable block, and then the main house appeared from the trees. Fooks' mouth dropped open. If Fooks thought sht Fairfield House was grand, Ardmaddy proved something else.

Swan smirked at his reaction. "I'm told it's Palladian," he said.

Fooks tossed a hand in the air. *Of course, that explains everything.*

The main house was built in a square, uniform on all sides. Except for the more ornate front façade. Four fluted giant pilasters framed three bays to the center and supported a triangular pediment. A pair of curved staircases led to the first floor and a triple arched terrace. In the precise middle of the terrace stood the main doorway, under a segmented pediment. The half-glazed double doors, with its oval tracery, had a transom light above.

The carriage swept around to come to a halt by one of the staircases. Cowdry alighted first.

"What's the matter?" Swan asked, when Fooks didn't move.

Fooks took his elbow from the window edge. He faced Swan, looking slightly sick. "I'm not sure about this, Tobe," he murmured.

Swan swotted Fooks' knee. "Takes a while to get used to but ya'll get there. I'll stay here and sneak out at the stables. Make m'way up to my suite from there." Swan laughed. "Don't worry. It'll be fine."

Fooks remained doubtful when Cowdry reappeared at the door.

"All is taken care of sir. Mr. Crane, shall I show you to your rooms?"

Fooks turned back to Swan. "Sure, you'll be safe here?"

"Yes. Police searched here last week. They won't come back."

"How can you be so sure?"

"'Cos this is Waltham, not Boston. Police here are different. Caroline told me their search was none too thorough." He held up a finger. "They have wives and families and dinners to go home for." When Fooks grunted, Swan added. "They won't be back. Trust me. Now get out."

As Fooks climbed out he hoped Swan was right but he had an awful feeling.

Cowdry burst through the door into Swan's suite at Ardmaddy the next morning. "Sir!"

"Cowdry, what the—" Swan started, collapsing the morning newspaper he'd been reading.

Cowdry hurried, breathing heavily into the main room where Swan and Fooks drank coffee.

"Police, sir." Cowdry stopped to get his breath back. "They're coming up the drive sir."

Swan and Fooks swapped glances. Swan dropped the newspaper and sprang up. Fooks rose more leisurely to his feet, taking a last slurp of coffee on the way. Rushing in situations like this led to mistakes.

"Quickly sirs. We can go by the back stairs, and I can sneak you out."

Swan paused to grab his hat. He'd dressed in range clothes today, denim pants and colored shirt under a leather vest. In contrast Fooks, once again in his suit, not so ruined as he thought. Cowdry had worked miracles overnight it seemed.

The back stairs were uncarpeted but functional. Their feet clattered down the short flights of wooden stairs at dizzying speed. Swan stopped suddenly when they emerged at the bottom. A disorientated Fooks stumbled into the back of him.

Cowdry edged out into the corridor, looking both ways, before signaling that the coast was clear. He opened the door to the outside slowly and silenced the bell above with a hand. Then he opened the door wider. Swan and Fooks hustled through. Cowdry repeated his actions in reverse as he closed the door.

"How many are there?" Swan asked, when they stood pressed against the outside wall.

Cowdry shook his head. "All Mr. Williams said was loads."

"Williams said that?" Swan frowned.

Cowdry wrinkled his nose, shamefaced. "Not exactly sir. He actually said the gate told him the police were coming up the drive, in considerable force."

"The Waltham police don't do considerable force. They only have nine officers, an' one of them is the Chief of Police. He's jus' a pen pusher."

"Maybe they've drafted in some help. Look, we can debate this another time," Fooks said, scanning hurriedly around. "Right now, we need to get you outta here."

Swan grunted and turned to Cowdry. "Can you saddle two horses?"

"Not without being seen sir."

Swan grunted. "We'll have to take our chances."

"I'm in your hands," Fooks said, with a shrug. He glanced at the sky. *Great, looks like rain.*

Cowdry cast nervous glances all around. Fooks laid a reassuring hand on the younger man's arm. "We've got this, Cowdry."

"I've an idea," Swan murmured.

"Uh-huh." Fooks' tone was ominous and he ignored the black look Swan gave him.

Swan turned to Cowdry. "Why don't you take my good friend Mr. Crane over to the stables and have him pick out a riding horse? Cream Puff'll do. While you provide a distraction, I'll saddle Striker. His stall is far enough away. No one should see me."

"Where will I meet you?" Fooks asked.

"Ride up the drive a way. I'll find you."

"Okay, quickly. C'mon Cowdry, show me this horse." Above, the sky continued to darken.

Let's hope this works. C'mon. Fooks bit down his impatience as he endured an explanation on the differences between Eastern and Western riding. He finally climbed aboard. Hands, knees, feet. So much to remember. Unfamiliar horse, strange stirrups, really weird saddle. Felt like he'd never ridden before. *Let's hope I can do this.*

He rode at a walk from the stables, trying to get used to the saddle. Fooks steered his horse, embarrassingly called Cream Puff, away from the house. He avoided the many police vans and carriages pulled up on the sweeping forecourt.

He kept to the edge of the woodland, which ran alongside the drive, until this gave way to open parkland. The odd bush grew here and there, and off in the distance, more areas of woodland. Not much cover for a way. He paused in the margins. Police swarmed over the drive. If he broke cover and made a bolt for it, he was sure to be noticed. He rubbed his cheek, pondering.

C'mon Fooks. This is no different from evading a posse, an' you've done that a time or two. Not on a strange horse and gear you haven't. He shook his head irritably. *Oh, shut up.*

His senses screamed at him to kick his heels and see what Cream Puff could do. Well, he couldn't sit here under the trees all day. He'd have to go for it and hope for the best. The only plus point, he was out of range of any gunfire.

He gathered the reins and moved slowly out into the open.

"Stop! You there stop."

CHAPTER TWENTY-THREE

Swan lay flat on his belly, watching the conversation taking place on the drive. He was lucky. Spring had come early this year. The bushes underneath where he hid enjoying a luxuriant growth. The trees above his head already partially obscuring the sky.

Like Fooks, Swan was all too aware of the implications of an interview by lawmen. Swan needed something to disrupt the conversation before the police hauled Fooks back to the house. Had to be something that would spook the skittish police horse but appear natural. A stone? A clod of mud? Swan dismissed both with a shake of his head. Throwing anything at the horse wasn't natural. No, he'd have to make a noise, but what?

He scanned around and then up. Overhead the sun burst through, casting its shadow briefly over the scene before disappearing once more behind increasingly ominous clouds. Whatever he was going to do, he had to do it quickly. He wanted to reach the safe place he had in mind before getting a soaking.

He could leave Fooks to his fate of course, hoping these local police wouldn't look more closely once Caroline established he was indeed a guest. That's not what partners did. Especially ones used to evading the law.

A noise it would have to be. He stood for a moment, listening to the natural sounds around him. Chirping and chattering of nesting birds. A distant tap, tap, tapping of a woodpecker. Scurrying of small creatures in the undergrowth. The wind got up, rustling through the leaves. The creak and groan of branches as they swayed together.

That's it.

Swan bent double and walked quietly. He needed a dead branch. One he could snap. The undergrowth, littered with twigs and leaves, but nothing big enough for his purposes. He carefully placed his feet as he moved, until he was far enough away from the gathering on the drive. He suspected they weren't listening, but no point in giving them cause to notice him.

A few minutes of scrabbling around and he found what he was searching for. A decent sized branch, dead a long time and brittle. He carefully made his way back and hunkered down. Fooks waved his hands, first one way then the other, using all his powers of persuasion to avoid going back to the house.

Swan chuckled quietly. *Haven't lost your touch, Flo, but let's help ya out.*

He passed the dead branch behind a tree, grasped both sides and pulled. He was rewarded with a loud crack. His horse, Striker, tethered some yards away, raised his head and twitched his ears, before lowering his head to continue happily cropping at grass around the base of a tree.

Not so the police horse. Its head shot up, ears alert, and bolted. The driver yelled. The policemen yelled. Cream

Puff sidestepped smartly out of the way as the van careened past.

Fooks raised an eyebrow at the sight of the policemen in pursuit, then spun his head around as something bounced off his arm.

Swan rose from behind a bush and beckoned him off the drive. Fooks guided Cream Puff into the tree margins as Swan untied Striker and swung aboard.

"C'mon, let's get out of here," he said, as Fooks joined him.

"Where are we going?" Fooks glanced upwards as rain started.

On the way Swan told him of a fishing shack, which hadn't been used for years. The place was part of the estate and isolated. Even local police wouldn't know about it.

"This is a shack?" Fooks queried, hands on hips.

Fooks stood under a dripping tree and surveyed the place where Swan had brought him through the driving rain. At one time, the wooden structure in front of him, although well-built, had seen better days. Its windows, once fully glazed, now mostly broken, stared back with foreboding. One of the dormer windows on the first floor hung lopsided by its hinges. The other banged in the wind.

Fooks arched his back and reflected on how sore his legs and backside felt. Lack of riding time. Not to mention how wet and clingy his clothes were. Cream Puff crowded under the tree with him. The horse looked as uncomfortable as he felt.

Swan, still on Striker, glanced back at the shack. Water dripped from his hat, cascaded onto his lap and ran down Striker's neck. His horse seemed unconcerned, shaking his mane.

"Yeah. It's what passes for a shack in these parts."

Fooks puffed. "It's bigger than Mary's house." Even though it was home for him now, he still thought of it as hers. Mary had owned it before their marriage and under Wyoming's property laws, still did.

Swan eyed the heavy sky. "This isn't letting up. Go an' explore. I'll see to the horses."

"Are we planning on being here awhile?" Fooks asked, preparing to make a run towards the shack.

"Figure once night's fallen, it'll be safe to go back."

Fooks ran for the porch and nearly lost his footing on the rotten deck. The door wasn't locked, and he went into a wooden floored hall. A musty smell pervaded the air. Rooms led off either side. In front of him was a staircase, to the sides stood two equipment racks, each containing fishing rods and other assorted fishing paraphernalia.

He couldn't go much further without a light. A lantern hung conveniently just inside the door on a hook. Fooks gave it a shake. Still had oil in it. He spied a box of matches on a nearby shelf. Damp of course, and he wrinkled his nose, doubting his success in making a spark. He gave it a go anyway, and the fourth attempt rewarded him with a flame.

With the lantern held high, he went off to explore. One of the rooms revealed itself as a fully equipped kitchen cum dining room. However, the ceiling had partially collapsed. Splintered wood and daub lay scattered over the furniture.

Fooks retraced his steps and crossed the hall to the other room, which turned out to be a lounge. Seemed to have fared better than the kitchen, although water dripped through the ceiling on the far side of the fireplace. When Fooks investigated, water penetrated down the chimney as well. Too wet for a fire. He sighed. He wasn't getting warm and dry any time soon.

He swung the lantern around and surveyed the rest of the room. The decoration, typically masculine in style. All dark wood paneling and leather button backed sofa and chairs. Mice had been at the sofa, ripping holes through which stuffing now poked. One of the chairs stood too near the dripping ceiling and now had a covering of mold and slim. The other wasn't too bad once he wiped the dust and grime off. He sat gingerly, then cursed himself at his care. His suit was already ruined by the rain. *Doubt I can make it any worse.*

"Haven't ya made a fire?" Swan asked, as he came in shaking water from his hat.

"Chimney's leaking." Fooks waved a hand in the air. "So's the ceiling."

"Sheesh, I didn't think it would be this bad." Swan went to the chimney.

"If this is being on the lam Eastern style, I don't like it," Fooks said. He shivered.

Swan grunted. "Which we shouldn't have to." He turned back. "We can't stay here without a fire. We'll catch our deaths."

Fooks shrugged. "What choice do we have?"

"Give me the lantern. I'll take a look upstairs. Must be some bedding we can use to dry off."

Fooks look up. "Don't like the look of the ceiling. Could collapse at any time. The ceiling in the kitchen has."

Swan frowned. "I'll be careful. Gimme."

Fooks handed over the lantern. He followed Swan into the hall. He didn't want to be in the room if, or when, the ceiling did collapse. Swan made his way upstairs while Fooks sat on the bottom. With the front door shut, he was soon in darkness. He hugged his knees to his chest, trying to generate some warmth. With the light gone, the place took on a creepy feel. The pounding of the rain, the ominous drips, the creaks and cracks as Swan moved about overhead. All that was missing were flashes of lightening and rumbles of thunder. *Don't conjure 'em up, Fooks.*

Swan returned with a couple of comforters over his arm. One he gave one to Fooks. "Here, these are dry."

"It's damp," Fooks protested.

"It's jus' cold. Quit complainin'. All I could find, an' it's better than nothing."

Tempted to strip off all their sopping clothes, but neither did. They'd only have to put them back on again when it was time to leave. Not something either wanted to contemplate. Fooks did take off his suit jacket and attempted to wring out some of the wet. With a sigh he hung it over the newel post, where it continued to drip. He snuggled into the comforter beside Swan.

They made a sorry pair sitting silently on the stairs with just the light of the lantern for company.

"Who does this place belong to?" Fooks asked, suddenly.

"Caroline's father. Hasn't been used since he died." Swan scanned the ceiling. "Might get it fixed up. It's a nice place to be."

Fooks scowled. "Yeah, on a different day," he muttered. He smoothed his hair back. At least it stopped dripping. "Reckon the police were tipped off?"

Swan shrugged and shook his head. "Dunno. They can't find me, so mebbe they're jus' checking places they've already searched on the off chance I've come back."

Fooks wasn't convinced. "Awful lot of law on the drive." He frowned. "As though they expected to find you."

Swan sighed. "Yeah, mebbe. Are you any closer to figuring this thing out?"

"Some. I don't have all the pieces yet." He scratched the side of his face. "I still need to see two of the tontine holders, Harvey Slocomb and Montgomery Whitlock. Maybe they will clarify a few things. And there's Ephraim Smith, Kinsey's business partner. I've a feeling he's avoiding me."

"So? Isn't that what ya'd do if ya murdered someone? Stay outta the way until it all blows over. The police have me in the frame. Perhaps Smith is waiting until they catch me."

Fooks twitched his head. "Yeah, that's what I'm worried about. You can't stay hidden forever."

Swan grunted. "Yeah, I do know." He paused. "What 'bout the guy in the theater?"

"Henry Downton? Doubt if interfering in the artistic direction of the theater is a strong enough motive—"

"Ya never can tell with these artistic types though Fooks. Keep him on the list."

Fooks rolled his eyes. "I am for now, but he's not at the top of my list."

"Who is?"

Fooks twitched his head. "Like I said, I don't have all the pieces yet. Gray has a motive I suppose. Must be hard being passed over, having worked so hard for the man, but he's not the type. I'm keeping him on for now until someone else firms up."

"What about the girl with the mouse? Kitty something?"

"Yeah, Kitty Miller." He shook his head. "I dunno if she's avoiding me on purpose." He sniffed. "Unlikely it's her. No, my prime suspect at the moment is Kinsey's business partner, Ephraim Smith."

"On what basis?"

"On the basis he won't see me!"

CHAPTER TWENTY-FOUR

Fooks jerked his head towards the darkened ceiling. "What was that?"

The rain seemed to have stopped, or at least slowed. Apart from the dripping from the lounge and scurrying feet on the wooden floorboards in the rooms above, no noise came from there. This had been something new.

Swan rang his fingers through his drying hair. "Aw, jus' bats."

Fooks raised his eyebrows. "Bats?"

"Yeah, I noticed 'em up there earlier. They're roosting, but I guess it's near time for them to come out for the night."

Fooks cursed under his breath. "You bring me to all the best places don't you?"

"I told ya. I didn't know it was gonna be this bad."

Fooks cast an eye above again and swallowed. Most things he could cope with, but flappy things appearing silently out of the darkness unnerved him.

"Relax. They won't bother us."

"How d'you know?"

"'Cos they don't need to come downstairs to get out."

No sooner said, when a black shape swooped over his head. Fooks squeaked. Both ducked and covered their heads with their hands. Fooks raised his head tentatively as the shape disappeared into the kitchen.

Swan blinked in surprise. "Since when have you got so jumpy? We've been in worse places before."

"Yes, but not for a good long while." Fooks gulped and pulled the comforter around his shoulders further. "Thought those days were over."

"Well, they ain't, so quit complaining. We'll head on back in a little while. 'Xpect Caroline is worried."

"Are you sure about Caroline?" Fooks asked, slowly, still nervously inspecting the ceiling and then the kitchen doorway.

"What d'ya mean?" Swan's voice hardened.

Distracted from death by bat, Fooks recognized the tone. He'd better tread wary. "Look what Kinsey did to her. Chased her all the way across the country." Fooks risked a glance at Swan. "He *was* after her money."

Swan's head snapped around, glaring at Fooks. "And he didn't get it." He rose abruptly, throwing off his comforter.

Fooks viewed Swan's stiff back. "I'm just saying—"

"I don't want to hear it."

Fooks stood, keeping his comforter firmly around his shoulders. "I know you don't, but there's still the possibility she's behind all this."

"No. There ain't." Swan stalked away. "Leave it Fooks. I'll get the horses." He wrenched open the door.

They rode back in silence until Fooks took it upon himself to be the first to crack. "Look I'm sorry," he said, softly. "We had to get away when the police arrived. It's just," he licked his lips, "an unpleasant reminder of how things used to be, that's all." He stared off into the blackness. "I suppose I'm scared for Mary."

"Mary? Why?"

"If anything should happen to me—"

"Nothing is gonna happen to you. It's me the police are after."

"Yeah. Here they are. If they catch you how long d'you think it'll be before they start looking into me? Loomis is already suspicious. He knows I'm not a Pinkerton detective."

"If you're that concerned, go home," Swan snapped.

"Well, mebbe I will," Fooks snapped back. He pulled Cream Puff's neck around suddenly and took off at speed back the way they'd come.

Swan growled. "Aw, Fooks. C'mon." He mumbled something uncomplimentary under his breath and took off after Fooks.

A short way along the trail, Fooks grunted as he hit the ground. His shoulder and hip took the full force of the landing. The saving grace, Cream Puff deposited him in a pile of leaves, cushioning his fall somewhat. Wet and sodden leaves. *Just about sums up my day.*

He rolled onto his back and stared at the sky. A late burst of sunlight peeked out behind a rain blackened cloud.

"Now you come out," he yelled at the sky.

He sat up and glared at Cream Puff's departing rump, making its way back towards Swan. By his jaunty gait, Fooks suspected the horse was laughing at him.

"Go on, run away. You no good excuse for a horse." In emphasis, Fooks flung a handful of wet leaves. He groaned, trying to shake the remaining leaves from his hand.

Swan found him still sitting there some minutes later. He'd caught Cream Puff along the way and he brought both horses to a halt.

"You all right?" he asked, trying not to laugh.

"Yeah. Guess so."

Swan dismounted, looping Cream Puff's reins around the horn of his saddle, and walked over. He offered his hand.

Fooks glowered at the hand, took a deep breath and took it. Swan hauled him to his feet. Fooks stumbled over a hidden tree root before finding his balance. He stood hands on hips as Swan brushed him down.

"I'm sorry we argued. I am grateful you're here, y'know," Swan said, as he brushed Fooks' shoulders.

"I'm sorry we argued too. Situation just got to me that's all."

Fooks tried a small smile, which Swan returned. He gave Fooks' shoulder a shake before turning away. "C'mon, I'll help ya get back on." He chuckled. "I did promise I would, didn't I?"

"Yeah, you did." He followed Swan to the horses. In the gathering twilight, Cream Puff appeared shamefaced. "How far is it?"

"Not far. Stables are a few hundred yards in that direction." Swan pointed the way.

Fooks went to unloop Cream Puff's reins. "In that case, I'll walk."

They stopped a few yards from the edge of the trees, approaching Ardmaddy from the back. "Looks like the police left someone here," Swan said.

He dismounted and left Striker's reins trailing. As Swan crept forward, Fooks draped Cream Puff's reins over a nearby bush, before joining him. They crouched to watch for activity outside the servant's entrance. Apart from one man, Fooks couldn't see anything amiss. "What makes you say that?"

"The fella in the shirt sleeves smoking by the door. He's not one of ours."

"Do you know all the staff?"

Swan's head snapped around. "'Course I do. Made it my business to find out 'bout everyone. Have coffee downstairs regular." He turned back. "Caroline hates it," he murmured.

Fooks pursed his lips. *Ah, so there is some disagreement between them.* "How we gonna do this?" Fooks asked.

Swan motioned to Fooks they should move back. Once back at the horses, Swan stood thinking, idly pulling Striker's reins through his fingers.

"Think we oughta leave the horses here until we see what's what."

"Is there another way in?"

Swan grinned. "Yeah, but you're not gonna like it."

CHAPTER TWENTY-FIVE

"What's this?" Fooks asked, as Swan pulled up a wooden door, set at an angle between the wall and the ground. They'd tiptoed around the house until they came to an inner courtyard of ancillary buildings.

"Coal chute. In you go."

Fooks stared at him wide eyed. "There must an open window somewhere."

"Yeah, possibly, but we ain't got time to look. We need to get inside and find out what happened."

"I know that. I wanna get warm and dry too, but this." He waved a hand at the coal dusty slope below the door, ending in blackness. Didn't look like a place he wanted to explore.

Unperturbed, Swan explained. "It leads into the coal cellar. It's right by the back door. Get down there and come open up for me. Don't forget 'bout the bell."

"Why me?"

"'Cos ya're still scrawny. Chute narrows at the bottom." He patted his stomach. "I won't fit."

"I'm not scrawny," Fooks said in protest. "I'm wiry. Lean. Svelte."

Swan glanced over his shoulder. "Whatever ya are, hurry up afore we're discovered."

With more glaring, Fooks stripped off his jacket and furiously flung it at Swan. "You owe me big time." He sat and edged to the slide. He held up a finger as he thought of an objection.

"How I'm gonna get the policeman away from the door?"

"I'll create a diversion."

"How?"

"You let me worry 'bout that."

"But I am—"

"Yeah, yeah. Get on with it."

Swan suddenly gave him a push. Fooks slid at pace. Not a steep slope thankfully, but fast enough before coming to a jolting halt, his feet in space. The narrow bit. Fooks tried to wriggle down. No purchase. He twisted, turning his hips first one way and then the other. To no avail.

"Sheesh." Stuck. He lay still for a moment, contemplating where he lay. Swan had already closed the outside door, shutting out any light.

He fumbled around, trying to work out what was holding him. Pockets. The seam of his pants tore as he forced his hand in the left one. He came out with a pocket knife. More squirming. Nope. Still stuck. He struggled to free his watch from the pocket on the other side. Now with enough room to wriggle, he slid down further.

Until his shoulders curtailed his descent. *Great. I'm gonna die in here.*

A slight shimmy and his descent continued, faster than he wanted. "Yeow!" Shooting out to land heavily on the pile of coal he'd hoped would be higher, but wasn't.

The only light came from the transom above the internal door. He lay for a moment, waiting for his eyes to adjust, as he tucked his possessions back in his pockets. Then he slowly crawled off the pile, feet skidding on the uneven lumps. Choking coal dust enveloped him. He coughed as softly as he could, but just made his desire to cough even greater. Covering his mouth with his hand didn't help. All he succeeded in doing was rubbing coal dust around his mouth. *That's it. I'm putting on weight when I get home.*

Muttering dire consequences to Swan when he next saw him, he made it to the edge of the room. Not before treading on the edge of something he couldn't see and sending it flying across the cellar with a loud metal ping. *Anyone hear that?* A moment later, he decided no one had. He put a hand against the wall and bent over, trying to expel the coal dust from his lungs. Shirt tails made a convenient cloth to wipe around his mouth.

Footsteps echoed outside the door and he froze. He paused in the shadows until the footsteps died away, then moved to the door. *Let's hope it's not locked.* He cautiously turned the handle and pulled. *Finally.* Only to close it again quickly when the footsteps came back. This time accompanied by two male voices.

"Cook says two buckets ought to do it."

Fooks flattened himself behind the door as it opened. *Please don't cough.*

"Where's the shovel?"

"It should be there. Let me look."

A thud as the metal coal buckets hit the ground. A man illuminated by the light from the corridor walked forward. "I keep telling... Ah, here."

He walked forward dangerously close to Fooks and retrieved the shovel. Heart pounding, Fooks listened as two buckets filled with coal.

"Leave it where we can see it." The shovel returned to the pile in view of the door. "That's it. C'mon, it's cold out here."

Fooks let out a breath as the door closed. *You're telling me. Now all I've gotta do is get out of here, get to the door without being seen, and hope Swan has found a way to distract the police officer.*

As it turned out, Swan hadn't needed to create a distraction. One was provided for him. In the shape of a flirting kitchen maid. She lured the police officer away behind a wall of an outhouse. They would be occupied for some time, judging by the amount of female giggling and male chuckling going on. Swan sneaked in through the open door without being seen. Earlier Fooks, after leaving the coal cellar, had a similar uneventful journey back to his room.

After much needed baths, the two of them along with Caroline regrouped in Swan's suite.

"We need a plan of action." Fooks sipped his coffee and waited for suggestions.

"I'll say," Swan said, his mouth around yet another sandwich, the last on the salver.

"Were the police here long, Caroline?" Fooks asked.

"No. They made a cursory search of the house and asked a few questions. They asked me who you were and where you went."

"What did you tell them?" Fooks was sharp.

"The truth." She pulled a face. "Mainly. I told them you were the detective I hired."

"They stopped me on the drive. I told 'em I was going for a ride. To think."

Caroline smiled. "I told them the same thing." Her face fell. "I'm not sure they believed me. They left officers at each entrance. How did you get in without being seen?"

Fooks leaned forward and slid the cup and saucer onto the table. "Best you don't know." He sat back.

"Talking of the police, did someone tip them off Sam is here?"

Caroline shifted in irritation. "It would appear that way."

"But how?" Swan asked. "I thought we were careful. Only Cowdry—"

"Williams guessed Sam was here," Caroline said. "Of course, it wasn't him," she added firmly, and when she noticed Fooks' doubt, said, "It wasn't, Mr. Fooks."

"Nah, weren't Williams," Swan said, shaking his head.

Fooks waved a hand, acknowledging defeat. "Someone did. Someone who knew you're at Ardmaddy..." He tailed off, biting his thumb nail.

"What?" Swan asked, taking a sip of coffee.

Fooks leaned forward, elbows on his thighs. He rubbed his thumbs as he considered his next words. With a brief glance at Caroline, he said, "After Mrs. Kinsey told Brook about the conditions of the codicil, he said something that's been puzzling me. I thought he was just lashing out at me. He don't like me, that's obvious, but...well after today, there may be more to it." He sat back, reluctant to say more.

Caroline had no such qualms. "Like what, Mr. Fooks?"

Fooks sat forward again. "Think he suspects I'm not who I say I am. That we're not who we say we are."

Swan pushed his cup and saucer onto the table. "Even if he does suspect, he can't know who we really are."

"True, unless Robert Kinsey found out and told Brook."

"He'da had the police on our doorstep within minutes." Swan shook his head. "Naw, he may've suspected something, but wasn't sure enough to do anything about it."

"Brook's not so clear headed," Fooks said. "And he's under a lot of pressure right now." He tapped his fingers on the arm of the chair. "Think I should go back to Boston tomorrow and ask him."

"I should leave well alone, Mr. Fooks," Caroline said. "Brook has a lot to think about at the moment. Aunt Anne and I want him to make the right decision about his future."

"Yeah, you go poking the bear an' he won't." Swan stood up. "You've other folks to see in Boston, so reckon ya oughta go, but leave Brook Kinsey alone."

CHAPTER TWENTY-SIX

Oh boy did he ache.
Despite Caroline wanting to stay at Ardmaddy with him, Swan persuaded her to return to Boston with Fooks. Although their arguing cost Fooks a day, he was grateful for the delay. His exertions over the last few days now haunted him with a vengeance.

Although frustrated by Swan's advice to leave Brook Kinsey alone, Fooks conceded Swan was probably right. When Caroline said she ought to go to Kinsey House to check on her aunt, Fooks jumped at the chance to go along. There was another reason to go to Kinsey House. He wanted to see the girl, Kitty Miller.

As Fooks stood in the doorway of the office, there she was: the girl who'd avoided him up until now.

"Miss Miller?"

The girl spun around. She was slim, brown haired, and even features adorned her face. She clasped the handles of a brown leather framed carpetbag, resting on the desk.

Fooks found himself smiling. "Joseph Crane. We met briefly at Mr. Kinsey's funeral. Before Mr. Gray dragged you away. Why did he do that?" He noticed her eyes dropped to the Pinkerton shield he held.

"The funeral was upsetting. Mr. Gray was simply trying to protect me from more unpleasantness."

Fooks walked into the room fully. "I'm investigating Mr. Kinsey's murder on behalf of Mrs. Martin."

"I-I don't know anything about his murder."

"Wasn't an accusation. I'm looking for some background, Miss Miller. That's all. Just a few questions, please?" He turned on his most dazzling smile.

Kitty swallowed and gave a nervous laugh. "Now's not a good time. I'm on my way home and," she looked at the watch pinned to her jacket, "I'm likely to miss my train if I don't hurry. There's not another one for an hour and Mama will worry if I'm not home on time." Her grasp tightened around the handles of her bag, as she prepared to pick it up.

"I must insist I speak to you now, Miss Miller." Kitty took up the bag and straightened to face him, preparing to argue. He added, "I'll walk with you. We can talk on the way." He held his hand out, smiling pleasantly.

"I walk very fast, Mr. Crane."

Fooks dimpled. "Oh, I'm sure I can keep up. In fact," he purred, "my carriage is right outside. Why don't I give you a lift to the station instead? Then you won't miss your train."

"I'm not in the habit of getting into carriages with men I've only just met," she said, tossing her head irritably.

"No doubt you'll be more comfortable with another woman present. I can assure you Mrs. Martin is accompanying me."

Kitty bit her bottom lip and swallowed. She graciously inclined her head in acquiescence. "Very well, you leave me no choice but to accept your kind offer." She came forward to join him by the door. "*If* Mrs. Martin travels with us."

"Of course, Miss Miller. I have *my* reputation to think of."

He followed her out, rolling his eyes.

Caroline watched with interest as Fooks held open the door of the carriage for Kitty.

"Miss Miller requires a ride to the station, Mrs. Martin. Hope you don't mind?"

"No, of course not." Caroline gathered her skirts and slid along the seat. "How do you do, Miss Miller?"

Kitty climbed in and sat opposite. Fooks handed in her carpetbag, which she placed on her lap. She nodded to Caroline. "Good evening, Mrs. Martin. I hope you'll forgive the intrusion. Mr. Crane insisted."

"Yes, Mr. Crane can be very insistent at times," Caroline said and looked with interest at Fooks as he climbed in to sit beside her.

"Which station do you need, Miss Miller?" Fooks asked, ignoring Caroline.

"The Fitchburg Depot please."

Oh no, not Haymarket Square again. Fooks reluctantly relayed the instructions to the driver. As he did, he caught sight of a woman pushing one of those newfangled perambulators, containing a baby of a similar age to Susan. *Doubt if Sue would like it.* He allowed himself a moment to reflect on the image as he closed the door.

"You were working late, Miss Miller," Caroline said.

"Yes, there's a lot of catching up to do."

"No doubt."

Fooks stared out of the window, chewing his thumb nail, still thinking about his daughter and how much he missed her. He started when Caroline nudged him. "Mr. Crane? Miss Miller is waiting to be quizzed. At your convenience of course."

Fooks flashed a quick glare at Caroline. *Why does she have to be so sarcastic?* He put his irritation with Caroline to one side and smiled pleasantly at Kitty.

"Tell me about the mouse, Miss Miller."

Kitty's lips parted and her back stiffened slightly. "The mouse?"

Fooks stared at her intently. "Yes, Miss Miller. On the night Mr. Kinsey was murdered you alerted Grieveson to a mouse in the office."

"Oh, yes," she murmured and swallowed. "It scurried along the wall. Y'know how mice are. They're fast, twitchy creatures. As I'm sure you'll appreciate, it wasn't something I expected. It frightened me."

"Folks don't usually expect vermin in such a fine house. What did you do?"

Kitty gulped, as if recollecting a bad memory. "I'm afraid to admit it but I screamed." Fooks nodded in understanding. "When Mr. Grieveson came to investigate, I told him what I'd seen." Kitty's hands tightly clasped the handles of her bag. "He summoned other members of the staff and initiated a search."

"And what were you doing while this search was underway?"

"I watched for a while, but I kept getting in the way, so I took my belongings and left."

"Did you see anyone in the hall as you left?"

"No. I told you. Mr. Grieveson supervised the search."

Her fingers jittered on the handles of her carpetbag. Fooks dropped his eyes to focus on the fidgeting fingers. Kitty stilled her hands. *Was he making her nervous, or was it the situation?*

"Did you hear raised voices coming from the study?"

"No. I heard nothing from the study."

"What time did you leave that evening?"

Kitty licked her lips. "Um, I'm not sure. Later than usual, I think."

"Any idea of the time?"

Kitty shook her head as she thought. "I think it must have been nearly seven."

"You didn't see Mr. Martin at all?"

"I'm not sure I'd recognize him."

"What exactly do you do in Mr. Kinsey's employ?"

Kitty blinked rapidly. "I'm employed to operate the typewriter."

As she readjusted her hold on her carpetbag, Fooks noticed how white Kitty's knuckles were. "Are you privy to confidential correspondence, Miss Miller?" he asked, in a low voice.

"Yes."

"You're aware of Mr. Kinsey's business affairs?"

"Some of them, yes."

"I understand they are many and various."

"Yes, they are."

"What time train did you take home, Miss Miller?"

Kitty widened her eyes at the sudden change of direction the questions had taken. She swallowed and gazed out of the window. "I missed the seven o'clock train, so it must have been the eight o'clock." She gave a slight smile. "Yes, that must be right."

"Rather late for a lady to be traveling alone—"

"I make sure I sit in the ladies' carriage." She took a deep breath. "And I only get on if there are other ladies present. I try and strike up a conversation if I can. My mother didn't raise a fool."

"Very wise," Fooks said, in a murmur.

Caroline leaned forward. "How do you come to be in Mr. Kinsey's employ?"

Fooks turned sharply to Caroline. He thought he was conducting this interview. *Good question, though.*

"My late father was a former business associate of Mr. Kinsey's."

"So, it's as a favor to your father Mr. Kinsey employed you?" Fooks asked, trying for control of the conversation again.

"I like to think I'm employed on my own merits. I doubt Mr. Kinsey would have kept me on if I wasn't up to scratch." She ended with a defiant raise of her chin.

Fooks gave a short laugh. "Please accept my apologies. I didn't mean anything disparaging, Miss Miller." He favored her with his dazzling smile. "Did Mr. Kinsey have any enemies?"

Kitty frowned. "No, I don't believe so." She shook her head. "Mr. Crane, I type. I do not conduct the business."

"Surely when you're typing you are also reading?"

"I do not retain what I read, Mr. Crane," Kitty snapped. "If I did, my head would be full of things which hold no interest to me." She drew herself up, point scored. The effect was lost as the carriage jerked, sending her scrabbling to prevent her bag sliding from her lap. She gathered it and for a moment hugged it tightly to her chest, before relaxing.

"But surely." Fooks stopped. Continuing to pursue that line of questioning would get him nowhere. Caroline's eyes were on him and his color rose. And *she* would step in. Of course, women can conduct business. He only had to look at his own wife. "My pardon, Miss Miller for my poor choice of words." He swallowed hard and was glad when Caroline relaxed. He cleared his throat and decided to proceed more cautiously. "Do you own a gun, Miss Miller?"

"A gun?" She stared at him. "Why would I own a gun?"

Fooks pursed his lips and shrugged. "I dunno. Self-defense maybe? Traveling alone on trains. At night."

Kitty laughed gently. "Mr. Crane I'm going to Waltham, and I can assure you I am perfectly capable of defending myself." She rummaged in her bag and brought out her incomplete knitting. She pulled one needle from the ball of wool and brandished it at him. "I know where a man's delicate places are, Mr. Crane." She raised an eyebrow. "Care to try me?"

Fooks gulped and fiddled with his collar, which suddenly felt too tight. "No, thank you Miss Miller. I'll, er, take your word for it."

Kitty gave him a knowing look before returning her knitting to her bag. Out of the corner of his eye, Fooks saw Caroline's smirk, before she turned away.

Fooks leaned forward and studied Kitty intently. "Now your employer is no more, what does this mean for you, Miss Miller?" His words held a hidden meaning.

Kitty stared out of the window.

Fooks glanced at Caroline, who glanced back when there was no answer.

"Miss Miller?"

Kitty started out of her thoughts. "Why, Mr. Crane, it will change my life."

CHAPTER TWENTY-SEVEN

The carriage pulled up on the opposite side of the road to the Fitchburg Railroad Depot. Fooks climbed out first and helped Kitty down. She all but shrugged him off, but covered her actions by smoothing her skirts.

"Thank you. I really must dash now."

She fled across the street, narrowly missing traffic, to the main entrance. Fooks watched her go until she safely reached the sidewalk. He glanced at the clock above the main entrance. Six-forty. *Hmmm, why did she need to run?*

"Fairfield House, please," he called to the driver.

He climbed back into the carriage. He sat opposite Caroline and slammed the door. The sudden movement of the carriage jerked him out of his thoughts. "What d'you think?" he asked.

Caroline raised an eyebrow. "She appeared on edge."

"I thought that as well."

"Did you notice her bag?"

"Yeah, it was heavy. Wonder what she has in there to carry back and forth," Fooks said, distracted.

"It has a rather unusual design."

Fooks frowned at her sharply. "Has it?" He shrugged. "A carpetbag. Pretty common, I'da thought."

"Yes," Caroline said, icily, "but I've not seen the red diamond pattern before."

Fooks gave it some thought. A brown leather patchwork frame. The material of the bag itself made of carpet. Bright red diamonds made of felt ran in decreasing sizes left to right along the width of the middle of the bag.

"And that's not all." Caroline gave an unladylike smirk when he jerked his head up. "On the other side the pattern is reversed, right to left."

"So? You ladies like quirky design."

"Don't be so petulant, Mr. Fooks," she snapped. "And listen. All the diamonds were machine sewn, except for the largest two. They were hand sewn, and the color red of the felt slightly different."

Fooks stared at her, trying to discern her meaning. He glanced out of the window, gave a short laugh and shook his head. *Woman's critical of everything.* "I'm sure it's nothing."

Caroline sniffed in a deep breath, not convinced. "Perhaps you're right," she murmured. "What's the next step?"

"I'd like to see Kinsey's business partner, Ephraim Smith. Shame he can't make time for me until later this week. I bet he can tell us a thing or two."

"You have your work cut out."

"I do." He sat with his hands clasped loosely on his lap. "How are you holding up?"

"I'm glad Samuel is safe."

"For the moment. Moving him to Ardmaddy was risky. Not sure we shoulda done it."

"I'm well aware of the risks, Mr. Fooks," Caroline snapped and then went on in a more delicate tone.

"Samuel thought it best and it was his decision. I thought you liked Ardmaddy. As a change from the city. Samuel tells me you are not liking Boston."

Fooks raised an eyebrow. "Not what I'm used to," he muttered. They were coming to Haymarket Square again. He braced himself for the traffic chaos.

"Samuel enjoyed spending time with you. Even if it was a little fraught." She hesitated. "This next week will give us a chance to know each other better. I fear we got off to a difficult start."

"True. Woulda been easier to meet under better circumstances." He grasped the arm rest as the carriage slew to the right and then stopped abruptly. *Sheesh.* Outside a horse shrieked. Angry men's voices, including their own drivers, rose over the general background noise.

"You don't entirely trust me, do you?" Caroline asked, continuing the conversation as if nothing had happened.

Fooks swallowed hard. "I-I wouldn't say that exactly—" When the carriage moved again, he slowly relaxed.

"Then what would you say?"

"Doesn't that bother you?" Fooks waved a hand behind him.

"No." Caroline brushed an imaginary piece of lint from her skirts. "Adams is an experienced driver. I have full confidence in him."

Glad you do. Fooks chose his words carefully. "I would say I'm out of my depth right now. Being here in a big Eastern city. It's a different world to the one I know. Not sure how things here work. I'm grateful for your help in opening the doors for me."

"It's in my interests to help as much as I can."

"I'm sure it is. I'll ask again. Why don't you call me Joe, or Joseph?"

Caroline inclined her head graciously. "I'll try. I find it difficult to be on first name terms with men I hardly know, but very well. Joseph."

"What do you know about Ephraim Smith?"

"Not much. My father had some dealings with him, which is how Robert became acquainted with him. Papa was surprised when they became partners."

"Why?" Fooks asked, sharply.

"Two very different men. An unlikely partnership, Papa said."

Fooks grunted and gazed out of the window. A sudden burst of evening sunshine made him screw up his eyes. "Smith has agreed to see me on Friday. Guess I'll find out then. In the meantime, I've still two of the tontine shareholders to see. Slocomb is the first on the list."

The next morning, Fooks was shown into a drawing room, belonging to Harvey Slocomb. On describing it to Caroline later, she said it sounded like Louis XV style. All spindly French furniture and gold leaf ornaments. In front of the huge white marble fireplace, more French inspired seating upholstered in rich silk brocades.

"You've lost her? Your nominee?" Fooks' eyes popped in response to the first thing he asked.

"Yes." Harvey Slocomb slapped the side of his legs and shrugged. "She's disappeared. Nobody has seen her for days. The police are out searching for her." He sank onto the edge of the sofa and sniffed. "I don't know what to do."

Harvey Slocomb was rather an effete young man, well dressed in the latest fashions. A white lawn shirt, crimson silk U-shaped vest, matching Ascot, tied in an overlarge knot. His light gray narrow trousers enhanced with crimson piping. On his feet house slippers covered with elaborate embroidery.

Fooks gulped and joined him on the other end of the sofa. "Has she ever gone missing before?"

"No. No. She's a mature sensible lady." He gave Fooks a weak smile. "That's why I picked her as my nominee for the tontine. She's not given to dangerous sports or risks of any kind. She takes care of herself."

"Mr. Slocomb." Fooks frantically searched his pockets for his notepad and pencil. "Perhaps this has something to do with the matter I'm investigating."

"But you're investigating murder!" Slocomb shook his head. "Oh no. That can't have happened to Lillian. No, no, no. This is all my fault. I should never have…"

Fooks watched uncomfortably as Slocomb folded over, rocking back and forward, clearly sobbing. *I thought only women did this.*

"Um." Fooks searched his pockets and found a handkerchief. He gave it a cursory glance. *Yeah, probably okay.* "Here, Mr. Slocomb."

"Thank you." Slocomb dabbed his eyes. "Mr. Crane, you must think I'm such a fool. Lillian is very dear to me. The thought of anything bad happening to her because of something I did. Well, it doesn't bear thinking about."

Fooks took back the damp handkerchief. "Not at all, Mr. Slocomb—"

"Harvey. You must call me Harvey," he said and sniffed. "You've caught me in a vulnerable moment. We can hardly be formal at a time like this."

"If you insist."

"You've been very kind. I trust this won't go any further?"

"No, I promise." Fooks leaned forward. "I do think Lillian's disappearance is somehow tied up with the case I'm investigating. I tell you this, the circumstances are very different. I'm sure we'll find Lillian safe and well. I'll keep an eye out for her while I'm about my business."

Slocomb gave a weak smile. "Would you? Thank you."

"Perhaps if you tell me about Lillian. What's her full name?"

"Lillian Emerson. She's sixty-five and she lives in Waltham."

Fooks eyes popped. "Waltham? Here in Massachusetts?"

"Why is this significant?"

Fooks pursed his lips. "Waltham has come up several times in my investigation. Popular place all of a sudden. What's her exact address?"

"Number 18, Highland Avenue."

"Has she lived there long?"

"She's lived in Waltham all her life."

"Do you know Waltham, Mr. Slocomb?"

Slocomb shook his head. "Me? No, hardly at all."

"Do you by chance know a woman by the name of Kitty Miller?"

"No. Should I?"

Fooks rolled his eyes as he tucked his notepad away. "No, you shouldn't." *You really shouldn't.*

A few minutes later, Fooks stood on the street outside and hailed a cab to take him back to Fairfield House. Tomorrow the last tontine holder, Montgomery Whitlock.

CHAPTER TWENTY-EIGHT

The next morning Fooks took a cab to the address of Montgomery Whitlock. He paid off the cab outside a large, double fronted house. When a woman opened the door, he tipped his hat.

"Sorry to disturb you ma'am. I'm Joseph Crane. I'm hoping to visit with Mr. Montgomery Whitlock. Does he live here?"

The shy middle-aged woman, half hidden behind the door, shook her head. She pointed across the street at the church and cemetery.

Fooks spun around. "I should try over there?"

She nodded and closed the door.

Fooks took himself across the street to the church. As he entered, he removed his hat and fluffed at his hair. He made his way along the nave, gazing at the high vaulted ceiling. *Wow, this is not like any church I've been in before.*

A man dressed in a black cassock hurried to meet him. "Can I help you, my son?" he asked, giving Fooks a non-threatening smile.

"Good day, Father. My name is Joseph Crane and I'm looking for Montgomery Whitlock. Lady across the street suggested I try here."

"I'm afraid you are too late. Much too late."

Fooks blinked. "I am?"

"Indeed, you are. The service was over two hours ago."

"The service?" Fooks winced. He sounded like an idiot.

"The service of internment." Fooks blinked. "For Montgomery Whitlock. That is why you are here isn't it?"

Suddenly all was clear. Sort of. "Er, yes. No. I mean…"

"Sit down my son." Before Fooks knew it he found himself eased into a pew. "I can see this has come as quite a shock for you. Was Montgomery a dear friend?"

"No, er, no. I-I didn't—"

"I quite understand. Sit there for a moment, until you feel like talking. My name is Father O'Brien."

"Thank you, Father, but you have it all wrong, I—"

"I'm quite used to grief and the different ways it affects us, Joseph. Take your time."

"No." Fooks rubbed his forehead in frustration. "I-I'm just looking for Montgomery Whitlock."

"Of course. I'll take you to see him in a moment or two."

"Oh, um, not why I've come Father."

"But you must. I can tell by your accent you're not from round here. You can't come all this way and not see him."

Give up, Fooks. Give up. "No, I suppose I can't. If it's not too much trouble, Father."

"No trouble at all."

Father O'Brien took Fooks outside, across the cemetery and led him up a slight incline. They stopped in front of a freshly dug grave. "He has a lovely view from up here."

Fooks smiled weakly. "Yes." He contemplated the bare heaped up earth. The temporary wooden marker bore the name of Montgomery Whitlock. "I'm sure he'll be very happy," he murmured.

"I'll leave you to pay your respects in private. If you need me, I'll be in the church."

Fooks remained standing silently, head bowed, hands and hat clasped in front of him for some time. The wind wiped at his hair and it wasn't long before he grew cold. So, Montgomery Whitlock is no more. *I think I can dismiss you as a suspect, but how did you die? And when exactly?* Fooks straightened his shoulders. He resolved to go back to the church and ask the over-solicitous Father O'Brien.

He had no trouble finding him, as the clergyman appeared to be waiting for him. "May I be of further help, Joseph?"

"Yes. How did Monty die?" Fooks cleared his throat. "Sorry, I mean Montgomery. I called him Monty." *Yeah, only to myself.*

Father O'Brien gestured to a pew. "A most peculiar accident. At the Boston Public Library. Do you know it?"

"Of course," Fooks lied.

"Then you know at times the place positively teems with crowds. I understand...Monty was descending the stairs. A group of young women came behind him, giggling and pushing as is their wont. One of their number stumbled and fell against...Monty. As you know, because of his condition, he suffered from a lack of balance." At this Fooks nodded, sagely. "I'm afraid to say, not expecting a shove from behind, poor Monty fell." Fooks gasped in horror. "All the way to the bottom, Joseph. Unable to save himself you see."

Father O'Brien put a hand on Fooks' arm in sympathy. "Hard stone steps are not very forgiving. Nothing could be done."

Fooks put his head down. "Poor Monty."

"I'm sure he's safe in the Lord's embrace."

"Yes. That is a comfort. Thank you for telling me. I should go now I've paid my respects."

Fooks left intent on finding out more about Whitlock's accident. Best place to start: the Boston Public Library. He hailed a passing cab and gave the address. "55 Boylston Street, please. The Public Library."

After a brief tour of Boston's attractions, Fooks arrived outside the library. He surveyed the brick building with sandstone trimmings. Four arched windows, two each side of the door, gave the building a church like appearance. Above a fake balustrade stood three clear glass arched windows. Empty alcoves on either side completed the façade.

Fooks walked up the few steps to the main entrance and found himself in a double height hallway. Flights of the fateful stairs hugged the walls on either side. If Whitlock had fallen from near the top. He shuddered. *Don't think about it, Fooks.*

Straight ahead lay a ramp leading into the lower library hall. He made for the lower hall indicator board, thinking he might find what he needed himself even if there was no one around to help.

A helpful woman with a name badge pinned to her left shoulder stood ready to assist with enquiries.

"Mr. Whitlock's accident? Dreadful. Poor man. I wasn't on duty myself, but my co-worker said the blood went everywhere. A number of women fainted. Fortunately, there was a doctor in the library. He gave what assistance he could, but no. The police came of course and shut the library. They questioned everyone here." She shook her head. "The poor lady who stumbled. What must be going through her mind?"

"Awful. An accident of course."

"Yes."

"Are there any newspaper reports?"

"Oh yes. The papers carried it for days."

"Here in the library?" Fooks smiled with both dimples, hoping the effect would work on her.

She flushed. "I'll show you."

Fooks followed into the reading room. She indicated he should sit at a large table, polished within an inch of its life, before searching in the stacks behind him. She brought out several broadsheets on wooden poles and placed these in front of him.

"These should get you started. If there's anything else I can find for you, please let me know. I'm here until four." She glanced at the watch pinned to her dress below the badge. "When I leave for the day."

"I might not have finished by then." His eyes twinkled mischievously. "But thank you."

She fled. Fooks watched her go, suddenly feeling guilty for flirting. *You shouldna done that Fooks. You're a married man.*

He soon put his qualms aside as he began to flick through the newspapers. He wanted more information on the group of women behind Whitlock. He rifled through several papers unsuccessfully; aware his rustling of pages was earning him irritated frowns from other library users. Determined to be quieter, it looked like his quest was going to remain unfulfilled. Until the final paper, the respected *Boston Globe,* ran the headline:

DEATH AT LIBRARY

Unnecessarily dramatic.

He read on. At first, it was just the same account of the unfortunate Mr. Whitlock's fall, the struggle to save him by an eminent doctor, the police investigation and then,

Police interviewed the somber group of four women, who were behind Mr. Whitlock on the stairs. One gave this account to our reporter, "It was Kitty who stumbled. We were jostling each other like good friends do. Maggie stopped her falling, but it was too late. Kitty had already knocked against poor Mr. Whitlock. Down he went, head over heels. The crack of his head when it hit the stone floor. I've never heard anything like it. So loud. And all the blood. Fiona fainted. Why, I almost took a turn myself. The police questioned us for ages and ages. We told the truth. An accident. Pure and simple."

Fooks scanned the rest of the editorial for more on Kitty but nothing. He made a fist and put it to his lips, thinking. Kitty. *Name keeps coming up, doesn't it?* Might be a coincidence. A lot of women were called Kitty. He tidied the newspapers and left them on the table.

On his way out a sudden thought struck him. He flashed his Pinkerton shield at the male librarian on the checkout desk. He explained he was investigating Mr. Whitlock's death for a client. *Almost true. I am kinda.*

"Did any of the women behind him borrow books that day?"

The librarian nodded. "Yes sir, I believe so. Would you like me to check?"

"Yes, please."

Fooks hovered as the librarian went off to check. He soon returned. "Three of the women took out books on Monday April 19, sir. Miss Rosemary Brown took out *Heidi*, by Johanna Spyri. Miss Margaret Wilson took out *The Portrait of a Lady*, by Henry James. And Miss Kitty Miller took out..." He widened his eyes, "a copy of *Gray's Anatomy*."

"Heavy going for a young woman." Fooks frowned. "Not that there's anything wrong with her reading it of course," he added, quickly.

"Each to their own. Will that be all?"

So, Montgomery Whitlock died three days before Kinsey's murder. A woman called Kitty Miller was responsible, albeit accidentally. What were the chances she was the same Kitty Miller who worked for Kinsey?

Fooks tipped his hat and left in search of a cab to take him back to Fairfield House. By the end of the day tomorrow, after seeing the hard to meet Ephraim Smith, he should have all the pieces of the puzzle he needed to work out what was going on.

CHAPTER TWENTY-NINE

"Mr. Crane, I can give you a few minutes." Friday morning finally dawned and Fooks could at last get to see Kinsey's business partner.

Ephraim Smith was a far younger man than Fooks expected. More Brook Kinsey's age. Caroline's father was correct. An unlikely partnership indeed. Smith sat in an easy chair in the middle of an orderly office. He gestured to the opposite chair, as he patted the pile of papers on his lap into a neat pile, then he stretched to lay them on the desk behind him.

"Thank you, Mr. Smith, I realize you're a busy man." Fooks crossed the room to take the offered seat. "You understand I'm investigating Mr. Kinsey's murder for Mrs. Martin? She's anxious to clear her husband of course so I may ask some direct questions."

"Yes of course. Although I don't know what else I can add to the answers I've already given to the police."

Fooks crossed his legs and took out his notepad and pencil, preparing to write. "The police have their job to do and I mine. I'll likely ask different questions. How closely did you and Mr. Kinsey work together?"

"Very."

"Are you fully apprised of what Mr. Kinsey worked on?"

Smith pursed his lips before answering. "Robert and I rarely kept secrets from one another. Not the basis for a good partnership."

"No." Fooks noted the hesitation and guarded reply. *Follow up on that later.* "Did you get on well socially?"

"We rarely socialized unless there was a business element to the gathering."

"How did your business relationship work, Mr. Smith?"

"Our business interests have two separate parts. He took care of his. I look after mine. We met once a month to swap progress."

"Interesting." Fooks wrote in his ubiquitous notepad.

"Why interesting?"

"The way people work, Mr. Smith. I've come across many different methods over the years. Always amazes me how some people chose to work."

"If it works, why change it?" Smith lifted his chin in challenge.

"I agree. Did Mr. Kinsey have any enemies?"

"Robert could be abrasive at times. Some parties didn't always appreciate his approach."

Fooks' eyebrows shot up in interest. "Who in particular?"

"No one in particular, Mr. Crane."

These Easterners are a cagey lot.

Fooks cleared his throat. "Where were you at the time of Mr. Kinsey's murder?"

"At home."

"Can anyone corroborate that?"

"My man served dinner at seven and after he had cleared away, I dismissed him for the night."

"Where do you live, Mr. Smith?"

"I live in Cambridge, near the university."

Fooks consulted the map of Boston in his head. "Mr. Kinsey lived on Mount Vernon Street, and he died before eight."

"Yes," Smith said, with a rueful smile. "Unless I can sprout wings, I couldn't possibly get there in the time. Does that take me out of the frame?"

"Mr. Smith, I am merely thinking out loud," Fooks said, quickly. "Do you own a gun by chance?"

"Um. An old hunting rifle but I'm not aware if it still works. I haven't used it for years." Smith frowned. "Why?"

Fooks hesitated, pondering on what to say next. "No, it doesn't entirely take you out of the frame. Were you embezzling from the business, Mr. Smith?"

Smith stared at him open mouthed. "What makes you—"

"I found certain documents in Mr. Kinsey's private safe—"

"What documents?"

"This, for starters." Fooks produced the note from his pocket and held it out. "But these are the most telling, Mr. Smith." He followed with a sheaf of documents.

Smith snatched at them. "What are these?" As he read his face fell. "These aren't what you think," he murmured.

"Really?" Fooks raised an eyebrow. "What *do* I think, Mr. Smith?"

"I can explain."

"Please do."

Smith stood and walked to the window. He stared out, arms behind his back.

"Do you have children, Mr. Crane?"

"Yes. A little daughter."

"How old?"

"Coming up to one."

"She is precious to you?"

Fooks thought of Susan. Given everything he'd been through to get her, oh yes, Susan was precious all right. "Yes."

"My daughter was three. Barely started her life." Smith spoke to the window. When he turned back to Fooks, his face was grave. "Her mother died in childbirth. Judy was all I had. She developed a serious illness. I needed money to pay for treatment that might save her. I went to Robert and explained I wanted to take more out of the business than usual. I thought he would agree when I told him my reason." Smith turned and pressed his lips together. "Do you know what he said to me?"

Fooks shook his head.

"Robert said Judy was my responsibility. Children die all the time, and I should accept it."

"Callous of him."

"It was," Smith agreed. His eyes watered and Fooks dropped his gaze. "I took three thousand dollars in total. Inflated my expenses, a little here, a little there. Gray didn't notice, so I thought I'd got away with it. I had every intention of paying it back of course, but then Judy...died."

"My condolences, Mr. Smith."

"Thank you. I went to Robert again and told him what I did. I suppose I expected more understanding this time." He laughed without humor. "I should have known better. Robert became angry. Shouting. Thumping the desk. I'd never known him like that before." He shook his head. "When Brook walked into the study unannounced, I took advantage of the interruption and left. This was shortly before.... I didn't see him again."

Smith sat and poked the documents on the table. "What you see here, in Robert's handwriting, are his attempts to uncover my misappropriations. I don't understand why he's done this. He knows I'm an honest man. Knew I intended to pay the money back. Surely Gray could put an extraordinary provision in the accounts? This would allow me to repay over time."

"Was he blackmailing you?"

"No, Mr. Crane, I was blackmailing him."

Fooks gawped at the revelation. "I don't understand. I thought the note was a draft of his."

"No." Smith smiled. "I sent it."

"Why were you blackmailing him?"

"Oh, it's quite simple," Smith said. "I had something on him."

CHAPTER THIRTY

Fooks opened his mouth. "What?"

"The business with Martin. Robert had his men shoot him." Smith paused. "I was present when he gave them their instructions."

Fooks leaned forward. "Mr. Smith, my client's husband is wanted for the murder of Robert Kinsey. The main motive being Martin took revenge on Kinsey for ordering his shooting."

"Yes, indeed. That's why I haven't mentioned this to the police. It wouldn't help Martin's case." He paused. "Mr. Crane, I don't believe Martin shot Robert. As far as I'm aware, he always dealt honorably with Robert, despite the provocation. I never understood Robert's antipathy to the man. Caroline appears extraordinarily happy with the marriage of convenience. By all accounts, the Martins' marriage is now a true love match. No, I don't want to assist in the prosecution of a man I believe to be innocent."

"Very commendable, but why tell me about your attempt at blackmail?"

"The police didn't uncover the note I wrote. You did." Smith sat back, tight-lipped. "You obviously have...talents, shall we say? That the police lack. I've no doubt this will not go any further."

Fooks pulled a face. Was this a thinly veiled threat? "Sounds like the police didn't ask the right questions. I'm not going to tell them the answers to questions they didn't ask."

Smith chuckled briefly. "I appreciate your candor, Mr. Crane."

Fooks dropped his voice. "The two men Kinsey hired; did they ever work for you?"

Smith stared at him hard. "No."

Fooks raised an eyebrow. "Were you *planning* to use them against Kinsey?"

Smith bit his lip as he considered his answer. Finally, he sighed, and said, "If I had to." He swallowed hard. "In the end I didn't need them."

Fooks wasn't convinced. "So, they had no idea what you had in mind?"

"No. I'd sounded them out about doing something for me but we discussed nothing in detail." He noted Fooks' look of interest. "And I certainly wasn't considering murder, if that's what you're thinking."

"I wasn't, Mr. Smith." He made a note in his pad and then regarded Smith thoughtfully. "Are you planning to keep quiet about your fiddling the books?"

Smith winced in irritation. "Yes."

Fooks rubbed the side of his face. "I checked the accounts, the ones Gray prepared, I didn't notice any differences."

Smith shrugged. "There shouldn't be. Gray paid my expenses as I gave them to him. He didn't query a thing."

"How did Kinsey come up with this set?"

"Robert knew what I should have spent. Gray does not. As far as Gray is concerned the expenses are legitimate." He paused. "I suspect Robert was trying to find out the extent of my misappropriations. Perhaps to use against me later, should he feel he needed to."

Fooks blinked. "And you were business partners? Where is the trust?"

Smith smiled. "It was there in the beginning. I can assure you."

"Did Mr. Kinsey have any other business partners?"

"When I first became involved, he had one other, but not now."

"And what happened to this other business partner?"

"His name was Chester Miller. He's dead."

"Chester Miller? The girl who types for Kinsey is Kitty Miller. Is she his daughter?"

"I believe so, yes."

"Were you aware of the tontine investment Kinsey held shares in for the building of the Hayes Theater?"

"Yes, but Robert told me it ceased some years ago."

"It had. Did you know Chester Miller also held a shareholding in the tontine?"

"No, I did not."

"What happened to Mr. Miller's business affairs after he died?"

Smith licked his lips. "There weren't any. I'm afraid Chester bankrupted himself. He left little of value."

Fooks chewed his bottom lip. "How exactly did Chester bankrupt himself?"

"Before my time, but as I understand it, a business deal went bad. He sunk everything into it and unfortunately things didn't work out how he hoped. He never recovered. I believe he tried a few other ventures, but he said he'd lost his touch."

Fooks moved his tongue around his mouth. All manner of things swirled in his brain. He resisted the urge to stand and pace. Instead, he rubbed his fingers together and stared into space.

"Mr. Crane?"

Fooks stared past Smith without seeing him.

"Mr. Crane, is something wrong?"

Fooks blinked rapidly and shook his head. "No, I-I." Now he did get up and strolled to the window. "Did…" He half turned. "Mr. Smith, was Kinsey involved in these business deals of Miller's?"

"Yes. He came out rather better; I believe."

Fooks swallowed hard and glanced away. Things were clicking into place. "Are you acquainted with Miller's daughter, Kitty?"

"Not really. Only by sight."

"What's your opinion of her?"

Smith laughed. "I hardly know her."

"Your impression then?" Fooks almost snapped, managing to catch himself in time.

"She appears a very confident young lady."

"Yes, she does," Fooks murmured, staring out of the window, not seeing the busy street below. A moment later, he crossed the room quickly, snatching his hat as he went. He paused at the door. "I'll leave those documents with you, Mr. Smith. For safe keeping." *I don't need 'em. Better off in Smith's hands.* With a meaningful nod he left a grinning Smith behind him.

Fooks walked along the street deep in thought. Some hostility between Smith and Kinsey, but would Smith kill him? He found Smith's explanation convincing, but didn't necessarily rule him out.

Fooks stepped forward, waited for a moment, before raising his arm to hail a cab to take him to the Fitchburg Depot. Train to Waltham, cab out to Ardmaddy. The blackboard awaited, and he was eager to get going, now he had the full picture. Perhaps he'd be able to make sense of it all now.

Okay, let's update this with what I've learned. Dawn the next morning found Fooks, still in his robe, scratching away at the blackboard Swan had set up in his suite. Swan's bed appeared hardly slept in. Fooks was alone, and gratefully so. He needed to think. While he found Swan's input helpful at times, he did ask questions and wanted explanations when Fooks needed to concentrate.

He'd already divided the board into two. On one half he'd drawn three boxes, labeled 'Tontine', 'Business' and 'Other'. These served as the connection to the victim. In each he'd written a list of names. The other half of the board he'd divided into three, each with a heading: Motive; Means; Opportunity.

"If the woman is to be believed, Eugene Camden has gone abroad. I'll dismiss him for now unless no one else stands out." He drew a line through his name. "The fella who fell down the stairs at the library, Montgomery Whitlock, is out, 'cos he died before Kinsey." He scratched out his name. "Who is left from the tontine? So that leaves them," he tapped the chalk at the Miller family, "and him." The chalk tapped at Harvey Slocomb. "No. No. He was so upset about Lillian Emerson being missing. Oh, but perhaps I shouldn't dismiss him 'cos I believe him. Okay, he stays for now. Who else?"

"Now Ephraim Smith has a powerful motive against Kinsey 'cos of the insensitive way he treated him over his daughter, but," he licked his lips, "if he lets things lie, no doubt things will sort themselves out. Guess that's his plan. If I'm keeping Slocomb on the list of suspects, I should keep Smith on as well. Only fair."

The next on the list. "Brook Kinsey. Is he the sorta man to kill his own father? He reacted badly when he heard Kinsey left most of his financial affairs to Caroline. Yet he couldn't know 'bout the codicil. By the same token, Caroline could also have a motive to kill him. All the aggravation he'd caused her over Swan."

"No. She doesn't."

Fooks jumped as Swan walked into the room, arms folded. He studied the board, as Fooks stood silently by.

"Give me the chalk, Fooks."

Fooks handed over the chalk stick and watched as Swan cross out Caroline's name. "It's true, Kinsey was a pain in the proverbial over our marriage, but Caroline wouldn't kill him over it. She's not that type of woman."

Fooks bit his lip.

"And ya still have my name on here!"

"I hadn't finished," Fooks said, defensively. "To do this proper, I have to consider everyone."

"Yeah, well I'm considered." Swan crossed his name through. He slapped the chalk stick into Fooks' palm and walked away a few steps. He ran his fingers through his sleep tousled hair. "Okay, what else ya got?"

"If you'd let me finish, I'm looking at motive next."

Swan waved a hand at the board. "Go on then. Look at motive."

Fooks let him off with a glare before turning back to the board. "The Miller family and Slocomb have a motive because they stand to come into money via the tontine. Gray was being passed over for his job. By all accounts he has a family to support, and losing his job isn't ideal. That's a motive. Then there's Henry Downton at the Hayes Theater. How much artistic interference could he endure until he cracked? Ephraim Smith is a possibility, but he lives too far away. Unless he got someone to do it for him."

"What 'bout those two fellas who shot me?"

Fooks considered. "Smith knows them." He sighed. "But I got the impression he didn't give them any instruction. Besides, I think they are more interested in not being picked up for shooting you, rather than Kinsey." He studied the board. "They're not even on my list."

"Thought ya said ya had to consider everyone." Swan tried not to grin.

"Shaddup." Fooks glared at Swan until he held up his hands in apology. He turned back to the board. "There's Brook Kinsey. Like I was saying before you rudely interrupted, he was upset his father left things to Caroline."

"No. You've met Brook Kinsey. You may be right about the way Kinsey planned to curtail his son's gambling habit. Brook was happy with life as was, and I don't think he'd murder his pa 'cos he wanted him to work for a change. Strikes me that's cutting off ya nose to spite ya face. Naw, Brook woulda wormed his way outta it, if it happened. Kinsey cutting him out of his will means he no longer has surety for his debts. I guess that's a mite worrying."

"Yes, I guess it would be." Fooks raised his eyebrows. "Surety? That's a big word for you. Know what it means?"

"Course I do. I live in a house with a library the size of a small town. I go in there, look stuff up." Swan tailed off. "Now if ya don't mind, like to get dressed." He headed for his dressing room.

"Now let's look at means."

Swan about turned. Fooks waited until he'd returned to stand in front of the board again.

"Kinsey was shot at close quarters with a 0.22. He musta known his killer to let them get so close. Must be personal—"

"Someone takes your life it's always personal."

"So," Fooks ignored him and glanced over the board, "doesn't rule anyone out. Not really."

"Opportunity?"

"Grieveson said Kinsey had no other visitors that evening." He stood hands on hips and walked slowly towards the board. "Could be true, but we'll have to assume no one sneaked in we don't know about. Means likely to be someone already in the house." He crossed through Slocomb, Downton and Smith. "Gray said he left about five and he was at his daughter's play all evening. Easy enough to check. If he lied, there are too many witnesses to say he wasn't there. Nah, not him."

Fooks crossed his name out.

"What's this Slocomb like?"

"Harmless, and he doesn't have a reason to kill Kinsey."

"His nominee is missing," Swan pointed out. "This tontine—"

"It doesn't work like that. It's not last man standing. The nominee has to be living, remember?"

"But if—"

"If she's missing, he can't prove she's alive. Can he? If he kidnaps his nominee, there's no benefit to him. No. He's so upset she's missing. He's coming off."

Swan watched as Fooks crossed through Slocomb's name. "Okay, but—"

"But nothing. He's off."

Swan folded his arms. "What's your conclusion?"

They both turned as the connecting door opened.

CHAPTER THIRTY-ONE

"*Have* you come to any conclusions?" Caroline came out to join them, immediately locking her arm through her husband's. She gazed at him fondly. "I heard you talking."

"Some." Swan gestured to a chair. "Fooks is jus' 'bout to tell me."

When all were seated, Fooks quickly brought Caroline up to date with the inquiry. She raised an eyebrow when he glossed over she had been a suspect.

"You are quite correct, Mr. Fooks. You do have to consider everybody," Caroline said.

Fooks inclined his head in acceptance and flashed a false smile in Swan's direction, who rolled his eyes.

"Who do you have in mind?" Caroline asked.

Fooks stood and paced to the window.

Caroline twisted in her seat to watch him and turned back to Swan.

"He really is the most irritating—"

Swan put a hand on her arm to silence her. Together they watched Fooks pace. He pumped a fist, frowned, and bit his thumbnail as he went.

Then Fooks suddenly stopped and stood arms akimbo. "It's gotta be the tontine."

"I don't understand." Caroline wrung her hands. "I thought the tontine was moot. Robert's nominee was my father, and he died four years ago."

"Yes, it is moot, as you say, with regards to your uncle's share. The tontine is wound up when the shareholders get down to the last two. With Kinsey out of the way, that leaves the Millers and Slocomb. Don't you see? Slocomb can't produce his nominee." Fooks tailed off and his eyes popped. "Lillian lives right here in Waltham."

Swan stood abruptly and snatched a newspaper from the top of a cupboard.

"The shareholders don't know who the other nominees are," Fooks said, in explanation. "Or if they're alive or dead. Whoever killed Kinsey didn't know your father was Kinsey's nominee."

Meanwhile, Swan rustled through the newspaper quickly. "Here we are." He folded the newspaper in half and half again. "Look." He showed Fooks, stabbing a finger on the page.

Fooks read. "Lillian Emerson," he murmured. "That's it."

Swan retook his seat. "Yeah," Swan confirmed.

Caroline looked from one to the other. "Who is Lillian Emerson?"

Fooks passed the paper over. When she finished reading, she frowned, still none the wiser. Fooks and Swan shared excited grins. With gritted teeth, Caroline repeated her question.

"Lillian Emerson is Harvey Slocomb's nominee," Fooks explained. "I have an idea." He levered up. "I'm going into town. Some of Lillian's neighbors might be able to tell us something about her disappearance. They might not be comfortable speaking to police, but they might just speak to me."

Swan puffed. "Wish I could go with ya."

Fooks tutted in sympathy. Swan was not the sort of man to sit idly by while others did the work. Must chafe. "So do I, but we can't risk someone seeing you. No." Fooks held up a finger. "Not even if you go in disguise."

Swan wrinkled his nose. "I know, Fooks, I know. Got ya gun?"

Fooks patted his pocket. "Yep."

"Okay then good luck."

After Fooks had departed, Caroline left Swan to get dressed. Cowdry brought his breakfast and when he'd finished, Swan stood in front of Fooks' blackboard, jingling change in his pocket. "Lillian Emerson lives here in Waltham. Hmmm." He stroked his chin thoughtfully. "Wonder if I can go downstairs without anyone seeing me?" He raised his voice. "Cowdry," he called, knowing his valet pottered about in the dressing room.

Cowdry appeared immediately. "Sir?"

"Need to go down to the library. What's the best way without being seen?"

"If you know what you want sir, I'll fetch it for you."

"Not sure I do. Looking for a book covering the local area that gives names and addresses."

"You'll want the Waltham Directory sir. It's mainly for businesses and advertising but also includes some individuals and their details."

Swan grinned. "Excellent. Sounds like what I'm after." He sat again.

Cowdry hesitated. "Will I get it for you sir?"

"Yes, please. And anything else about the town might help. A map say? I'm not too familiar with all the side streets."

"I'll go right now sir."

Cowdry took a long while. Long enough to have Swan arranging the ornaments and trinkets on the side tables. Straightening pictures on the wall. Desperate, he contemplated organizing his closet. Not something he'd done before, and no doubt he'd be told off for, when Cowdry finally returned.

"Ah, Cowdry, glad you're back. I very nearly gave you a heap of work."

Cowdry frowned. "Really? Why sir?"

Swan shook his head. "Never mind. What have you got for me?" He noticed Cowdry held two books, and he snatched them away before Cowdry replied.

"The Waltham Directory as requested, and a history of the town. It has a fairly up to date map in the back."

"Well done. Thanks. Any trouble?"

"No sir. Should there have been?"

"No. Jus' checking, that's all." Swan waved him away and returned to his chair to study the books. He flicked through the contents of both immediately. For a further hour he became fully absorbed in the detail. Cowdry brought him a pot of coffee, which he drained unconsciously. Later, when Cowdry came to collect the tray, Swan chuckled at his valet.

"Cowdry, how'd ya like to go with me on a secret mission?"

"Me sir?" Cowdry's eyes popped. "What sort of secret mission?"

"Ya can drive a carriage, can't ya?"

Cowdry twitched his head. "If I must," he said, with reluctance.

"How well d'ya know Richard Bailey?"

"Mr. Bailey, the stable master?"

"Is there another?"

"No sir. He's the one I meant."

"So? Do ya know him?"

"Not well sir. He rarely takes his meals in the servant's hall."

Swan licked his lips as he considered his next question. "If ya asked him to take out a carriage, would he think it odd?"

"Yes sir, probably. It's not something I usually do."

"Hmmm, exactly what I thought," Swan murmured, with a frown. He brightened. "I'll jus' havta think of something convincing, won't I?"

"What do you have in mind sir?" Cowdry asked, doubtfully.

Swan tapped his fingers on the Waltham Directory. "There's a local woman missing. She might be connected to Kinsey's murder. Her name's Lillian Emerson and I've found out where she works. It's in this here book. She does some part-time bookkeeping for Pullman's Ice Dealers. I wanna go take a look around. My guess is the place is full of isolated buildings. Being Saturday afternoon, I bet there's no one there right now. Perfect time to poke around. Mr. Crane has gone to where she lives. He won't figure this yet."

"Won't he find out?"

Swan pursed his lips. "Probably, but I've gotta do something, Cowdry. All this sitting around is driving me crazy." He nodded. "I'll be covering all the bases. We can't wait for Joe to find out about this. I'll be there doing it. What d'ya say? Will ya help me?"

"So let me get this straight sir. You would like me to acquire the use of a carriage and take you to Pullman's Ice Dealers?"

"'Bout the size of it, yeah."

Cowdry gulped. "How would I convince Mr. Bailey to allow me to take out a carriage?"

Swan took on a thinking face, before snapping his fingers. "I've got it Cowdry, I've got it. Mr. Crane had someone drive him into town earlier. You tell Bailey Mr.

Crane asked for you to go get him at," he glanced at his pocket watch, "at three o'clock."

"Why me sir?"

"Because he...has tailoring to pick up an' he needs ya advice. You being qualified in such matters an' all." He sat forward in his chair. "I don't need to tell ya, as far as this household knows I ain't here. Ya have to give Bailey a plausible reason an' it's the best I can do on the spur of the moment. If ya come up with something better, feel free." He looked at Cowdry expectantly. "So, Paul, what d'ya say? Will ya help me?"

Cowdry still appeared doubtful. "Mrs. Martin—"

"Oh, you leave Mrs. Martin to me." Swan levered up. "Let's get to it. Times a wasting."

CHAPTER THIRTY-TWO

Once in Waltham on a busy Saturday morning, Fooks consulted his notes for the address of Lillian Emerson. Deciding he'd arrived at the correct one, he pushed open the gate. His eyes strayed to the upstairs windows as he walked the short path. All quiet and uninhabited.

He knocked on the front door and waited. When predictably there was no response, he stepped back and first surveyed up and then around. He contemplated breaking in. The left of the building, too close to the dividing fence. To the right, bushes grew in the space between the building and a substantial brick wall. No way through there either. *Nope, street's too busy.*

He retraced his steps to the gate, paused and glanced back. *No sign of anyone about.*

The house to the left showed signs of occupation. He would start there, knocking smartly on the front door. He waited for an answer, which he knew would be coming by the yelling between occupants to "Get the door." He pulled the Pinkerton's detective shield from his pocket. The door opened to reveal a middle-aged woman, drying her hands on her apron.

"Excuse me ma'am. Sorry to bother you." He politely tipped his hat. "My name is Crane and I'm a Pinkerton detective." He showed her the shield. "I'm investigating the disappearance of your neighbor, Lillian Emerson."

The woman raised her eyebrows at the mention of Pinkertons. "Oh my, such a fuss. The police have already been here."

"Ma'am, I'm afraid her sudden departure has caused great consternation for certain parties." When he realized she was about ask who, he added, "I'm not at liberty to say, ma'am. You understand, our clients demand the utmost confidentiality."

"Oh dear. What can I do to help?"

Exactly what he wanted to hear. He took out his pencil and notepad. "I'd like to ask a few questions if you don't mind, Mrs. ..." Fooks gave her his most dazzling smile.

She reddened, wiping her already dry hands on her apron again. "Dingwall, Clara Dingwall."

"Mrs. Clara Dingwall," Fooks murmured, noting the name, seemingly unaware of the effect he was having on her.

"Do you know Lillian well?"

"Of course, we've been neighbors for many years."

"And when did you see her last?"

"On Monday. I was taking Mikey to school. He's my son. He rolled his hoop into her. I haven't allowed him to play with it since. Children should learn their manners and respect their elders. Don't you think, Mr. Crane?"

Fooks dimpled at her, setting off a deeper flush to her neck. "I agree totally, Mrs. Dingwall. Now, did Lillian say anything to you about going away?"

"Not exactly, but she has a sister in Maine who she hasn't seen for a while. She's mentioned to me several times lately she should go for a visit."

Fooks pursed his lips. "I'll follow up of course. If you spoke to her before her disappearance, I'm surprised she didn't tell you."

"Yes, so am I, but perhaps spur of the moment—"

"She wasn't ill or worried about anything?"

"No, no, she was her usual chatty self. Oh, Mr. Crane, do you really think something bad has happened to her?"

"I'm sure she's fine, Mrs. Dingwall. Perhaps my client is worrying for nothing. Now, is Lillian employed?"

"She does some bookkeeping for Pullman's Ice Dealers. They have an icehouse on the other side of the river by the Prospect Foot Bridge."

"Interesting." He paused for a moment. "Have there been any callers at Lillian's house? Any strange callers? Ones you don't recognize. Perhaps acting suspiciously?"

Mrs. Dingwall frowned. "No, I can't say there's been anyone there. Well, apart from the police of course. They came through here and climbed over my fence to get round the back, you know."

Fooks twitched his head. "Usual police procedure. I hope they didn't inconvenience you too much." He flipped the notepad closed and clipped the pencil on to the side, before tucking it away. "Thank you for your help, Mrs. Dingwall. I'm sure we'll find her soon." He tipped his hat.

"I do hope so. Goodbye Mr. Crane."

Fooks tried the house on the right but there was no reply. Neither did he have any luck at two more nearby houses. He'd resolved to give up, when he glanced across the street. An elderly gentleman watched him from his doorstep. Fooks crossed the street.

"Excuse me sir, I wonder if I may trouble you for a moment?"

"Hold it right there mister, and state your business," the old man growled, raising his stick, halting Fooks at the gate.

"Of course." Fooks held up the Pinkerton shield. "Name's Crane. I'm investigating the disappearance of your neighbor, Mrs. Emerson." He tossed his head behind him.

The old man grunted. "Who isn't these days? Woman is more popular now than when she lived there."

"May I come in and speak with you, sir?"

The man waved his hand and went inside. "Come on in if ya want."

Fooks accepted the gracious invitation, appearing in the doorway. "Do you know Mrs. Emerson, sir?"

The man sniffed. "Can't say I do."

If Fooks was any judge of character, this man was one of those who kept an eye on everything going on in the neighborhood. Even though he rarely spoke to anyone.

"Any comings and goings over there out of the ordinary?"

"Police have been there nosing around."

"I mean apart from the police?"

The man sniffed again. "Pinkerton are ya?"

"Yes. For my sins." *Sheesh, why do I say these things?*

The man grunted. "I suppose someone has to be. Police ain't up to much these days. Don't ask the right questions."

"And what are the right questions?"

The man cackled. "Ya was almost right, young man. When ya asked if I seen anything outta the ordinary."

Fooks widened his eyes. "Have you seen anything outta the ordinary?"

The man cackled again. "Depends what ya mean by ordinary. I seen Pullman's ice van pull up outside."

"Pullman is the local ice dealer. Lots of folks have ice deliveries."

"Yep, 'tis true, an' I hear tell Lillian does some work for Pullman from time to time. An' she has ice from him. Except the delivery is usually done by ole Roy Abbott and his boy, Gordon." The man pointed across the street. "Last time, it was a woman on her own. Now that's outta the ordinary."

"Yes, it sure is." Fooks rubbed his chin. "When was this?"

The man considered. "Must be..." He raised his head skyward, "Must be last Monday. Yeah, Monday. In the PM. The Dingwall brat had just come home from school. So 'bout four o'clock I'd say."

"This is very interesting, Mr...."

The man sniffed. "Culpepper."

Fooks fumbled in his pocket and brought out his notepad and pencil. He scribbled what Culpepper said. The old man craned his neck to see what he'd written.

"Only one L in Culpepper."

Fooks dutifully scribbled out an L and continued questioning with high expectations. "Can you describe this woman, Mr. Culpepper?"

Culpepper grunted. "Youngish. Slimmish." He shrugged. "Young woman. They all look alike to me these days. What can I tell ya?"

"What was the color of her hair? Did you see her face? What was she wearing?"

"Whoa, slow down mister. What was the first question?"

"Did you see the color of her hair?"

"Nope. Darkish I suppose."

"And you didn't see her face?"

"Nope. She didn't look this way. Jus' saw the back of her."

"What was she wearing?"

Culpepper pulled a face. "Not well up on women's apparel." He grinned. "Not these days anyway." Fooks smiled, strangely warming to the old man. Culpepper puffed. "Longish, darkish skirt I guess."

"What about her hat?" *No doubt, hatish.*

"Roundish, plainish." Culpepper shrugged. "Nothing outstanding."

"Okay." Fooks took a deep breath. He'd try a different tack. "This woman, what did she do?"

"She went into the house."

"Did she come out?"

"Nope, not that I saw, but the van went."

"When did you notice it gone?"

Culpepper scratched his head. "Weren't there when I shut m'curtains."

"What time?"

"'Bout seven I guess."

Fooks reviewed his notes, pencil poised. "So let me get this right. A young woman turns up in Pullman's ice van, goes into the house around four o'clock but the van is gone by seven. You didn't see or hear anything in the intervening period?"

"Nope. Come five o'clock this street is that busy with folks going to work. And again, in the hour after six when they come back. Shift change at the watch factory y'see?"

"Ah, yes." Fooks flipped his notepad closed. "That's all, Mr. Culpepper. Thank you very much for your help." He tipped his hat.

"Ya got any leads?"

"Possibly, Mr. Culpepper, possibly. About to go and follow one up right now."

Curious Lillian Emerson should go missing right after a woman appears in a Pullman's Ice Dealers van. Fooks walked slowly along the main thoroughfare of Moody Street. Pullman's Ice Dealers was the logical next place to visit, but where were they?

"Excuse me, ma'am," he said to a woman passer-by and smiled. "I'm looking for Pullman's Ice Dealers. Can you tell me where I can find them, please?"

"Yes sir. They're on the riverside, at the other end of the Prospect Street Foot Bridge."

That meant nothing to Fooks. "Is it far?"

"About a mile and a half sir. If you walk up Moody Street." She pointed out the direction. "Until you get to Maple Street. Take a left and keep walking until you hit the river. The bridge is straight ahead. The ice houses are on your right as you go across."

Fooks winced. He still ached from a few days ago. A mile and a half hike would be too much.

"Is there somewhere I can get a cab?"

"Mayweather's will sort you out. You can telephone from the Post Office across the street."

Fooks blanched. "Telephone? Er, I've never used a telephone."

The girl appeared surprised. "Oh, it's quite easy. Ask for Sally. She'll help you," she said, and swept away.

Fooks gulped, pondering how different life was back East with all this newfangled technology he didn't understand.

Fooks regretted his decision to walk after two blocks. Before setting out he went into a stationer and purchased a map of the town. He sat on a bench studying the map and realized he still had a long way to go. As he sat there wondering what to do, along came an omnibus with the sign for City Hall. A quick glance at the map again told him City Hall stood on the other side of the river. A short walk to the main train station for Waltham, one stop away from Riverview, where he wanted to go. Pullman's ice house stood opposite. Chuckling, he joined the queue for the omnibus.

He decided not to attempt the climb on top. Instead, he found himself crammed on to one of the long seats inside. Opposite, a man struggled to read a newspaper. Apart from thinking him foolish, Fooks gave him no thought. Until, that is, the man shook the newspaper out to turn a page, when a headline caught his eye.

He thought the headline had read:

NOTORIOUS OUTLAW SPOTTED IN BOSTON

How can you go hot and cold both at the same time? Yet he did. His first instinct was to run. Not an option. The omnibus moved at a fast clip. On one side, a big woman wedged him into place. She wore an ostrich feather hat, intent on tickling his nose. To his other side, a man carrying an outsize bag, the corner of which kept digging into his thigh. Nope, he wasn't going anywhere until the terminus at City Hall.

Fortunately, the omnibus made no more stops and when it did, he pried himself from the seat. His anxiety levels had decreased significantly, and now he could think rationally again. He might have misread. Only a glance after all. The paper may have meant someone else: unlikely, but not improbable. Even so, he turned the collar up on *that* jacket, cursing himself again for not getting rid of it when able, and tipped his homburg forward over his eyes.

He disguised his Western accent with one that he hoped would pass as more local and purchased a ticket to the next station along, Riverview. On the track stood a self-service newspaper stand. He obtained a copy of the paper the man on the omnibus was reading. With a few minutes to wait until his train, he tore through the pages until he found the headline. It did say what he'd thought.

He read on in horror. A short editorial, but still made his heartbeat faster.

A man answering the description of Florian Fooks was seen abroad in Boston on several days last week. Florian Fooks is described as brown haired, brown eyed man of average build. This man is the leader of the Guardian Wall Gang, who has terrorized the western states in recent years. Why such a notorious figure should be seen in Boston, far from the land of his exploits, is anyone's guess. The Boston police are investigating this sighting.

Who was the source? The description on his wanted posters was vague at best. Who knew Florian Fooks well enough to positively identify him? He didn't know anyone in Boston who knew him as Florian Fooks apart from.... Fooks swallowed hard and finished his thought. Swan and Caroline. *No, surely not? But why? Why would she do it?* Fooks shook his head. He didn't understand it. Surely if Caroline tipped the police off, all she'd do was draw attention to Swan? The last thing he needed right now was for Samuel Martin talked about in close proximity to Tobias Swan. *No, no, if it wasn't Caroline, then who?*

Fooks ran his fingers nervously through his hair as his thoughts turned to Mary and Susan. What would happen to them if he was caught? How would they cope? Fooks shook his head. Mary would be okay. She knew who he was before they married. Knew there would always be the possibility he could be arrested and she'd accepted the risk. *I really don't deserve her.*

Fooks, busy mulling things over, nearly missed his train, just managing to jump on in time and take the nearest seat. With a deep sigh, he resolved to concentrate on the matter in hand first. He couldn't leave Swan to his fate. They'd known each other too long and been through too much together. Once this was over, then he would ponder who might have potentially betrayed him.

CHAPTER THIRTY-THREE

"Right here. This is it," Swan yelled, to Cowdry up top on the carriage.

Cowdry slowed the vehicle, Swan already half out before they came to a complete stop. He called up. "I'm gonna have a scout around. Park somewhere where ya can see the entrance. I'll signal to you when I'm done."

"Yes, sir but what should I do if someone comes?"

"Can ya whistle?"

Cowdry puckered his lips together and blew. He emitted a soft sound, which drew an indulgent glare from Swan. Cowdry's chin dipped, and he bit his bottom lip.

"Jus' do ya best, Paul. I'll likely hear someone coming anyway." Swan darted away, leaving Cowdry to trot on.

The icehouse building sat on a sizable plot. Bordered by the Charles River to its south, the train tracks to its north and the approaches to the rickety Prospect Street Foot Bridge to its east. Other industrial buildings were arranged someway off to the west. The icehouse building dominated the site, sitting askew on its plot. Several buildings clustered by the bridge approach. At a distance stood a further set of wooden shacks.

Between January and March, the icehouse, its environs and the river foreshore would be a hive of activity. Now, in early May, the ice harvesting season had finished. Daily deliveries accounted for the only activity on site now. Today being Saturday, work finished for the day at lunch time. Midafternoon, all was quiet. Perfect time to poke around, as he'd said to Cowdry earlier. Even better, the place didn't look as though it had any security. Swan wasn't sure what he expected to find. *Sure, feels nice to be outta the house though.*

He wasn't entirely familiar with the workings of a commercial icehouse. Common sense told him he wouldn't find anything of interest in the main building. The single brick building on site had a chimney sticking out the top. This likely housed the hoisting engine. Used for pulling the ice cakes up the wooden ramp and into the icehouse. Swan smiled. He was right. No one around any of the buildings.

He glanced in at the wooden buildings by the bridge as he passed, but they proved to be what he thought. Tool rooms, repair shops and other equipment stores. With the ice harvest not long finished, these buildings were still in use, repairing and maintaining equipment for next season. No, he needed somewhere more remote. The shacks at the rear would be ideal for hiding something, or someone.

Soon lost from sight of a casual observer, he headed for the three shacks arranged in a semi-circle. One, on the far right, beyond use, its roof caved in and the bowed in front wall, collapsed under the weight. The middle shack, locked with a rusty padlock. No expert at locks, Swan left that to Fooks, but even he could tell the lock hadn't opened recently. A circumnavigation of the walls showed him no other way in, not even a window to peer through.

He tried the third shack. This appeared more promising. The biggest of the three, this had a window, but a rough curtain of burlap was pulled across, obscuring any view inside. What really caught his eye was the padlock, shiny and new. In truth, he hadn't really expected to find anything. Just wanted an excuse to get out of the house and do something.

A noise came from inside, a faint mewing. This was something. He put his ear to the door and listened intently. When it came again, he banged on the door.

"Anyone in there?"

As Fooks sat on the train steaming towards Riverview Station and the ice house, George Jones was on his way to work at the watch factory. He kept a nervous eye on the fast-running river beneath his feet while walking across the Prospect Street Foot Bridge. Ice had long since broken up during the spring melt. Yet the river remained swollen with melt water from the White Mountains, now massing in the lower stretches of the Charles River here in Waltham.

Mildly relieved to be nearing firm ground again, he began to take notice of his surroundings. A carriage parked on one side of the road ahead. As he drew closer, a man exited, spoke briefly to the nervous looking man up top. Then he darted into the grounds of the icehouse. George frowned. Curious. Pullman's Ice Dealers were shut for the day. The carriage drove on, across the railroad tracks. At the triangle of land beyond, the carriage turned around and stopped. George frowned again. Definitely suspicious.

George turned his attention back to the first man. He was squinting in at the tool room, and as George continued to watch, he moved on to peer in the equipment store window.

Reaching the entrance of the Thompson Pleasure Boat House, George turned in and leaned on the reception desk.

"Say, Abe, is anything going on over at the icehouse this afternoon?"

"Going on? What d'you mean? Everyone cleared out," Abe glanced at the clock, "two hours ago."

"I jus' seen a man skulking around over there. Kinda familiar too."

"Show me." Abe lifted the counter and joining George in the entrance.

They watched from behind the boat yard sign, as the man George had seen earlier disappeared behind the main icehouse building.

"What d'you suppose he's up to?"

Abe's turn to frown. "Dunno, but you're right, he does look kinda familiar." Abe pondered, while George continued watching. A moment later Abe clicked his fingers in triumph. "I've got it! D'you know who it is?"

"No. Who?"

"Samuel Martin. Y'know, him who married Caroline Fairfield all of a sudden? Him, who I hear tell is wanted in connection with the murder of that Kinsey fella from Boston."

George's eyes grew round. "No."

Abe nodded in confirmation and nudged George. "Say, who's this girl?"

He pointed to the track on the far side of the icehouse, the original entrance, now superseded by the one from Prospect Street. Along the track walked a young slim female figure.

"Dunno. Don't recognize her. What's going on, Abe?"

Abe shrugged, but he hunkered next to George to watch some more. When the girl disappeared from their sight, she was going in the same direction as the man.

"Reckon we oughta call the police?" George asked.

"Yeah, I think we oughta. Whatever's going on ain't right."

They made as if to go when George put his hand on Abe's arm. "Now who is this? Don't recognize him either."

A slender man, wearing a red and green plaid jacket and a dark homburg, crossed the train tracks. As they watched, the man came closer on to the approach of the bridge and stopped. He regarded the icehouse, hands on his hips. After a moment's deliberation, he retraced his steps and stepped into the grounds.

Abe and George swapped glances.

The man went through the same actions as the first man, peering in the front buildings. George and Abe jumped when a shot rang out. The man's head snapped around. George and Abe gasped as they saw the man draw what appeared to be a gun. He took off at a run in the direction the shot had come from.

"Yeah, we'd better call the police. C'mon."

"Hold on. I'll get ya out."

A noise answered him. Although he couldn't make out words, it sounded human. Swan turned his attention back to the padlock. He couldn't pick it and he searched around for something to break the clasp. He found a rusty but still robust crowbar in the broken-down shack. Swan struggled with it. The curved end, too big to fit between the clasp and the plate. Reversing it, he tried the end for removing nails, managing to wiggle one of the claws into position. He heaved and heaved.

At one point he put both feet up on the door jamb, only to end up on the ground when the claw lost its grip. But it had moved. More finagling and the padlock parted from the plate.

Swan undid the fixing and threw open the door. There on a filthy palette lay a woman, trussed up to an iron peg concreted into the earth floor and gagged with a filthy rag.

"Hey," Swan cried, dashing to her side. He crouched beside her and gently removed the gag. "Don't be frightened. I'm here to help you. Are you Lillian?"

The woman nodded. "Who...?"

"I'm Sam Martin. Can ya sit up?"

She struggled to move but she found her bounds too constricting.

"Okay, okay, lie still. I'll get these—"

"I wouldn't do that if I were you."

CHAPTER THIRTY-FOUR

Swan spun around on his toes. *Sheesh. I must be slipping. Letting someone sneak up on me like that.*

In the doorway stood a young woman, holding a gun pointed at him. He rose slowly to his feet.

She gestured with the gun. "Move away."

He complied, with the all too familiar pose of raised hands.

"Now miss, you be careful with that gun. Could go off."

"Don't patronize me, mister. Who are you?"

"Name's Sam Martin."

To his surprise, she gave a harsh laugh.

Swan twitched his head. "Didn't know m'name was that funny. Seeing as how we're getting acquainted, mind telling me who you are?" He edged closer, his eyes flicking to the small gun she held. Curiously, her hand didn't shake. In his experience, females holding guns shook with fear. *Whoever she is, she's a cool customer.*

"You don't need to know," she snapped, and gestured for him to move back.

Swan held his ground. His eyes widened. "Is that a Rupertus?" He whistled. "Never seen one of them before. Heard about 'em though."

"You know about guns." She said it as a statement of fact, rather than a question.

"Yes ma'am. Kinda required in my previous line of work." *Better watch my step. She's no push over.* "Pepperbox too. What is it? A 0.22?" He took a step forward. *Almost, Tobias. Just one more step.*

"Don't you come any closer!" She cupped both hands about the grip of the gun. Her thumb rested on the hammer; one finger coiled around the trigger.

Swan stopped and raised his hands. "Your move, ma'am. Can't stand like this all day. I've got a lady to rescue."

The girl responded by cocking the gun. Swan took advantage of her momentary distraction. Barreling into her, knocking her arm high.

A loud crack sounded as the gun went off. Followed immediately by the splintering of the wooden roof.

Lillian gave a cry of pain as a roof shard hit her.

Swan pressed his hand hard on the girl's arm, keeping the gun held high. She struggled furiously, one foot kicking at his shins. He cursed but didn't let go. His other hand found her shoulder, and he pushed her back against the wall.

"Mighta known." A new voice momentarily distracted the girl, and Swan wrenched the gun from her. He stepped back, breathing heavily. "Here you are grappling with a young lady. And you a married man now." The voice tutted.

Fooks stood in the doorway of the shack. "Hi." He flashed a grin at the girl. "We meet again, Miss Miller."

Swan nodded. *Why am I not surprised?*

"Go to hell." She glared at Fooks, as she tried to restore some order to her clothes, the carpet bag over her shoulder hampering her efforts.

Fooks sidled into the shack, keeping his gun leveled at Kitty and stood beside Swan. They exchanged glances. "You okay?"

"Am now." Swan frowned at the small gun. "Never thought one of these little 'uns might finish me off," he murmured. "A Rupertus Pepperbox. At least it's rare."

"Here," Fooks handed over his Schofield, "have this *big* gun and keep an eye on her, while I release Mrs. Emerson."

"This thing again? We're gonna have to have a serious talk when we get outta here 'bout decent firearms, Joe." Swan tucked Kitty's gun into the pocket of his vest.

Fooks crouched beside the prone woman. "'Tis Lillian Emerson, isn't it?"

"Y-Yes. W-Who are you?" Her voice was a whisper. Dehydration, fear and pain will do that to you.

"We'll soon have you outta here, Mrs. Emerson," Fooks said, inspecting the chain, attaching to the iron peg.

Swan kept the Schofield leveled at Kitty as Fooks picked up the padlock. "Hmmm." Fooks swiveled around on his haunches and frowned at Kitty. "Have you got the key for this?"

Kitty stood with folded arms. She regarded him, sullenly.

"Suppose I'll have to do it the hard way," Fooks murmured, finding his lock picking tools. A fair amount of wiggling and face pulling later, and the padlock eventually snapped open. "There you go, Mrs. Emerson." He untangled her wrists.

"Thank you," she breathed.

"Can you sit up?" He steadied her as she tried, resting her against the shack wall. He noticed she shivered. So, he took off his Mackinaw jacket and draped it around her shoulders.

"What are you planning on doing with me?" Kitty asked, tossing her head, defiantly.

"Well now Miss Miller, depends on how co-operative you are," Swan flung a hand in Lillian's direction. "What's this all about?"

Kitty licked her lips. "I'm not saying anything."

Fooks stepped forward. "I can understand that."

"I can't," muttered Swan.

Fooks tossed his head. "What about Montgomery Whitlock? Somehow I don't quite believe he really had an accident?" Something flickered over her face. What? Regret? Sadness? "Might be a different matter when it's the police asking." He paused. "Kidnap and false imprisonment of an innocent woman is a serious charge y'know."

"Like I said to him, go to hell."

Swan grinned at Fooks. "Prickly, ain't she?"

Fooks shrugged. "Dunno why, seeing as we aren't the police."

"You're a Pinkerton." Kitty tossed her head at Fooks. "Same as the police." She sniffed. "Or that's what you claim to be. I've had my doubts since the first time we met."

Fooks and Swan swapped glances, before Fooks dropped his voice to take on a menacing tone. "What do you mean, Miss Miller?"

Kitty regarded him with a baleful eye. "You'll find out soon enough," she said, with a confidence not matched by her body language.

"Don't mess with me, Miss Miller. You're not coming from a position of strenght."

"What d'you want to do with her?" Swan asked, steering them back to the matter in hand.

Fooks turned to him. "Do you reckon her treatment of this poor woman should go unpunished?"

"No, I don't."

It was Lillian who answered. Fooks winked at her and Swan smiled. They were trying to bait Kitty into telling them what this was all about. At the same time, reassure Lillian she hadn't fallen out of the frying pan into the fire.

Kitty looked from one man to another and appeared to have a realization. "I know who you two are." She took a step towards the door. "I read the newspaper, but I thought no. What would Florian Fooks be doing in Boston of all places? But the description fits, and you know each other. That must mean you're Tobias Swan."

Swan tutted. "Now, now, Miss Miller, I'm holding a gun on you, don't forget." He waved the Fooks' Schofield in emphasis. "Like I say, I'm Sam Martin and he's Joseph Crane. No one else, and certainly not," he gave a short laugh, "guys with crazy names like those two desperados."

Fooks closed his eyes and shuddered at Swan's choice of words.

"You won't shoot me." A faint tremor in Kitty's voice. "Not if you're who I think you are. Not your style." She took another step towards the door. Then she made a bolt for it.

Swan quickly followed her.

"Kitty!"

CHAPTER THIRTY-FIVE

The pair skidded to a halt. Three police patrolmen faced them, guns drawn, intent on creeping up on their position but now in the open.

"What's going on here?" the first demanded.

"Er." Swan realized it looked bad for him. Wanted for murder and now found holding a gun on a woman.

"Put the gun down, mister. Kick it away and get your hands up."

Swan had no choice. He carefully laid the Schofield on the grass, kicked it deliberately towards the door of the shack, before straightening with raised hands. *Story of my life.*

"Thank heavens! You got here in time. He was going to kill me, I'm sure," Kitty cried, hugging her bag to her chest and running towards the police. One patrolman came forward and put his arm around her shoulders.

"Now, now miss, don't take on. You're safe now."

"Sarge! Do you know who this is? It's Samuel Martin," the other patrolman yelled.

"What?" Sarge did a double take at the speaker and back at Swan. "That true? You Samuel Martin?"

"I can't deny my name is Samuel Martin. Sergeant, ya don't know what's going on here. We've rescued Lillian Emerson, who she held hostage in here all tied up."

"That's not true!" Kitty burst out. "He and his friend in there were trying to do the same to me." Kitty ended in fresh sobs into the chest of the patrolman who held her.

Sarge motioned Swan out of the way and moved closer to the door. Just as Fooks appeared, holding Lillian on her feet.

"Who are you?" Sarge asked.

"Joseph Crane, Pinkerton detective. I'd show you my shield, but I've kinda got my hands full right now. This is Mrs. Lillian Emerson. She's a missing person."

"Yeah, she's been missing for a few days," Sarge agreed. "McKenna. Help, Mrs. Emerson."

McKenna stepped forward and took Lillian from Fooks.

Fooks pulled the Pinkerton shield from the pocket of his Mackinaw jacket as Lillian passed by. He held it in front of Sarge. "Mrs. Martin hired me. Samuel Martin didn't kill Kinsey, Sarge, and I'm working to prove it."

"That's as may be, Crane, but until I hear different, he's still a wanted man." Sarge stepped forward, handcuffs at the ready. "Samuel Martin, I'm arresting you for the murder of...what's the man's name, Lombard?"

"Kinsey, Sarge. Robert Kinsey."

"Samuel Martin, I'm arresting you for the murder of Robert Kinsey. Turn around and put your hands behind your back."

Swan locked eyes with Fooks. An unspoken conversation took place between them. Both aware there was nothing Fooks could do. "Always wanted a ride in a Black Maria," Swan joked, weakly.

Swan put on a brave face, all too aware Fooks knew he didn't cope well in confined spaces. A Western jail was one thing. A brick-built cell was another. *Fooks'll get me out somehow.* Fooks nodded and shrugged, signaling he didn't know how right at that moment.

Swan submitted to a robust search of his person and, not surprisingly, they found the gun. The patrolman held it up.

"Give me that. Take him away Jones."

"Don't you let the girl go, Sarge. She's not what she seems," Swan said, as the cuffs tightened around his wrists.

"Don't you worry Martin. I'll be having a long conversation with all of you at the station house. Now move."

As the police led Swan away, Fooks bent to pick up his Schofield at the same time as Lombard went for it.

"It's mine, Lombard. I'll take care of it." Fooks' tone of command made Lombard back off.

Kitty, still sobbing seemingly uncontrollably, Lombard and Fooks followed. They tramped across the grass to the waiting police vehicle. As Swan predicted, a Black Maria. Swan inclined his head at Fooks, directing his attention to the road across the train tracks. In particular, he drew Fooks' attention to the carriage waiting there.

As they watched, the carriage started forward. Fooks delayed climbing into the front of the Black Maria to give the carriage time to catch up. He wasn't surprised when the carriage driver was Cowdry. Fooks gave a brief nod in his direction. The banner emblazoned on the side of the vehicle told Cowdry exactly where to go. An answering nod told Fooks he understood.

At the police station, Fooks expected an anxious time. Kitty correctly guessing who he and Swan were gave him palpitations. He had a hard time thinking through the answers to the questions directed at him, in a calm rational manner.

Kitty gave an entirely plausible and heartfelt account of events. Worming her way out convincingly. Her brother had worked at the icehouse for a time. He'd told her about the disused shacks on the site. She said he suspected Lillian might be there and rather than tell the police, she went to investigate for herself. Yes, she knew her actions were foolhardy. Sometimes ideas run away with themselves, and you must act on them. Her ramblings were so convincing, the police believed her. After her tale, Fooks had a hard time persuading the police he and Swan weren't responsible for kidnapping Lillian Emerson. And not about to do the same to Kitty.

Fortunately, the patrolman who took Lillian home returned in time. He'd taken her statement. Lillian hadn't seen her abductor's face. Someone grabbed her from behind and pressed a cloth to her face. She'd woken up alone in the shack. Occasional food and water delivered at night by someone who didn't speak. Yet Lillian would swear this was a woman. On this basis, the police allowed Fooks to leave. The question of his Pinkerton credentials did not come up in all the confusion. Nor did he volunteer the information.

Kitty keeping quiet on her suspicions of them surprised him. What was she up to? She's a cunning one. *Doing exactly what I would do in her situation.* Keeping information for later use.

The Waltham police telephoned their counterparts in Boston. Later that day, armed police would transport Swan to the larger metropolis. *Telephoned.* Fooks couldn't get used to it. *Good job me and Swan gave up crime when we did.*

Fooks finally left the police station, exhaling a long breath as he tripped down the steps. Cowdry, having idled away the hours in a cafe across the street from the police station, fell into step beside Fooks as he approached. Fooks gestured to the saloon on the corner of the street. A confused Cowdry followed him in.

Fooks ordered a whiskey, threw a few coins on the counter, received his drink and knocked it back in one. Satisfaction crossed his face.

"That's better." He placed the empty glass on the counter. "Let's get outta here."

This isn't gonna be easy. Fooks took a deep breath before he climbed the stairs. Caroline would not be pleased the police had Swan.

"How could you let the police take him?" Caroline cried, when Fooks finished telling her what happened. Caroline turned on Fooks, her face red and puffy.

"What was I supposed to do?" Fooks stalked towards her. "Not preventing the arrest was the only way. Tobe understood that. I didn't have my gun. And even if I did have it, I couldn't shoot 'em. I'd be arrested and then we'd *both* be in serious trouble. Wouldn't have helped any, would it?"

"At least he wouldn't be in prison!"

Fooks came close to her, his eyes cold and hard. She took a step back and swallowed. "No, he'd be on the run. Have you any idea what that's like? Have you? We know all about being on the run from the law. Only this time, he'll be hunted with a little more enthusiasm now the charge is murder!" He stomped away.

Caroline wrung her hands, shaking her head in despair. She sank onto the sofa in tears. "I don't know what to do anymore. Sam told me he didn't kill Robert and I believe him." She regarded the rigid back presented to her. "What do we do, Joseph?"

Fooks took a deep breath. He didn't like dealing with crying women. Especially when this one was usually calm and confident. He turned and took a seat next to her.

"Tobias didn't kill Kinsey," he said, quietly. "Sure, he was angry when he went to see him. He had every right to be. The man ordered his men to shoot him. I told you before, Tobe would never use a 0.22. No, someone else killed Kinsey." He hesitated. "And I have my suspicions."

Caroline seized on his words. "Who?"

Fooks shook his head. "Need to think on it more."

"You can't just say something like that. You have to tell me."

"Okay. Look, every alternative lead we've found is leading us nowhere. Except one. To Kitty Miller. After today, she's shot to the top of the list. The police were all too willing to accept her story, but I sure as hell don't. She kidnapped Lillian Emerson, I'm sure of it." He shook his head. "Not enough to hold her though. She's real sneaky. Talked her way outta it. Right in front of me." He shook his head and puffed. What she said next, took him by surprise.

"Could you...could you break him out? Samuel told me you're good at it."

Fooks widened his eyes, sniffed and twitched his head. "A jail cell in a one-horse town with a part-time sheriff is one thing. A professional high-security establishment like a Boston police station is another."

"What about using your alter ego?"

Fooks stiffened.

"Samuel says he can do anything."

Fooks shook his head. "No."

His black alter ego let loose unchecked wasn't something he wanted to think about. He did too much damage. To himself and other people. It scared him. He would only consider it if the situation became so desperate, there was no other way. Right now, not the way forward.

He paced.

"But couldn't you at least try?"

The welling up of her eyes matched the desperation in her voice. He had sympathy for her. This was hard. Nothing like anything she'd ever encountered before. He understood her feeling of helplessness. Right now, he shared it.

"I can't, Caroline." His voice shook.

"But—"

"No." He turned away. "You've no idea what you're asking." He gulped. "I can't control him on my own, and with Swan not..." He put his head down and shook it. "I'm sorry Caroline, I can't do it. I have Mary and Susan to think about. I've a lot to lose."

"Don't I have a lot to lose too?" Caroline snapped.

Fooks turned away and then immediately turned back. "Have you forgotten? Neither of us are who we say we are. We can't draw too much attention on ourselves."

He moved to his Mackinaw jacket from where he'd draped it over the back of a chair. From the inside pocket he took a folded newspaper. "Here. Read that." He tapped the folded report. "Captain Loomis is already sniffing around me. The description is a tad vague, but it won't take a lot for Loomis to realize I *am* Florian Fooks. In which case the police will come for me. It'll only be a matter of time before Loomis pegs Samuel Martin for Tobias Swan. We're partners, remember?"

Caroline gave a whimper, took a deep breath and steadied herself. "Then what do we do? We can't leave Samuel in prison. He could be hanged."

"I know that!"

Fooks saw the shock on Caroline's face and moderated his tone. He returned to sit beside her. "Look Caroline, we'll get him out. Don't worry."

"How?" Caroline sniffed. She pulled out a handkerchief to dab ineffectively at her nose and eyes. "I've come to love him, Joseph. I can't bear to lose him."

Fooks clasped her hands. "I love him too. He kinda does this to you. Gets under your skin." He patted her hand. "I can't use my alter ego. It's too risky. The police have guns in Boston, and I suspect they know how to use them too." He became serious. "I promise you I'll come up with something else."

Caroline seized on his words. "What?

"We have to prove Tobe didn't kill Kinsey."

"How?" Caroline raised her head. "How do we do that?"

Fooks pursed his lips. "I don't know exactly how right now. Trust me. I'll think of something." He gave a faint chuckle. "I'm supposed to be a criminal mastermind. Remember? What's the point of having a reputation if you don't live up to it, huh?"

CHAPTER THIRTY-SIX

"Did you ever discover if someone tipped off the police about Tobias being here?" Fooks asked, the next morning over breakfast. "Or did the police come back on the off chance?"

Fooks still hadn't thought of a plan of action. Well, he had a bit of a plan, but he wasn't entirely pleased with it. *Not my usual standard.* As a distraction he thought around the problem. Let his brain quietly work on a plan in the background. Usually the best way. Forcing himself to think on a solution rarely worked.

Caroline took a deep breath as she folded her napkin. "I'm afraid to say it must be a member of staff."

"Is anyone new?" Fooks asked, in a low voice. "Say in the last six months?"

"Most of the staff have been here for years." She shook her head but shifted uneasily. "I've only taken on two staff since Father died."

"And who are they?" Fooks demanded.

"An apprentice gardener and a footman."

"Tell me about them."

"Joseph, I really don't think—"

"Tell me about them."

Fooks was firm. Caroline stiffened her back. "I trust my staff, Mr. Fooks."

He gritted his teeth. "You may trust them, but do they trust you?"

"Whatever do you mean?"

His tongue explored his mouth. "I'm sorry I was sharp Caroline, but this is important."

Mollified, Caroline inclined her head. "Very well. The gardener is straight from school. His father also works on the estate." She paused. "As did his father before him. I know the family well."

Fooks lifted his chin. "And the other?"

"A junior footman, and he came recommended."

"By who?" Fooks snapped.

Caroline flashed a look of annoyance at him. "By whom."

"Caroline, this is serious." Fooks scraped back his chair and paced, biting his thumb nail.

"Very well. My uncle recommended him to me."

"Robert?"

"Yes."

Fooks groaned loudly and put his hands behind his head. He continued to march up and down. "I can't get it," Fooks cried. "It's there. I can't..."

Suddenly Fooks stopped pacing, turned and rushed back. He perched on the edge of his chair and leaned towards Caroline. "When Robert recommended this footman to you, what did he say about him?"

"He was the son of a business associate of his, who died, and the family had fallen on hard times. I interviewed Alfred. He's a pleasant young man and I've heard no complaints about his work."

Fooks chewed his bottom lip. "At the time did you need a new, er," he waved his hand as he thought of the occupation, "junior footman?"

"Yes. Samuel promoting Cowdry to his valet created the vacancy. I should have dealt with it sooner. Remiss of me."

He began to pace again. Caroline watched him for a while and then reached for the tea pot.

"This business associate of Kinsey," Fooks said with his back to her, "was it Chester Miller?"

"I believe so yes."

Fooks turned on his heel, stalked back and stared at her.

Caroline frowned up. "Is something wrong?"

The muscle in Fooks' cheek twitched. "No. I've figured out the connection."

"What connection?"

"Miller." He paused, waiting for realization to dawn. "Your new junior footman, Alfred. He's Kitty Miller's brother."

Caroline summoned Alfred Miller to the drawing room of Ardmaddy after breakfast. She and Fooks regarded the young man as he entered to stand in front of them, arms behind his back. A slender man, with tousled hair.

"Alfred." Fooks forced the man's attention on him. "Robert Kinsey recommended you for this job. Is that correct?"

"Yes sir."

"Had you previously done this type of work before?"

"No sir." He shrugged. "He knew I was seeking alternative employment and suggested I apply for this position."

"How were you employed previously?"

Alfred swallowed hard. "At Pullman's Ice Dealers. It's hard work and cold, especially in the winter. I-I struggled. When Mr. Kinsey told me about the job here, I jumped at the chance."

Fooks nodded with smug satisfaction. *Yes, Kitty said as much to the police.*

Fooks had never worked at ice harvesting, but he knew the principle. Not something he wished to do.

"Alfred, have you heard of Lillian Emerson?"

"Yes. She does the bookkeeping at Pullman's."

"She lives here in Waltham. On Highland Avenue. I understand your family also live in Waltham. Where exactly?"

"On the corner of Ash Street and Moody." Alfred frowned. "May I ask why you want to know sir?"

Fooks ignored the question and pursed his lips as he consulted the map in his head. "Not far from Lillian," he said, in a murmur.

Alfred shrugged. "It's a residential part of Waltham, sir. I don't know her well."

"Have you always lived in Waltham?"

"No sir." He hesitated before continuing. "We moved here from New York after my father died."

"Tell me about your father."

Alfred blinked in surprise. "My father?" He turned to Caroline. "What is this about, Madam? Have I done something wrong?"

Caroline and Fooks swapped glances. He raised his eyebrows. *You can answer, Madam.*

Caroline rolled her eyes and shot Fooks a look of disgust. "That depends, Alfred. Were you aware of Mr. Martin presence here?"

Alfred reddened. "Yes Madam," he said, quietly.

"How did you know?" Fooks demanded.

Alfred bit his bottom lip. "I saw Mr. Cowdry preparing a tray. He said it was for you, Mr. Crane, but you dined with madam that night."

Fooks winced. *Fundamental error.*

"I followed Mr. Cowdry, and he took the tray into Mr. Martin's suite." His head went down and took a deep breath. "I put my ear to the door and heard voices. One I recognized as Mr. Martin's." He swallowed and looked from one to the other.

Fooks and Caroline swapped glances.

"Did you tell anyone?" Fooks asked, softly.

Alfred put his head down.

"Alfred." Caroline was sharp, and Alfred's head shot up.

"Not...not exactly."

"What do you mean?"

Fooks sat back and waited for the answers. *Okay, she's getting more out of him than me right now. Let's see where we go from here.*

"On my last evening off, I went home to have supper with my mother. It was the day after Mr. Kinsey's funeral. Kitty was there and she and Mama talked about it. Mama wondered where Mr. Martin could be all this time and I said..." Alfred put his head down. "I didn't *actually* say he was here, Madam," he added, quickly.

Fooks bit his lip. *Ah, but you inferred it.*

Caroline stiffened. "That was very indiscrete of you Alfred."

Fooks noticed her hands clasped tightly in her lap, her knuckles white.

Alfred swallowed and his eyes flicked to Caroline. "I'm sorry Madam. Am I dismissed?"

Caroline appeared to be having a battle with herself. "No, Alfred, not this time. However, I expect all my employees to have loyalty to me in the first instance. Please remember."

Alfred nodded.

"Alfred, did Kitty ask you specifically about Mr. Martin?" Fooks asked.

"Yes sir, but I realized I shouldn't have said what I did and I changed the subject."

"Okay, Alfred." Fooks said. "Now tell me about your father. How did he die?"

Alfred put his head down. "It was...sudden, sir."

"Was there anything suspicious about his death?"

"It was—" Alfred stopped and gulped, before continuing in a quiet voice. "It was suicide."

Fooks hadn't expected that. "I'm sorry Alfred." He rubbed his cheek. The questions he'd planned would seem harsh under the circumstances, but he had to ask. He leaned forward.

"Alfred, I realize this is difficult. Why do you think he felt he had no other way out?"

Alfred bit his lip. "He made some bad decisions. Business decisions. Lost a fortune. I don't think he could live with himself, sir."

Fooks pursed his lips. All was becoming clearer. In his mind at least. *Just one more thing.* "All right Alfred. Thank you. How is your family managing? Financially I mean."

Alfred wiped his face. "As you can imagine it was a shock at first but we're doing better now. Mama is able to keep a small house and take in laundry. Kitty has a job with Mr. Kinsey in Boston, and I'm here."

Fooks uncrossed his legs and stood, indicating the interview had finished.

Alfred looked to Caroline, who nodded. "Thank you, Alfred. You may go."

Alfred leapt up and headed for the door.

Fooks joined him by the door. "Oh, one more thing. Your father held shares in a tontine. I believe you and your sister inherited."

Alfred widened his eyes in surprise. "Yes sir. How did—"

"Who is the nominee?"

"Mama, but I don't—"

Fooks gave Alfred a tight-lipped smile, and showed Alfred out. "Thank you."

As the door shut on Alfred, Caroline stood and faced a grim faced Fooks.

"What are you thinking?"

He walked forward shaking his head. "The tontine ties everything together. Alfred and Kitty's pa was a business associate of Kinsey, until he died. Kitty and Alfred inherited their father's share of the tontine. The nominee is their mother." He glanced at Caroline. "Who is still alive." He paced.

"Under the terms of the agreement, when the shareholders get to the last two, the tontine is wound up. With Kinsey out of the way, that leaves the Millers and Slocomb. Slocomb's nominee, Lillian Emerson went missing.... I said I thought Kitty kidnapped her." He trailed off, watching understanding flicker over Caroline's face. "Now I'm certain she did."

"You think she killed Robert for the tontine dividend?"

"Kitty had the opportunity. She was there that evening. You said yourself how on edge she was when I questioned her about it."

"But she's a woman."

Fooks turned on his heel. "So? Women can be murderers too."

CHAPTER THIRTY-SEVEN

After Alfred left, Fooks raced upstairs to Swan's suite to stand in front of the blackboard again. There was something he wanted to check. He tapped a chalk dot beside Kitty's name. "Caroline said something about Kitty's bag. She said…"

He walked away frowning hard. "Why did no one hear the shot? Even a 0.22 makes a noise. And she had a gun at the icehouse. A 0.22. I thought as everyone was looking for this mouse, but of course." He whooped. "Makes perfect sense." *Mrs. Miller certainly didn't raise no fool. That's brilliant.*

The rest of his plan to get Swan out of jail suddenly clicked into place.

He hurried back to the drawing room, intent on telling Caroline, arriving at the same time as the mail. Caroline received several white envelopes and to his surprise there was one for him. He recognized Mary's writing straight away. Couldn't be anything urgent else she would send a telegram.

Fooks walked away to the window and tore open the letter impatiently. He quickly scanned the pages. In the main, Bronze Canyon gossip. Until Mary finally got around to telling him the important things he wanted to know. She and Susan were fine, although Susan missed her pappy. She kept pointing at his desk chair and whimpering. She got hold of one of his shirts and Mary found it hard to take it away from her. Almost as an afterthought Mary wrote:

> *Susan took her first steps today. I walked into the living room and caught her toddling across the room to your desk. Of course, when she realized I watched her, she plopped to the floor. She squealed in delight when I picked her up and made a fuss of her.*

Fooks lowered the letter, disappointed. He knew before he left it wouldn't be long, but he hoped he'd be there to witness her first steps. He'd missed another pivotal moment in his daughter's life. With a sigh, he stuffed the letter back into its envelope.

"Not bad news I hope," Caroline said.

He turned to face her. "No. Letter from Mary. She says Susan's walking now." Regret was written all over his face.

Caroline was sympathetic. "I'm sure you'll be back with her soon and then you'll wish she wasn't walking."

Fooks glanced at her. "Yeah, 'xpect." He tapped his fingers on top of the letter. "I've made a decision Caroline. About how we can get Tobe out of jail."

Caroline leaned forward eagerly. "How?"

"I think the best thing to do in this situation is tell the truth."

"The truth? The truth about what?"

"Everything." He paused and winced. "Nearly everything." He paused again. "The only way I can see

Loomis letting Tobe out is for me to outline to him all the evidence I have."

"I sense you have reservations."

"Yeah, some. Not easy for a man in my position to willingly go into a lawman's office, y'know? Even if this is nothing to do with my, er, own circumstances. And Loomis is already suspicious of me."

Caroline took a deep breath. "Would it help if I came with you?"

Fooks glanced at her and away. "I dunno." He shook his head. "No. No, I don't think it would. Tell you what though, you can help by going to your uncle's house. You could ask if anyone found the key to the study. I'm going to suggest to Loomis he conduct a search, but if it's already found..."

"How is the key relevant?"

"Because whoever handled it last must be the murderer. If I can persuade Loomis to search for it and he finds it, he might just believe the rest of my story."

Willingly walking into a Boston police station was one of the hardest things Fooks had ever done. So unlike the Western jails he was used to. *If this goes badly, I might never get out of here.* Hoping Loomis would be out, he pulled back his shoulders and asked for the captain. Told to take a seat, he still hoped. Right up until Captain Loomis pushed through the door from the station interior.

"Crane, what d'you want?"

Fooks smiled, restricting the dimples, and uncrossed his legs. He rose. "I've come about the Kinsey case. I've information that will help."

Loomis chewed on his unlit cigar. With a grunt, he inclined his head. "Follow me and let's hear what you've got."

Fooks followed along meekly to a sparse room, devoid of furniture except for a center table and a few chairs. A large clock hung on the wall. *Ticking away my freedom?* He took the seat indicated, leaned his forearms on the table and knitted his fingers together. Loomis pulled a notepad towards him, found a clean sheet and licked the end of his pencil.

"What you got?" he growled, around the cigar.

"The key is the, er…" Fooks took a deep breath. *This'll better work.* "Well, it's the key to this case." He finished with a nod.

"The key? What key?"

"The key to Kinsey's study. Samuel Martin locked the door when he left."

"Yeah, I don't understand why he did that."

Fooks shook his head and held up his hand. "Just accept it's one of those things folks do on the spur of the moment. The fact is he did. Martin says he threw it away. Look, whoever murdered Kinsey got into the study somehow. No other way in apart from through the door. I know, I looked. They musta found the key. Surely—"

"Murderer might've taken it with him," Loomis pointed out.

Fooks nodded. "Yes, it's a possibility, but if you don't search for it, we won't know for sure. Anyone in the house at the time is a suspect. Keeping it is a sure-fire way to look suspicious. If the police found it on someone or amongst their possessions…well, that's as good as a confession."

Fooks went on pursing his lips and shaking his head. "Naw, they hid it and if we can find it and check for fingerprints, we might find those of the real murderer. Analyzing fingerprints is new. Not everyone knows about it—"

"How do you?" Loomis removed the cigar from his mouth and jabbed it at Fooks. "And don't tell me it's because you're a Pinkerton, 'cos I know that's not true." He stuffed the cigar back in his mouth and chewed it.

Fooks gave Loomis an indulgent smile. "I read a lot. Are you telling me a metropolis like Boston don't have the facilities to analyze fingerprints?"

"Yeah, yeah, we have a small experimental lab." Loomis raised a finger in Fooks' face. "Might also point to Martin as the killer. You're theorizing someone entered the room after Martin and killed Kinsey."

Fooks bit his lip. "Yes, true, but it's the only logical explanation. If Martin didn't kill Kinsey, then someone else had to get into the room to do it. Didn't your men scour the room looking for another means of entry?"

"Yeah, no forced entry via the window, no secret door, the fire was alight, so no way down the chimney."

"Exactly. How else would a person gain entry? They had to use a key."

Loomis drummed his fingers on the table. "I've heard about fingerprints. It's use in criminal cases isn't proved. Not even Scotland Yard is using them yet."

Fooks shook his head and waved a hand dismissively. "I'm not talking about what you can provide as evidence in a court of law. I'm talking about giving you a reason to arrest the real murderer. There's enough evidence in other ways to convict her. What d'you say?"

"You said her. Do you know who did this? If you're holding out on me, Crane—"

Fooks swallowed hard. "I have my suspicions about Kitty Miller, but—"

"Kitty Miller? The girl who worked for Kinsey?"

Fooks nodded. "Yeah, she's not what she seems. Look, I don't want to accuse an innocent woman before I'm sure." He raised his eyebrows. "Loomis, you'll be the first to know when, or if, I can confirm my suspicions."

Loomis sat back as he considered. "You think finding this key is important?"

"Yes." Fooks paused. Perhaps he'd been a little too insistent. "What do you have to lose? Apart from an hour or so of a couple of your officers' time. Samuel Martin was wearing gloves. If," he tapped his forefinger on the table in emphasis, "you find fingerprints other than Kinsey's on the key. Won't that give you cause to doubt Samuel Martin is the killer?"

Loomis couldn't meet Fooks' intense stare. He struck a match and puffed his cigar alight. Fooks wrinkled his nose as Loomis sat back, sending clouds of smoke into the room. Fooks tried not to cough as they stared at each other intently. Then Loomis appeared to decide.

"Mrs. Martin's late father was an ardent supporter of the Boston Police. I've no doubt his daughter feels the same. I suppose," he sighed, "I can extend my view to her husband, mysterious though he is." He scraped his chair back. "Very well. I'll take a couple of men to the Kinsey residence and search." Puffing on his cigar, Loomis fixed Fooks with a hard stare. "You'd better come along."

Fooks stood and offered his hand. "Thank you, Captain Loomis." *You've no idea how relieved I am to hear you say that.*

First thing on arriving at Kinsey House, Fooks went to see if Kitty was in the office. Gray informed him she'd requested the day off to care for her sick mother. *Convenient.*

Returning to the hall, he paced up and down as two police patrolmen on hands and knees inspected the whole area outside the study door. This including the darkest recesses of the hall corners and under the stairs. Loomis watched on from the center of the hall, smoking his ubiquitous cigar.

Caroline came down from visiting her aunt as they arrived.

"Any sign of the key?" Fooks asked, in a low voice.

Caroline shook her head. "No." She took a seat to one side. "I doubt if the police will find it after all this time. The servants have cleaned here since the police left."

"But wouldn't they have mentioned it to someone if they'd found the key?" Fooks asked.

"Perhaps they wouldn't think it important enough."

"It's lack of presence at the time caused this to happen." He waved a hand at the splintered door surround. "I would have thought—"

"I don't know, Mr. Crane. This is your theory. Let the search proceed."

Caroline arranged her skirts and sat up straighter. She wrinkled her nose at Loomis' cigar smoke when it wafted near her. She alternated between waving her hand in front of her nose and fiddling impatiently with her gloves.

Fooks stood at her side and then walked forward to stand next to Loomis. "Mr. Martin threw it away. How about under the edge of the rug? Coulda got kicked under there in all the confusion."

"Let them do their job, Crane."

"Sorry." He retreated to sit beside Caroline.

As he watched the police search, Fooks thought back over what Swan told him happened that night. He closed his eyes and envisaged the scene. Swan'd come out of the study, noticed the key, locked the door and thrown it away. Fooks recognized it for what it was. Knowing his partner well enough; the act pure frustration on Swan's part.

Fooks suddenly gasped. Caroline regarded him sharply as Fooks leaned forward. "He's left-handed," he breathed.

"Joseph?"

Fooks jumped to his feet. "You're looking in the wrong place."

Loomis regarded him. "What did you say, Crane?"

"Samuel Martin is left-handed. Look, I'll show you."

Fooks crossed to the study door. With his back to it, he walked quickly further into the hall. He held up his left hand as if he held something. "The key, Loomis." He made a tossing motion, and his eyes followed the flight of the imaginary key. He pointed to the long case clock ticking away against the wall. "If Swan was the last person to have the key, your men should be searching over here," he said, in excitement and stalked away.

Loomis directed one of the two searching police officers to where Fooks peered at the floor. The other he detailed to continue searching where he was.

"Are you sure about this Crane?" Loomis asked, scouring the floor. Fooks, on his hands and knees, lifted the edge of the rug.

"This is exactly the direction a left-handed person would throw. If you find it somewhere else, then doesn't that prove Mr. Martin's innocence?"

"Not really. Martin coulda—"

"It does." Fooks was insistent. "Look, Mr. Martin left here in a hurry. In no frame of mind to think 'bout deliberately locating the key. He jus' threw it away." Fooks spoke quickly, his diction suffering in his haste to convince Loomis.

"I suppose," Loomis said, begrudgingly. "There's been so much activity in this hall of late, coulda gone anywhere. If it's here."

"It's here." Fooks was confident.

Ten more minutes and even he was beginning to admit defeat.

"Found it, Captain."

"Ha." Fooks gave an involuntary gasp. The call come from the other side of the hall.

"Don't touch it, Pearson," ordered Loomis. "If Crane is right, there may be valuable evidence on it."

Fooks came to stand by Loomis' side. Together they gazed at the spot illuminated by the lantern Pearson held. Wedged under the skirting board shone the bow of a key.

"It's on the right, Loomis. This isn't the direction Martin woulda thrown it, so someone else musta put it there, after he threw it away. Now d'you believe me?"

Loomis shifted uncomfortably. He chewed his cigar furiously. "Let's say, there's a check in your favor."

CHAPTER THIRTY-EIGHT

"What? Let Martin out on bail? He's wanted for murder!" Loomis stuffed his lit cigar into his mouth.

Fooks and Loomis regrouped back at the police station. Loomis persuaded his superior he had an ideal candidate for the police's evaluation of the merits of finger print testing. The longer they waited for the results of the testing, the more anxious Fooks became. What was taking so long? Would the results, when, if, they came, support his assertion someone else handled the key?

He'd plenty of time to think as they waited. After this he wanted to confront Kitty Miller once and for all, and he needed Swan out to help. *He* needed out of here. Loomis was already far too suspicious of him. The newspaper report hadn't helped. Loomis musta seen it. Only a matter of time. Surely?

"Yes. Yes, I realize it's a stretch, but hear me out." Fooks leaned forward to press his point.

Loomis chewed his lit cigar furiously and gestured for him to go on. Loomis listened hard, as Fooks explained. Fooks knew his story hit home when the cigar moved less and less.

"Kinsey was shot with a 0.22. Right?"

"How do you know that?"

Fooks waved his hand in frustration. "Right?"

"Yes, he was shot with a 0.22. So?"

"We took a 0.22 from Kitty Miller at the icehouse."

"The Waltham police found it on Martin."

"Yes, because he'd taken if off her. It's a Rupertus Pepperbox. Easy enough to check who bought it. Can't be more'n two, three-gun shops in Boston who'd sell one."

"There's more gun shops than that in Boston."

"Yes, probably, but not everyone will sell a Rupertus. It's rare, Loomis." Fooks paused. "And the other thing, I need to get a look at her bag."

"Her bag? Crane, you're the most—"

"Mrs. Martin pointed it out to me. The design is unusual. A row of red felt diamonds, decreasing in size across the middle of the bag. The pattern is reversed on the other side. The interesting point—"

"Oh, so there is one."

Fooks chewed his lips, swallowed an irritated repost and carried on. "The interesting point is the largest two diamonds have been replaced recently by hand. I think she shot Kinsey through the bag, to muffle the sound, and sewed the two diamonds on to cover the holes."

"I don't believe it."

"Kitty had the opportunity, Loomis. She was there that evening. Remember the mouse? An invented story if ever I heard one. And no one saw her leave in all the confusion. I guess you can check what train she caught home, but probably only gonna confirm what she told me." He sat back and waited. "Well, what d'you think?"

Loomis sat and stared back, the cigar threatening to fall from his lips. In a quiet voice he said, "The autopsy found traces of red felt and carpet in the wound. Examiner couldn't explain how they got there. There's no red felt in the room and the carpet fibers didn't match the rug."

Fooks widened his eyes. "So? What more d'you need? I'm telling you. Kitty Miller is our man, or woman in this case. I asked for her at Kinsey House earlier. She's away today, taking care of her sick mother. They live in Waltham."

Loomis slowly stubbed his cigar out.

"Okay, I'll send some men out there."

Loomis made to rise but Fooks stopped him. "No Loomis, we haven't got time. Waltham isn't in your jurisdiction, is it? Think of all the paperwork if you sent officers out there without telling the Waltham police first. And we don't have time to explain. She'll get away, and it'll be anyone's guess where she'll go."

Fooks stared at Loomis hard, willing him to understand. "Mrs. Martin hired me to find her uncle's killer. Let me handle it, but I need Martin's help. If Kitty sees him out of jail, she'll wonder why. She'll talk to us, but this should be handled quietly."

"Why?"

"As a private citizen, I can do things you can't. I can offer her a solution to her problems."

"You mean lie to her."

Fooks twitched his head. "I mean gain her trust."

Loomis gave him a hard stare.

"How can I be sure the three of you aren't in cahoots? The moment I let Martin out, you all take off and I never hear of you again."

Fooks smiled. "Mr. Martin has a wife, Loomis. Caroline Fairfield as she used to be known. Man doesn't run out on a woman who looks like that, and certainly not one with that kinda money."

"What's the other reason?"

"Kitty's mother. Whatever happens, she still has to continue living in Waltham. Steaming in with loads of police is going to make that impossible for her. Mr. Martin and me can do this without any fuss. Show her some respect and let her keep her dignity."

Loomis considered, but Fooks realized not yet convinced. He glanced at the clock, ticking loudly.

"Y'know sometimes Loomis you just need a little faith. I suppose I can appreciate you have suspicions about me, given the circumstances. I'll tell you what I'll do. I'll give you the name of someone who can vouch for me."

"Who?"

Fooks licked his lips. "A sheriff."

He swallowed. This was a gamble. Fooks and Swan had first settled in Bronze Canyon with the agreement of Sheriff Wash Turner. He'd accepted their word they wanted to go straight and needed a safe place to do it. He hadn't said he'd protect them. Fooks and Swan both knew if the law came for them, Wash would give them up. He had his own family to take care of and the lives of two outlaws easily sacrificed.

That was then. Fooks was in a much better place now and Wash knew how hard he was trying. If Loomis only asked about Joseph Crane, Wash would probably answer truthfully. Anything more searching, well it was a gamble.

Fooks took a deep breath. "Sheriff Washington Turner, Bronze Canyon, Wyoming. He'll vouch for me."

"Can he vouch for Martin as well?"

"He hasn't lived there for a while, but yes, Wash can vouch for him too."

Loomis raised his eyebrows. "Oh, so you do know Martin?"

Ouch. Clever Loomis. Fooks winced and nodded. "Yeah, I know Mr. Martin."

Loomis glared at him hard, then shuffled his papers into a neat pile, tucked them in the file and closed it. He sat still, hands resting on top. He glanced at the clock on the wall, and he stood. "Wait here. It'll take time to check. If your sheriff answers."

"He'll answer."

Fooks sounded confident but inside a bundle of nerves. As Loomis went out, Fooks pursed his lips. Well, in his heyday he was known as being a gambler, and a good gambler always looks at the pot. Swan being released represented the pot, and he did like that pot.

A long wait. Given the time difference, Fooks knew what he was in for. Didn't help with his uncertainty over what Wash would make of Loomis' request. All depended on what Loomis asked. Fooks wasn't party to that, and he tried not to think about the consequences. What will be, will be. He folded his arms, tilted his head down. In situations like this, only one thing to do. He dozed.

He was well away when the door opened suddenly. Fooks all but leapt from his chair, hand to his chest.

Loomis came in with a rueful smile at the start he'd given. He held the door open, and a sheepish Swan walked through.

Fooks bounded to his feet, grinning with pleasure. "Sw...Mr. Martin."

"Mr. Crane, I presume?"

Loomis dragged forward another chair for Swan and sat on his own. He gave an exasperated growl. "Don't give me that. You two know each other."

He opened the papers, before seeing the two men swapping grins. Clearing his throat had the desired effect. He got their attention.

"Mr. Crane has convinced me that the two of you can apprehend Kitty Miller, safely and quietly. Are you prepared to try?"

Swan nodded. "Oh yes indeedy. This murder rap you're holding over my head is becoming a tad irritating, Captain. I'd like an end to this, and Kitty Miller holds the key to removing it."

Fooks smirked. *Oh, if only you knew what you said.*

Loomis scowled. "Whether she does, or doesn't, remains to be seen. The fingerprint analysis confirms there are prints on the key." He paused. "They ain't yours, Martin."

Fooks and Swan swapped glances.

Loomis continued. "As yet we're unable to determine whose they are." He looked from one to the other. "No doubt Miss Miller can help us with that line of inquiry."

"I do hope so," Fooks agreed.

Loomis spun out a document from his file.

"Under the circumstances, I've set bail at fifteen thousand dollars. No doubt your wife will cover it?"

Fooks pondered the irony of the bail being more than the price on both their heads combined.

"I'm sure she will."

"Very well. Sign here."

He pushed the document towards Swan and pointed to a pen in the inkwell. Swan scratched a signature with his left hand. Fooks and Loomis glanced at each other, the former with a knowing smirk. Swan pushed the document back.

"Are we done? Can we go find Kitty Miller?" Fooks used the table as a lever to push up.

"There's another condition."

Fooks sat again.

"Two of my men will follow you." Loomis stilled Fooks' protest. "You will go about the business of finding Miss Miller as if they weren't around. They will hold back and won't interfere unless she tries to escape. Their names are Beamish and Gomez."

With a glance at Swan, Fooks reluctantly nodded.

"Given the severity of the charge against you, Mr. Martin, I could do nothing else. It's my job on the line if you abscond. You may go now. Beamish and Gomez will be waiting for you outside."

"Thank you, Captain."

Swan and Fooks scraped back their chairs and shook hands with Loomis.

"Oh, by the way, Crane," Loomis said, as they were about to leave. "Your Sheriff Turner gave you a glowing report."

Fooks beamed the full double dimple. *Good ole Wash.*

CHAPTER THIRTY-NINE

"Thanks for getting me out," Swan said, as they trotted down the steps of the police station. "I knew ya would somehow."

"Yeah, well, don't thank me just yet. There's still the little matter of finding and hanging onto Kitty Miller."

"Ya got a plan?"

Fooks stopped, hands on hips, and chewed his cheek. "When I spoke to Alfred, Kitty's brother, I got the impression their ma was important to both of them. Kitty said something similar as well. I'd say her house is a good place to start, don't you?"

"Hope so." Swan stroked his throat. "I've gotta do something. It's my neck that'll stretch if we don't, an' I kinda like it the length it is."

Fooks grinned. "Then it's a good job I know where she lives. Corner of Ash Street and Moody, Waltham."

Swan walked away. "Post Office over there." He pointed across the street. "I'll telegraph to Ardmaddy. Have Cowdry collect us from the train," Swan said, over his shoulder.

"While you're doing that, I'll tell the boys there what we're doing." Fooks nodded to the two trying-to-be-inconspicuous men lurking behind a newspaper stand.

Swan twitched his head doubtfully. "Yeah. Dunno how much help they'll be, but I guess we need all the help we can get."

The house was small but appeared in good repair. Unlike most others in the street. Out of tune music seeped from the bar on the opposite corner. Litter blew along the sidewalk. A laughing child ran barefoot, chased by a barking dog, to an older brother, judging by their similarity of looks. Fooks' eyes narrowed as the child handed something over, quickly pocketed by the other. He could recognize a pickpocket racket when he saw one. As the elder child walked nonchalantly away, whistling, hands in his pockets, the younger child calmly bent to pet the dog. A puffing, middle-aged man turned the corner, stopped, threw off his cap and dashed it to the ground.

"Who does the knocking?"

Swan's question focused Fooks back on the task in hand.

During the train journey to Waltham, he'd brought Swan up to date with developments. As promised, Cowdry met them at Waltham Station with a carriage and brought them here. To stand outside Mrs. Miller's front door.

Swan motioned to the door in front of Fooks. "You're right there."

"Who's good with the ladies?"

"You've got the silver tongue. Smile that smile of yours at her, you'll have her eating outta ya hand in no time."

Fooks gave him a doubtful glare before reaching for the knocker.

As they waited for the door to open, both heard the hushed voices and the hurried movement from inside. Swan stepped to one side. Sheer curtains covered the bottom half of the nearest window. He stood on tiptoe to peer in, cupping his hands either side of his face to offset his reflection.

"She's gone out the back," he cried and bolted for the side of the house.

Fooks prepared himself to follow when the door opened. He swept off his homburg at the sight of the middle-aged woman.

"Yes?"

"Excuse me ma'am but I need to use your back door," he yelled, pushing passed her and entering the hall.

"Hey! You can't just—"

"Sorry ma'am," Fooks yelled as he crashed out of the back door.

He took the three steps in a leap. Swan joined him a stride or two in front. They raced along the path. The slim figure of Kitty Miller reached the gate. Beyond in the lane a buggy waited. She all but dived into it and set the horse forward at a fast clip.

Swan skidded to a halt. Fooks careened into him. Together they tumbled to the ground. Swiftly untangling themselves, they bounded smartly to their feet. Fooks ran up a slight mound. From there he watched over the garden wall, locking his eyes on the buggy as it made off. Swan in the meantime ran across the garden in the other direction. Until he could see Cowdry waiting in their carriage out front. Another carriage containing Beamish and Gomez waited along the street.

"Cowdry! Round the back. Quick."

When Cowdry flicked the reins, Swan returned to Fooks.

"Ya still see her?"

"Yep."

As Cowdry pulled up at the back gate, Swan gave his partner's arm a nudge. Fooks took one more look and followed. Swan climbed into the carriage. To Cowdry's surprise, Fooks climbed on top next to him.

"Go! It'll tell you where." Map in his hand, he pointed with the other. "Left onto Lowell Street." A moment later, he yelled, "Right onto Taylor."

Fooks puffed as he consulted the map.

"Do you know where she's going?" Cowdry managed to ask, his face a study in concentration.

"Not exactly. Can't you go any faster?"

"It's not exactly open country here sir," Cowdry protested.

"Here." Fooks stuffed the map into his pocket. "Let me."

Fooks snatched the reins from Cowdry and flicked them on, compelling the horse into more speed.

"Hold on!" he roared as they came to the end of the lane. Turning left across traffic. No time to wait for a break. Fooks forced them out on to the road. Causing havoc. Screams, whinnies and angry yells sounded behind them. Unfazed, they continued at breakneck speed. Edging ever closer to their quarry.

Off to the left a whistle blew. The sound of chugging echoed. Steaming around the bend, a train. Kitty made it across the tracks in front of the train. Fooks with a determined face, flicked the reins again, urging the horse faster.

"Sir!" Cowdry screamed.

"Not now."

CHAPTER FORTY

Kitty was across the railroad tracks. Fooks glanced at the approaching train. Then at the distance to the crossing. *Nope.* He pulled up hard. The horse jumped in the traces. Snorting and bucking. The train passed inches in front of its nose.

No sooner had the train passed, Fooks set them off again. Kitty remained in sight. Already heading out over the bridge across the Charles River. The traffic on the opposite approach snarled into a bottleneck. No room to overtake. Forced into a slow pace.

Once across the bridge, Fooks set the horse into a fast trot. Consulting the map now in his head, a major intersection lay ahead. Fooks took advantage of the clear road and the horse's willingness to run.

Nearly catching up when they hit the intersection. Kitty forced her way into the stream of traffic. Frustrated, Fooks had to wait for a slow delivery van to pull off to the left. Kitty went straight on. Over another set of train tracks, mercifully free of trains and on. Another main intersection. Kitty forced to slow allowed Fooks to came to a halt behind her.

Tossing the reins at Cowdry, Fooks prepared to get down. But no. Kitty glanced back and urged her horse left. Fooks cursed. He snatched the reins back, hoping to replicate her move. Not so. No room to pull out. Yet pull out he did.

"Maniac."

Leaving chaos in their wake, they sped on. Fooks gave no quarter to other vehicles. He concentrated solely on Kitty. Slewing left around the Town Hall corner, carriage tilting at an alarming angle. No sooner straightened up, then turning right. This time the opposite wheels left the ground, slamming back when the carriage righted.

Up top, Fooks yelled at Cowdry. "Any idea where she's going?"

Cowdry clung to the side of the seat, his knuckles as white as his face. "Going? No sir."

"Come on Cowdry you know this town. How would she get back to Boston? She's going the wrong way now to drive all the way."

Kitty forced them into another sharp left. And another right.

Inside, Swan found himself in a whirlpool. Nothing much to hold on to, try as he might.

"Sheesh, Flo, do ya mean to kill me?" He cursed when a particularly violent jolt sent him sprawling to the floor of the carriage. He groaned and decided he was better off where he was. Getting back on the seat would be impossible at this velocity.

"Train!"

"Huh?"

Cowdry panted as a sharp turn to the left nearly pitched him over the side. "She's trying to lose us."

"You don't say."

"Train, sir. We've nearly at Riverview Station."

"Must be it."

"The road bends round." Cowdry groaned as another lurch threw him so hard against Fooks, he nearly dropped the reins. With one hand, Fooks pushed Cowdry back into the seat. Cowdry clapped a hand on his hat, and he gulped. "As I was saying sir, the road bends round and on to the approach. There sir." Cowdry pointed at their quarry stopped outside the entrance of the train station.

Kitty already dashing inside as they pulled up. Fooks briefly considered the irony of being back where it all began a few days ago. The ice houses clearly in view across the bridge. No time for reminiscing. Cowdry caught the reins as Fooks clambered down. Fooks snatched the door open and blinked.

Swan sprawled on the floor, looking up at him. He groaned.

"Nice of ya to stop an' see how I am," he grumped.

"She's gone in the train station. C'mon, stop messing about."

Swan struggled into a sitting position.

"Can ya help?"

Fooks grabbed under his arms and pulled until Swan could put his feet on the ground. The moment he could, they took off in pursuit.

"Am I coming sir?" Cowdry called after them.

Swan half turned as he ran. "No. Go on home."

"Hey! You can't come through here without a ticket."

As they attempted to race onto the platform, the ticket collector stopped them. His arm barred them entry through the gate.

"Why not? She did." Swan waved at the disappearing figure.

"I know her. That's Kitty Miller. She has a season ticket."

"I have this." Fooks held up his Pinkerton shield. "We're in pursuit of a murderer and they're getting away. Now let us through."

The ticket collector gulped and pulled the gate smartly aside.

Fooks and Swan raced along the platform. The conductor yelled at them to jump on if they were going to.

"Did she get on?"

"Think so."

The train dispatcher blew his whistle. Fooks leaped onto the rear viewing platform. Swan delayed long enough until he was sure Kitty didn't break from hiding. He clambered up beside Fooks as the train jerked to a start. Then the train shuddered to a halt again as Beamish and Gomez pushed their way on. Fooks bundled them out of the way. He and Swan kept watch until the train cleared the station platform.

"Nah, nothing." Swan shook his head. "Ya sure she's on here?"

"No," Fooks said, firmly.

Swan did a double take. "No? I thought ya were watching her?"

"I was," Fooks protested, hunching his shoulders and opening his hands.

"How can ya not know if she's on the train or not?" Swan waved his hand dismissively. "Awh, let's get inside."

"We'll come through in five minutes," said Beamish. Or Gomez, Fooks wasn't sure.

Fooks followed Swan inside and down the aisle. They made their way through the car, glancing at each side. Studying the passengers for signs of Kitty. Both well aware of the drill. Both had experience hiding on trains in plain sight or when they were doing the hunting. With two pairs of experienced eyes, if she was there, one of them would spot her.

It was a long train. Unusual for a Monday afternoon, even in this part of the country. They emerged onto the viewing platform after the first car and faced each other.

No need for words. Neither saw her. Swan sighed, turned, and stepped across the gap between cars.

Two, three cars further on they stopped again. Swan climbed down when the train pulled into Waltham main station.

Fooks hovered in the rear of the viewing platform. He skimmed along the train on the far side. Running off across the other track was something he'd done. A dangerous move. Yet he'd probably do it again given the circumstances.

Swan walked away from the train. Much to the disgust of fellow passengers, he stepped onto a bench. His eyes swept behind, to the side and in front. Hoping to catch a glimpse of a woman moving away fast. No one a likely candidate. Then the possibility Kitty was watching him. He scanned around for likely hiding places. Catching Beamish and Gomez doing the same.

"All aboard!"

With the last of the passengers boarded, the train dispatcher blew his whistle. Swan had no choice but to scramble back on. He shook his head at Fooks' unspoken question. Fooks slapped the handrail and motioned for Swan to lead the way again.

Another car searched with no luck. Then the train slowed. A train steaming from their left converged on them. The trains ran in parallel, for a short time. Before the other train gathered speed and pulled ahead. Their train slowly came to a halt in Clematis Brook station. Fooks and Swan repeated their actions from earlier.

Once under way again, three more cars moved through, and still no sign. They slumped disconsolate in the foremost seat in the foremost car.

"She ain't on this train, Flo." Swan stated the obvious to avoid any misunderstanding.

Fooks crossed his arms and his legs. "She could be, and we didn't see her."

"She coulda got off. The main station was pretty crowded."

"Yep." Fooks stared at a spot on the floor. "'Tis a possibility."

Swan sniffed and mirrored Fooks' body language. "What do we do now?"

"Look out at every station until Boston I suppose."

"I've never been on the slow train. Are there many stops?"

Fooks shrugged. "Who knows?"

Swan cursed under his breath. He rested his head back and tilted his hat over his eyes. Only to sit up straight when Beamish and Gomez slid into the seats across the aisle.

Fooks silently asked the did-you-see-her question and received a slight shake of the head from Beamish. Or Gomez? What were they gonna do if they hadn't found Kitty by the time they got to Boston? Fooks groaned. Just have to think of something. Simple. *Yeah right.*

CHAPTER FORTY-ONE

"How did we miss her?" Swan said, in frustration. "She was on the train. I know she was."

The train terminated at the Fitchburg Depot terminus in Boston, where they'd hovered on the platform, until all the passengers alighted. A flash of the Pinkerton shield and they were through into the headhouse. They now sat slumped on a bench. Beamish and Gomez took a watching position further away.

"We didn't miss her. She missed us."

"Huh?"

Fooks gestured at the next track over. "The express is in."

Swan frowned at him. "So?"

Fooks swallowed. "Remember when we had to slow? Where the track is double? Musta been the express which came alongside us." He sighed. "She crossed onto the other train then."

Swan widened his eyes in realization. "Heck, I wouldn't try that."

Fooks twitched his head. "Trains do about eight miles an hour when they come together. Perfectly feasible she could cross from one to the other." He shook his head. "Only explanation which fits." He shook his head again. "Takes some guts, I grant you."

"We've lost her and no idea where she is going. Great."

They sat for a moment in silence, until Fooks suddenly stood. "Not necessarily," he muttered, as he walked away.

Swan watched his partner disappear for a moment, before following him. Out of the corner of his eye he saw Beamish and Gomez. They lurked behind their favorite place of concealment, the newspaper stands.

Fooks had waylaid the concierge. As Swan joined them, Fooks flashed the Pinkerton shield and described Kitty Miller. He waved his hand at the express train, indicating where she had come from.

"I believe a woman of that description boarded the Cambridge Street railroad. Number 9."

"Where does it go?"

"It's a circular route. Links all the Boston railroad depots."

"Did you happen to notice which way round?" Swan asked. When the concierge looked doubtful, Swan flicked a hand between himself and Fooks. "I'm with him."

Fooks acknowledged the truth of this.

The concierge drew himself up. "In that case, she went counter-clockwise."

"Thank you."

"Yeah, thanks." Swan took Fooks by the elbow and led him quickly away. "Listen, I've an idea where she's going," he said, out of the corner of his mouth.

"Where?"

"I think she's gonna catch a train to New York. If she went counter-clockwise, I bet she's gone to the Park Square Depot. If she was going to one of the other depots she'da gone the other way round."

Fooks twitched his head. *Not entirely convinced, but I guess this is your patch now.*

"Let's take a cab and go look-see. It'll be quicker than the streetcar."

Fooks trudged after him around the corner of the headhouse to the cab rank, where they were confronted by a long queue of waiting would-be passengers. To his surprise, Swan marched to the head of the queue and greeted the dispatcher by name. "Hi Owen, any chance of a cab? I'm in kinda a hurry."

"Hey!"

Fooks felt guilty as he waited. The queue would likely become mutinous any minute.

With a pleased grin, Owen opened his mouth to greet him by name but Swan stopped him with a raised hand. Instead, "How are you sir?"

"Fine, fine, and Mrs. Owen?"

"Bearing up sir. Bearing up. Cab to Park Square y'say?"

He beckoned the first cab in line forward. When the cab drew up, Owen opened the door and ushered Swan and Fooks inside. Fooks noticed Swan press a bill into Owen's hand as he climbed in. A quick word with the driver and they were off.

As they paused to turn out onto The Causeway, Fooks glanced back at Beamish and Gomez, having an animated conversation with Owen. Fooks bit his lip in amusement as their cab moved away into the traffic. *Said you could come, but never said we'd make it easy for you to keep up.*

Fooks and Swan sat side by side not speaking for some minutes. The traffic as usual was chaotic on The Causeway, and slow. Once through they proceeded along at a fair clip.

"Go on then, say it," Swan snapped.

"Say what?"

"What ya gonna say."

Fooks blinked innocently. "I wasn't gonna say anything." He stared out of the window for a moment, chewing his bottom lip, a smile threatening to creep over his features. Swan chuckled and playfully slapped his arm. "Okay, why are we going to the Park Square Depot?"

"Alfred told ya the family used to live in New York, right?"

Fooks nodded.

"So, if ya running, wouldn't ya want to run to where ya'd feel safe?"

"I guess."

"What have we got to lose? We're here now an' on our way."

The pair sat in silence for a few moments. When Fooks glanced out of the window, he blanched. Haymarket Square again. *Sheesh.*

"What do we do if we don't catch her at Park Street?" Fooks asked, trying to distract himself from the free for all outside. "We can't chase her all the way to New York."

"Look, Flo, you know how these things work. Things appear stymied, and then you think of something." When Fooks rolled his eyes, Swan added, "You always do. Why should this time be any different?"

"Lots of reasons."

"Such as?"

"Those guys behind us for one." Fooks turned to peer through the rear window. "I take it they are still behind us?"

"Yeah, they're still there. A long way behind us, I might add."

"They don't know Kitty comes from New York. Or why we're going to another railroad depot. What's Loomis gonna think if we get on the long-distance train? And the train doesn't go all the way to New York, does it? Isn't there a boat somewhere?"

"Going this way, yes at Stonington. Have to change there and take the steamer down the Long Island Sound all the way into New York." Swan sniffed. "Good route."

"You've been to New York?" Fooks eyes popped.

"Yes, Caroline and me went for our first wedding anniversary."

Fooks stared at him in silence for a moment, then shook his head.

"What?"

"Nothing."

"Yes, there is. I know you Fooks."

Fooks continued to stare out of the window.

"Flo—"

"What's New York like?"

"Too glitzy for me, but Caroline seems to like it."

Fooks swallowed the lump in his throat and kept his face turned away. *Why does this hurt so much? Am I jealous? I shouldn't be. Is it 'cos Swan's having adventures I'd like to have? Come on Fooks, you have a beautiful wife and a gorgeous baby at home. Isn't that enough for you?*

CHAPTER FORTY-TWO

Their arrival at the Park Square Depot interrupted his thoughts. Now they would find out if they had truly lost their quarry. Fooks climbed out of the cab. He stood on the edges of a wide concourse. Hands on hips, he regarding the Park Square Depot, while Swan paid the fare. He'd thought the depots in Chicago impressive. This was something else again.

Constructed from red brick, the building loomed large, the details picked out in sandstone, in a modern Gothic style. There were four high vaulted archways, one more elaborate than the others. Above, a series of windows, and above those an ornate central window with a triangular molding. It even had a cross at its peak. To the left of the main façade, an overly high clock tower. When Fooks craned his neck, he saw a weathervane sat up top. Fooks gulped. The whole edifice resembled a cathedral.

Swan came to stand next to him, tucking away his money. "Impressive, huh? They say it's the biggest in the world."

"I'll say."

Swan swatted him with the back of his fingers. "C'mon, we haven't got time for sightseeing."

Fooks followed blindly, still in awe of the magnificent architecture. Under the *porte cochere*, with its resemblance to a Turkish bazaar, and into the great marble hall. High above, a hammer-beamed ceiling. Part way down the walls ran a balconied gallery, allowing access to the railroad offices. To one side stood the gentlemen's waiting room, on the other another for ladies. Fooks trudged the length of the hall to join Swan at the ticket office window.

Swan pulled Fooks to attention. "Show him ya shield," he whispered, *sotto voce*.

Fooks jerked his mind back to the matter in hand and produced the Pinkerton shield. He described Kitty Miller. The ticket vendor confirmed their suspicions. A woman of that appearance had indeed purchased a ticket to New York. "On the four o'clock." He pointed in the direction of the train shed.

Swan took off immediately. Fooks turned more slowly from the counter, consulting his pocket watch.

"Wait up," he called.

Swan furrowed his brow in irritation at his tardy partner.

"Train leaves in fifteen minutes," Fooks said, as he caught up. "We go tearing onto the platform and she's liable to get spooked."

"What d'ya suggest?"

Fooks raised an eyebrow at the sound of running feet behind them. Beamish and Gomez clattered in and skidded to a halt. On seeing Fooks and Swan standing in the middle of the hall, they tried to appear nonchalant. Fooks and Swan swapped grins. The former stepped forward, inclining his head for the detectives to join him in a quiet alcove.

"She's got a ticket for the four o'clock New York train," he informed them quietly.

"What are we waiting for? Let's get after her," said Gomez. Or might be Beamish.

"Not so fast." When Swan joined them, Fooks pulled them into a tight huddle. "She knows us." He flicked a thumb between himself and Swan. "But she doesn't know you. I suggest you scout around in the train shed and locate her. Come back here and we'll discuss a plan of action. Okay?"

Beamish and Gomez swapped glances and one of them nodded their agreement. As they watched the two go ahead, Swan put his hand on Fooks' shoulder. "They sure do stand out as police to me," he said, in a whisper.

Fooks rolled his eyes. "That's 'cos you're you." His grin became broader. "Why d'you think I sent them? My guess is she'll see 'em, realize she's being tailed, and not by us, and make a run for it. Is there another way out of there?"

Swan shook his head. "Not that I know of. Unless you're a train."

Fooks grunted. "Let's hope she doesn't become one. I don't fancy running along the tracks."

Things happened fast. One moment Fooks and Swan were loitering unconcerned by the doorway of the men's waiting room. The next the doors to the train shed crashed open. Beamish and Gomez tore out, running full pelt.

"She went out the ladies' waiting room window," Gomez panted. Might be Beamish.

"Sheesh. She's a..." Swan didn't finish as he took off after the detectives. Fooks brought up the rear.

They came to a halt outside on the concourse, scanning around for a fleeing woman. Swan went to the corner of the building to see down the length. He squinted for a moment. "There she is," he yelled and took off.

The others followed. With the New York train about to depart, the concourse was full of hurrying passengers. Friends and relatives huddled in groups saying their goodbyes. Lots of general milling around hindered their pursuit. The running men sidestepped frantically, tripping over luggage and yelling at porters who weren't moving out of their way fast enough.

At the end of the head house building, activity became quieter. They stretched their legs as they ran the length of the train shed, ignoring the raindrops threatening to become a significant downpour. Kitty got to the end of the train shed some way before them. She ducked out of sight.

"Where's she going?" panted Gomez. Might be Beamish.

"There're the tracks. Sheesh." Swan cried.

They rounded the corner and Kitty's route became clearer. The separate building of the engineering workshop stood off to their left. No public access. Kitty had already scaled the low fence demarcating its boundaries. Juggling her carpet bag, she ran on. She headed between the workshop and the tracks. Her heels kicked up. She hitched her skirt higher, showing off red and purple striped stockings.

Interesting choice.

Swan and Fooks powered after her, the two detectives some way behind. One stopped and retreated, leaving Beamish, or might be Gomez, to follow on alone.

"Hey! You ain't allowed in here," a railway man called as Kitty streaked by him. Nearly flattened by Fooks and Swan as they tore in pursuit. Placated by the now lone detective flashing a Boston police shield in the railway man's face.

The distance between the train tracks and the workshop narrowed considerably. Alarmingly so when a train approaching the depot steamed feet from where they ran. The men checked their pursuit and slowed. Kitty ran on regardless.

Up ahead, steps led up to the road bridge that crossed the tracks. A closed wooden gate stood at the top of the flight. The rain made the narrow treads of the steps slick. Not a staircase intended for general pedestrian use. Railway workers wanting to access the bridge without walking all the way around back passed the workshop.

Kitty reached the head of the stairs and tugged open the gate. She glanced back. Fooks and Swan struggled to maintain speed on the narrow steps. Fooks stumbled and nearly fell. *What is it with me and steps in this town?*

Swan ran out on the bridge first. A delivery van impeded his view across. He hopped in frustration waiting for it to pass. Kitty was across the road, moving more slowly. She glanced back, saw Swan and stopped. An anxious expression crossed her face.

"Kitty!"

Kitty leapt up onto the bridge parapet. "Don't come any closer. I swear I'll jump." Her bag hindered her attempt to balance, and she dropped it back onto the roadway.

Fooks, by now caught up, and Swan stopped their advance.

"Now, Miss, ya don't wanna do that." Swan moved closer.

"Get back! I mean it."

"Why don't I jus' come on up there beside ya and we can talk about this nice and calmly?" As he spoke Swan climbed onto the parapet some feet from her. The rain increased.

"Tobe!" Fooks breathed.

Swan waved a hand in Fooks' direction. He had this. Fooks bit his lip. Swan was always the one with a head for heights and seemingly disregard for his own mortality.

"Nice view ya get from up here," Swan said, starting the conversation.

"Get back. I don't want you here."

Swan shrugged nonchalantly. "Free country ain't it?" He took a sidestep towards her.

"Go away," she gasped, taking a step away. Noticeably, a smaller one than his.

"Sooo." Swan drew out the word and pursed his lips. "What's this all about Kitty?"

"You chased me. You must know why," she shot back.

Swan cocked a thumb over his shoulder. "I do what he tells me."

Kitty risked a glance in Fooks' direction. "Oh, yes, Mr. Crane, who can't keep his nose out of another person's business."

Fooks winced. Licking his lips and swallowing hard. *What is Swan going to do?*

Swan gave a quick laugh. "Yeah, I'm afraid he's always like that. But I'm glad he took an interest. Y'see the police have me figured for the murder of Robert Kinsey." He paused and glared at her. "Now I know, and you know I didn't do it." He took a step closer.

"Sorry about that. D-Don't come any closer."

Swan saw her peer down.

"Best not to do that, Miss. Easier to keep ya balance if ya don't look down." He raised his voice over the torrent of water descending upon them.

"Thanks for the advice. What are you?" She swallowed. "Some kind of high wire act?"

"No ma'am, jus' someone who's used to being on high things." He paused and twitched his head. "Course usually they're moving," he said, innocently.

Fooks shuddered.

"M-Moving?"

"Yes, ma'am. Kinda occupational hazard in the line of work I used to do."

Kitty's eyes widened. "Then it's true. You two are Florian Fooks and Tobias Swan."

Swan laughed gently and took another step closer. One more step and he would grab her. This time she couldn't move away. The central pilaster rose higher than the top of the parapet. Too high and wide for her to step over.

"I can't believe…" she panted. Her eyes flicked everywhere, searching for an avenue of escape.

"Kitty, look out," Fooks yelled, over the sound of a rapidly approaching train.

The lone detective panted to a halt at his side and bent over, hands on his knees. Spent.

Fooks already smelt the coal smoke turning acrid in the damp air. The roar of the engine deafened him. Metal wheels protested their compliance on the rails. A cacophony of sound echoed around. An ear-splitting whistle sounded. Hot, sulfurous steam enveloped the bridge and everyone on it. High above the rattle of the train, a female scream, an anguished male cry. Fooks saw nothing.

Heart in his mouth, Fooks raced forward. The billowing white steam took ages to clear, and when it did, Kitty was gone. And so was Swan.

CHAPTER FORTY-THREE

"No! Tobe," Fooks wailed.

"Help!"

Kitty clung to the top of the brickwork, her legs dangling in mid-air.

Fooks reached down and grabbed her arms, just as her hands began to slip from the wet bricks. His wiry build hid unsuspected strength. A fact that had often caught out an unruly gang member in the past. With the parapet for support, he held on. He frantically searched the ground below. He fully expected to see the broken, mangled body of his partner laying on the tracks. But no, he wasn't there. Where?

"Here."

Five feet below and to one side, Swan hung from the string course of brickwork. His feet, finding purchase on an out of line brick of the arch, sloping away below him. When their eyes met, Swan nodded slightly. His silent gesture told Fooks he had a good hold. He wasn't going anywhere in a hurry.

"Pull me up," Kitty screamed.

Fooks forced his attention back onto her. He grunted. "Seems you're in a bit of fix, young lady."

"Pull me up," she screamed again. "Please." Kitty raised her anguished face to him, rapidly blinking back the rain that fell into her eyes.

Fooks tightened his grip on her. "You found the key, didn't you?"

"What?" Kitty eyes widened.

"The key to Kinsey's study. After Mr. Martin threw it away. You found it, didn't you?"

"Yes," she whimpered, and swallowed hard. Kitty gasped. "Please. Pull me up."

Fooks peered at Kitty. "If you believe I'm the man you think, then you'll know he has a certain reputation," he said, in a hiss. Then more urgently, "Tell me what happened in Kinsey's study."

Tears coursed down her cheeks and her nose ran. "Pull me up!"

Fooks released his hold on one of Kitty's arms. Just a little. Kitty screamed.

"Talk."

"I saw Mr. Martin throw the key away."

Fooks tightened his hold on her arms. "Go on."

Kitty sobbed. "It was laying on the rug." Kitty's breath came in short, sharp gasps. "Please, Mr. Crane. I'm begging you."

"What happened then?"

Kitty gasped. "Please..."

Fooks loosened his hold on her again.

"Okay. Okay. I'll tell you. Please pull me up."

"Let's hear it first. Then I promise," Fooks said with a pleasant smile.

"I opened the door. Kinsey thought I was Mr. Martin returning. Please."

"I'm getting tired Kitty," Fooks said, in a bored voice. "The rest of it."

Kitty sobbed harder. "I pulled the trigger."

"Here! On the bridge."

Fooks snapped his head around at the shout from Beamish, or Gomez, frantically waving on a coterie of police, slashing through puddles as they ran. Several uniformed patrolmen skidded to a halt. One man in plain clothes ran forward. Captain Loomis. Of course. That's where the other detective, whatever his name, went. To telephone for help.

"I killed him!" Kitty screamed loudly. "Is that what you wanted to hear? I killed him! I killed him!"

"That's enough Crane. Pull her up."

Fooks braced his feet against the side of the parapet. Loomis helped, and together they pulled her up in a rather undignified scramble. Once on the bridge, Kitty's feet went from under her.

"Captain, there's a man here too," one of the patrolmen called.

Loomis hurriedly waved the man to deal with it.

"Did you get that Loomis?" Fooks faced Loomis.

"Yeah, I heard."

Fooks sped away.

A lone patrolman stood on the bridge above where Swan clung. "Pearson's gone for a rope," he said, as Fooks dashed up.

Fooks checked on Swan. "You okay?"

"Been better," Swan said, with a grunt. "How's Kitty?"

Fooks regarded the scene behind. Kitty folded over. Loomis stood by her side, concerned. The other patrolmen clustered around.

"She'll be okay too."

"Watch her. She's slipperier than a pig in butter."

Agonizing minutes ticked by. Fooks paced up and down huffing at the delay. The patrolman drifted off to join the crowd around Kitty. Then the rope arrived, courtesy of Pearson.

"Here, will this do?" Pearson held out the end of a length of rope, the rest coiled around his waist.

"Yes." Fooks glanced over the parapet again, to reassure himself Swan still clung there. "Hold on. We're gonna lower a rope."

Fooks pulled on gloves. Pearson uncoiled the rope, leaving enough still tied around his middle. Together they braced their feet against the parapet and Fooks called to his partner. "Okay, grab hold. We've got you."

Mercifully the rain slowed to a misty drizzle. Both men grunted as they took the strain.

"I'm on," came the disembodied voice from below.

Fooks felt tempted to say "we know" before deciding to save his strength for pulling. *Swan must've put on thirty pounds since I last did this. Sheesh.* Swan rolled over the top of the parapet, huffing and puffing and with a fair amount of groaning.

"Thanks fellas," he gasped when he found safety. Pearson coiled up the rope.

"What on earth d'you think you were doing?" Fooks' eyes flashed angrily as he stood hands on hips, glaring at Swan.

Swan shrugged. "Rescuing a damsel in distress. It's what I do in all those dime novels written 'bout us. Didn't bank on the train nearly doing for me."

Fooks grunted. Now was not the time to go into the merits or otherwise of Swan's preferred reading matter. Especially not with Pearson by his side and Captain Loomis stalking his way over. Fooks tapped Swan's arm and shot him a look which said, *I've got this.*

Fooks plastered on a smile. "Captain Loomis, this is a fortuitous meeting. How did you happen to be here?"

Loomis growled. "I might ask you the same question, Crane. You nearly lost Beamish and Gomez at the depot. I thought I told you to keep 'em in sight."

Fooks pressed his lips together. He shrugged. "What can I tell you? Things were moving on apace and we had to keep after her. Didn't want to lose her."

Loomis raised a finger, about to issue a sharp rebuke.

"Get the cuffs on her quick, Loomis," gasped Swan.

"She's under arrest, Martin." Loomis jabbed his cigar at Fooks. "As for you. I don't like your methods, Crane."

Fooks shrugged and fixed Loomis with a level gaze. "Neither do I, Loomis, but it worked. You heard what she said."

Loomis stuffed the cigar in his mouth. "Under duress. Doubt if it'll stand up in court. Lawyers get picky about that kinda confession."

Fooks shrugged and swapped glances with Swan. "You've got enough to hold her for now."

"Yeah. We're taking her back to Hanover Street." He fixed both with an uncompromising glare. "You two should come along."

Fooks and Swan swapped glances. A polite invitation to visit police headquarters was one they didn't want to accept, but couldn't refuse.

"Did anyone pick up Kitty's bag?" Fooks asked, suddenly.

"I've got it," said Gomez. Or Beamish? He held it up the bag. "Thought it might be important."

"Well done, Officer Gomez," Loomis said around his cigar.

"Beamish, sir."

"Ah," Fooks nodded. *At last, I know who's who.*

"Spill it," Loomis ordered, when they sat around a table at the police station. All except Kitty. Pearson had taken her away already. Glasses of water provided for each of them didn't bode well. The afternoon would prove to be a long one. Fooks' eyes went to the glass in front of him. *Surely that wasn't what Loomis meant?*

Loomis puffed his cigar alight. He blew out a cloud of smoke and leaned back. "Let me have your explanation for all this."

"I thought I told you everything the way I see it earlier?"

"There's a stenographer here now." Loomis indicated the woman setting up a type writing machine in the corner. "This is your written statement."

Fooks glanced at Swan. Of course. Nothing else to do but comply. At least Swan wasn't under arrest this time. Well, not yet. They sat side by side, across from Loomis. A file containing papers lay open in front of him. Fooks, ever the more curious of the pair, couldn't make out what they were. He had an awful feeling they weren't related to this case.

The partners swapped glances, before Fooks said, "Probably best if I begin—"

"At the beginning," Loomis said, with a snarl.

Of course, Captain, where else would I start? No, no, don't say it. "Depends what you call the beginning." *Why can't I listen to myself?*

Swan came to his rescue before Loomis blew a gasket. "Tell him 'bout the tontine thingy, Joe. That's what this is all about."

Loomis frowned. "What the heck is a tontine?"

Swan gave Fooks a nudge with his elbow and gestured for him to explain.

Fooks took a deep breath. "It's a financial instrument. In this case used for investment. Y'see..." Now he was up and running he couldn't stop. The stenographer had a hard time keeping up as Fooks gabbled out the whole story. About how the tontine worked. Who the shareholders were, the nominees, and the secrecy surrounding them. Swan chipped in now and then, adding details Fooks stumbled over.

"Kitty found out about the tontine when her father died. His nominee was her mother. The accident with Montgomery Whitlock may have set her thinking. My guess is she found out about the other shareholders and their status. Kitty realized she stood a chance of the whole thing. Killing Kinsey did two things for her. She killed the man she thought responsible for her father's death, and moved the Miller family one step closer to the tontine pay out. Only Lillian Emerson, Harvey Slocomb's nominee, stood in her way. My guess is Kitty had a pang of conscience, couldn't kill her, so took her hostage instead."

Fooks licked his lips and glanced at Swan.

"Unfortunately for her, Martin and me found Lillian in the icehouse at Waltham. You know the rest."

As he finished, there came a knock on the door and Beamish entered. He carried Kitty's bag and a note, which he passed to Loomis. The detective read and grunted.

"One of the fingerprints on the key belonged to Miss Miller," he said. "Appears there is some substance to your story after all."

Fooks gasped. *Incredible! You still don't believe me.* "Y'mean—" Swan forcefully nudged his elbow. Fooks bit his bottom lip. *Yeah, he's right. Shut up Fooks.*

Loomis chewed his lips. "We have Miss Miller's bag here. Let's find out if your story really stacks up."

Loomis nodded to Beamish, who upended the bag onto the table between them. They dismissed the effects typical for a young woman and pawed through the rest. Loomis unfolded half-finished knitting, revealing a neat hole. Fooks wouldn't have seen the hole before, the knitting being tightly wrapped. Fooks shook out the book of anatomy and several notes flew out. When he read them, he swallowed hard and passed them to Loomis.

"If this is Miss Miller's handwriting, these are damning," Loomis said, when he'd read. "Why would she want to know exactly where the ribs lie in relation to the heart?"

"Because she wanted to know where to aim," Swan said, quietly.

"You had a theory about the bag." Loomis turned the bag inside out. The largest diamonds covered holes, one slightly bigger than the other. Loomis fingered them thoughtfully. "Could have happened innocently," he murmured, but without conviction.

"Look like holes made by a 0.22 to me," said Swan.

Loomis licked his lips. "Yes, they do," he agreed. "While you were gone, I checked on the Rupertus. You're right, there are only a few gunsmiths in Boston who deal in them." He paused. "One remembers repairing one for a woman of Miss Miller's description." He pushed the contents and bag to one side. "Here Beamish, inventory all this stuff. I'll have our science expert analyze the fibers from the bag against those found in the wound. If they're a match..."

The realization Kitty Miller was responsible for these crimes didn't sit well with any of them. The evidence proved indisputable. A few formalities left. Fooks and Swan signed the statement produced by the stenographer.

Fooks and Swan watched as the stenographer packed her equipment. Fooks appealed to Loomis. "Can we go now?" In emphasis, they rose together.

"Not so fast," Loomis barked.

CHAPTER FORTY-FOUR

As one, Fooks and Swan retook their seats, swapping nervous glances. Loomis glanced over his shoulder to make sure the stenographer had left before he turned to them.

"I have a few more questions for the two of you." To their surprise, Loomis' first question was to Swan. "Who are you?"

Swan blinked in surprise. "What d'ya mean who am I? I'm Samuel Martin, husband to Caroline Fairfield as was. Don't tell me ya don't know that? The court case made plenty of newspaper headlines a few months back."

Beside him, Fooks snorted water. *What? He didn't tell me 'bout a court case!* He cleared his throat and pointed at it. "Sorry, wrong way." Swan's guilty expression said *I'll tell you later*.

"No, you aren't. The only trace I can find of a Samuel Martin before you came to Boston, is from the sheriff in that hick town in Wyoming. What's it called? Bronze Canyon?"

"That'll be me. Not sure Wash will appreciate his town being described as hick. Do you Joe?"

Despite the dangerous ground Swan had admitted to, Fooks smiled. "Nope. Bronze Canyon is a nice, quiet small-town Loomis."

"Sheriff Turner says you live there."

"Everyone has to live somewhere." Fooks shrugged. "Why not in Bronze Canyon?"

"You planning on staying in Boston long?" Loomis asked around his cigar. He directed the question at Swan.

Swan took a moment to consider his answer. "Like I said, I'm the husband of Caroline Fairfield. This is where she lives, so I guess this is where I live too."

Loomis grunted and turned to Fooks. "And you?"

Fooks licked his lips and shook his head. "I've got a family and a business in Bronze Canyon. I'll be going back soon."

Loomis stuffed his cigar in his mouth and rifled through papers from the file in front of him. He held one up and read:

"A brown haired, brown eyed man, of average build." He peered at Fooks over the top of the paper. "Florian Fooks." He set the wanted poster aside and turned to the next. "Brown curly hair, blue eyes, medium stocky build. Tobias Swan."

Fooks twitched his head. "I told you before Captain. Those descriptions could match a lot of men. They're pretty vague."

"Yes, they are." Loomis paused. "So vague, in fact should I come into contact with two men of those descriptions here in Boston." He licked his lips. "What are the chances they *are* Florian Fooks and Tobias Swan? Two thousand miles away from their stomping ground."

"Remote, I'd say." Fooks pursed his lips. "There's a rumor out West they're trying to go straight," he said, brightly.

"Yeah, and why would Fooks and Swan help you bring in a murderer?" Swan said, with a laugh, which earned him a sharp glare from Fooks.

Loomis set both posters aside. "Unlikely, I admit." He took a deep breath and suddenly closed the file. "All right. I guess it's just a coincidence these descriptions match you." He pursed his lips. "I'll let you go, but before I do, *Mr. Crane.*" Fooks noticed the emphasis on his name. "I'll confiscate the Pinkerton's shield. I doubt you have a *legitimate* reason to use it."

Fooks reached into his pocket. "Sure, Captain. Guess I won't be needing it anymore."

He placed the shield on the table in front of them. They all studied it for a moment, before Loomis slid it towards himself.

"Goodbye Mr. Crane, Mr. Martin." As they stood, trying not to make it too obvious they were glad to escape, Loomis added, "Mind how you go."

Upon release, Fooks and Swan adjourned to the nearest saloon. It was the end of the working day, and the place heaved. They were lucky to find space at the bar.

"He knows," Swan said, as he and Fooks stood backs to the counter, sipping restorative whiskeys. One whiskey already downed in one go; now on their second. This time drinking more slowly.

"Course he knows," Fooks confirmed. "You'd better watch your step. He'll be watching you."

"Uh-huh." Swan sniffed. "I'll get Caroline to write a big check to the police department. Should keep him off my back for a while."

Fooks regarded him askance. "Money isn't everything, y'know?"

Swan smiled. "No, but it sure helps." He folded his arms. "What will happen to her?" He didn't need to stipulate, Fooks knew he meant Kitty Miller.

"I'll guess there'll be a trial."

"Evidence we dug up is overwhelming, isn't it?"

Fooks bit his bottom lip. "Yep."

"Will she—"

"I don't know. Up to the jury," Fooks said, quickly. Neither man wanted to think about the fate of the woman. The fate they'd been instrumental in deciding.

"Yep." Swan drained his glass and set it on the bar. "You done?"

"Nearly. What's this about a court case?"

"Oh. That."

"Yes. That." Fooks turned to face him, determination on his face. "Wasn't it a tad risky?"

"Didn't get no choice in the matter. Robert Kinsey didn't believe Caroline married me willingly. He'd thought I'd coerced her in some way. He took us to court in a bid to overturn our marriage and have himself declared Caroline's guardian. And getting his hands on her fortune in the process."

"And he didn't dig into your past?"

Swan pursed his lips. "Didn't really come up. Judge wanted the case to focus mainly on our relationship and how we felt about each other. Say, did you ever find out who thought they saw…." He scanned around at the crowded bar. Customers at his elbow, cheek by jowl. everyone having their own loud conversations, didn't discount theirs being overheard. He dropped his voice and leant closer to Fooks. "That ornery ole outlaw in the paper ya read?"

"Don't change the subject. What was the court decision in the end?"

Swan grunted. "That me and Caroline were legally married. No grounds to dissolve the marriage. Sure, put ole Kinsey's nose outta joint."

Fooks cracked his jaw, considering. "You said it was in the newspapers?"

"Yeah. Pictures as well."

"Pictures!" Fooks' eyes popped, and dropped his voice still further. "Someone coulda recognized you. Passengers on trains come from all over, y'know?"

"Relax. I made sure they didn't print my face. Swept Caroline into a passionate kiss, right at the top of the steps to the courthouse." Swan grinned. "*That* was the picture the newspapers printed."

Fooks glowered doubtfully at first. Then as Swan's grin became infectious, his features slowly softened. "Well, I guess the editorial in the newspaper wasn't 'cos someone recognizing *you*. Guess a passenger from a train some time *thought* it was me. There sure were a lot of 'em." He tossed back the remaining whiskey. "Now I'm ready."

"Great. I'll go telephone a cab."

Fooks caught Swan's arm as he turned away. "You can use a telephone?"

"Of course," Swan replied, in surprise. "Can't you?"

Fooks waved his hand dismissively. "Yeah. Doesn't everyone?" As Swan walked away, Fooks' face fell. If telephones became part of everyday life, he'd better learn how to use one. And quick.

Fooks stayed at Ardmaddy until the following Sunday. Would take him a week to get home, and he should be in plenty of time for Susan's first birthday. Nice spending time with Swan openly now he was in the clear. With Swan and Caroline, Fooks visited the theater and opera. Swan took him for the promised round of golf. Fooks picked it up quickly, but not something he would be doing regularly. He didn't know of a golf course near to Bronze Canyon.

He spent a happy afternoon browsing the collections in the Boston Public Library. He finally had to be dragged away.

All too soon it was time to leave Boston. Swan walked in on Fooks as he packed his bag. He paused, holding open the door for a moment, and closed it.

"Ya know Cowdry woulda done that for ya."

"Yes, but I wanted to do it myself."

Swan wandered over to the bed, jingling change in his pants pockets, while Fooks packed his bag. A flicker of annoyance crossed Fooks' face and he turned away in search of shirts.

"Caroline and me have had a talk," Swan said, breaking the silence.

Fooks folded his freshly washed and pressed shirts into a shape that he could pack. "Oh yes?"

"Yeah, a real honest, hands on the table kinda talk y'know?"

"Uh-huh."

"Ironed out a few things out. Told each other how we felt an' all that slushy stuff."

Fooks bit his bottom lip to hide his smirk. *Don't tell Caroline what you said. Women just don't appreciate plain speaking.* "So?"

"So ya do know I'm not going back to Wyoming with ya don't ya?"

Fooks sucked in a deep breath. "Yeah. It's pretty obvious—"

"I love her, Flo." Swan shook his head. "Can't really explain. She's not my usual type."

"No, she's far too good for you."

"I suppose," Swan went on as if Fooks hadn't spoken, "its only to be expected with us being married an' all. In every sense of the word." He paused. "Turns out she loves me back." He blinked, surprised at the thought.

"There's no accounting for taste."

For a second, Swan scowled. When he saw his partner's face, they swapped grins.

"It's a different life for you, Tobe. I hope it'll work out for you."

"Yeah, but it gets me away from guns. I know ya had concerns. I did too an' I had to do something to get away. I'm kinda used to it all this now. I've got a business. Who'da thought it? Friends. Social life..." He drifted off to stare into the distance. "Family." He pulled a face. "Mebbe."

Fooks beamed and held him by the upper arms. "Is Caroline...?"

Swan gave a wry smile. "Possibly. She's not sure yet."

"Hey, partner. Congratulations." Fooks pounded Swan on the back. "Being a father is the greatest feeling."

"Wish we were free and clear though, Flo," he said, sadly. "Is there anything we can do 'bout it?"

Fooks shook his head and sighed regretfully. "You know Wyoming doesn't have statute of limitations." He gripped Swan's shoulder and gave him a shake. "One day when we're too old for the law to bother throwing us in prison."

"Long time to wait." Swan brightened. "Mebbe something'll come up. Unexpected."

"Yeah, mebbe." Fooks returned to his packing. They were both getting slushy, and he kept his head low as Swan moved around the room.

Swan held a stack of papers. "Are these the documents from Kinsey's safe?"

"Yes. You'll have to put 'em back."

"An' jus' how am I supposed to do that?"

Fooks shrugged. "Dunno. Ask Caroline. She's a resourceful woman. And I can give her the combination." *Doubt if she'll need it though. I bet she can crack the safe.*

"Yeah, you're right. I'll give 'em to her."

An awkward silence fell before they both spoke at once.

"Will you—"

"I'm—"

Fooks gestured for Swan to go first.

"I was going to say, I'm glad things are working out for you with Mary."

"Thanks."

"What were you going to say?" Swan asked.

"Gonna ask if you'll be all right, but you've already answered me. I reckon you will, but y'know you'll always have a home in Bronze Canyon."

Swan grinned. "Sure, as long as you don't peeve Wash off too much."

Fooks grinned back. "I'm trying real hard not to."

EPILOGUE

Leaving his partner behind was hard. Swan furnished Fooks with money and purchased first-class train tickets for him. He'd be traveling home in comfort.

Yet as the miles rolled by, he began to reflect on Swan's new life, far different from his previous one. A world away, in fact. Not for him of course. Mary and their daughter filled his life. He was happy in Bronze Canyon, working in his hardware store.

He didn't blame Swan for wanting a different life. Something about Caroline attracted his partner to give up everything he knew. He could certainly appreciate why Swan fell for her. Outwardly she exuded confidence. Yet once or twice, he caught a glimpse of vulnerability.

He doubted if he and Caroline would ever feel entirely at ease with one another. The fraught circumstances under which they first met would forever have something to do with it. Apart from Swan, he and Caroline had nothing in common. At the back of his mind, Caroline would always be the cause of the partners' separation.

Ah, but it was inevitable once he and Mary married. With the decision to go straight, their lives had already changed. Of course, there would be wives and families. Now they both had a wife, and he had a family. *Looks like Tobe is getting one too shortly.* Good luck to him.

While Fooks would never be entirely reconciled to Swan being so far away, he respected his right to make the decision. He could stop worrying now he knew where he was and what he was doing. He doubted if either of them would write much. Just knowing he could, and where to, proved to be a balm for his worries. He would fully relax into his new life with Mary and Susan.

Well, not fully relax. Still the little matter of being wanted. But who knows? Perhaps it would resolve itself in the fullness of time.

Fooks relaxed into the homeward journey. Once taking in the changing scenery ran its course, he struck up conversations with his fellow passengers when it suited him. Able to take advantage of his own personal space, he would retire to his compartment to sleep or read. He'd purchased a book for the journey, *The Adventures of Huckleberry Finn*. He'd read others by Mark Twain before, and he was delighted to find a new publication by his favorite author.

He'd almost finished the book by the time the train pulled into Bronze Canyon. On reflection, he enjoyed the journey, but glad to be home.

In Bronze Canyon, the short walk from the train station to the little house he now called home became fraught with delays. The townsfolk, knowing he had gone to Boston to visit Samuel Martin, stopped him at every opportunity to ask about his journey. About Sam. How did he like Boston? He answered all questions politely but briefly. However, by the time he finally reached his home, he was beyond fractious.

The feeling disappeared as soon as he opened the door. He'd sent a telegram from Cheyenne, alerting Mary to the train he'd be on. So, he was surprised when she wasn't in the living room waiting for him.

"Hey Susan, is that Pappy?" Mary's voice came from Susan's bedroom. When the door opened, Fooks saw his family. Mary pulled down Susan's dress and gave her a nudge forward. "It is Pappy. Go and say hello."

Fooks dropped his bag as the excited child toddled towards him. "Hey, look at you."

Susan appeared steady on her feet at first, firmly clutching her cloth rabbit by its long ears. Speed caused her to stumble. Fooks saved her from embarrassment. He snatched her before her face hit the floor. Susan squealed as he kissed her cheek. "No stopping you, is there?"

"Everything important has to go up high now." Mary joined them. "I mean really high. She can climb."

Fooks put an arm around Mary's shoulders and drew her close. He smacked a kiss on her cheek and gave her a fond squeeze. A proper hello would have to wait until they were alone. "How are my two best girls? Did you miss me?"

Mary gave him a playful swot. "Of course, we missed you. How was your trip?"

Fooks took a moment to consider. "Good." He nodded. "Resolved a lot of things. Swan's staying in Boston. I'm not happy 'bout it, but he's made a life for himself there now. I'll tell you all about it later." Mary patted his shoulder. "How are things here? Is the store okay?"

Mary rolled her eyes. "Yes, the store's fine. Ted and Russ managed fine without you."

Fooks grunted. *Do they really need me?*

"Craig printed your latest Florian Fooks mystery. I think he called it *Fake or Fortune*."

"Really? How did that go down?"

Mary laughed. "Wash wasn't too pleased as usual, but readers liked it." She turned to him and put a hand on his chest. "The real news is Wash has broken his leg."

Fooks gaped. "How did he do that?"

"Janet had him nailing the loose shingles on the back porch. The ladder slipped."

Fooks made an O with his mouth.

"He'd like you to stop by."

"Yeah, I will." Then he tightened his hold on Mary's shoulder. "Tomorrow. The rest of today is reserved for my two girls."

He leaned towards her, intent on a kiss, when suddenly Susan thrusting her toy rabbit in his ear couldn't be ignored. Neither could the child's high-pitched squeal of "Pappy!"

If you enjoyed The Elusive Key, please share your thoughts by leaving a review on Amazon.

Historical Note

In 1863, President Lincoln gave an executive order that the eastern terminus of the planned transcontinental railroad should be at Council Bluffs rather than Omaha. This was further clarified in 1864, when Lincoln amended the railroad act to include financial incentives to facilitate construction.

Union Pacific had already started construction and by 1865 ran the first passenger service west from Council Bluffs. In 1867, the first railroad to reach Council Bluffs from the east was the precursor to the Chicago and Northwestern. This is the railroad Fooks takes from Council Bluffs.

By 1869 the Transcontinental Railroad was complete. The lack of a bridge over the Missouri River, the only missing link. For three years, through passengers were obliged to continue their journey by ferry across the river. It wasn't until 1872, that a bridge was built and at last passengers could complete their journey without risking life and limb crossing the treacherous Missouri River.

The Union Pacific's Council Bluffs Transfer Depot and Hotel opened in 1878. This building is long gone now. While I could find several old photographs of the exterior, I was unable to discover any of the interior. A description appears in Robert Louis Stevenson's *Across the Plains,* written in 1879-80 but this wasn't published until 1892. A further description appears in Ryan Roenfeld's little book, *The Development of the Union Transfer Grounds at Council Bluffs.* Undoubtably the most useful in describing the interior of the transfer depot was the original architects' drawings held in the Library of Congress' digital archives. These gave a detailed layout of each floor.

In Fooks' time, 1886, eight railroad companies had their main terminus in Boston. By 1900, these had consolidated into the North and South Union Stations. Railroading was an industry the financiers of Boston were keen to take part in for two main reasons. As the country rapidly spread westward, Boston's geographical location meant it was rapidly losing out to more accessible cities like New York. Previously its location had proved ideal for oceangoing trade but now Boson found itself increasingly remote. The race was on to link up Boston with the rest of the country. Once that was established, Boston financiers found they had a liking for railroad construction. Boston money backed a notable number of railroads across the country and beyond.

Richard C Barrett's *Boston's Depots and Terminals* was invaluable in describing the various buildings, with photographs and comments pertaining to their construction. Timetables, ticket prices and brochures, all give a sense of how much railroads were important to society in the later part of the 19th century.

The Hoosac Tunnel was first conceived as a canal in 1819 to connect Boston with Albany in New York State. This project was quickly killed off due to the exorbitant cost only to be resurrected in 1841 as a way through the Berkshire Hills in western Massachusetts. Work began in 1851 and took 24 years to complete. This was partly due to slow and dangerous tunnelling methods. Work sped up with the first use of nitro-glycerin as a blasting agent, electric firing and the development of compressed air drilling machinery. Even so the tunnel did not enter service until 1875, but at the cost of 196 lives. At 4.75 miles long it remained the longest tunnel in North America until 1916.

In the mid-19th century, the use of ice to keep food fresh was an important commodity, almost as important as coal in winter. The icehouse in Waltham did stand in the position on the Charles River as described, although I have changed the name of the proprietors. In winter, a wide, shallow bay allowed for the river to freeze easily, creating an ice field. As Alfred says, ice harvesting was a cold and brutal occupation. It was not unusual for men to slip into the freezing water, sometimes with dire consequences: frost bite or death. Once frozen the area was scored into a grid, often by horses pulling an ice-plow. Men would labor to separate these blocks, or cakes. These would be floated along a channel up to the icehouse. A wooden framework, built on the outside of the icehouse, allowed for the cakes to rise by steam powered elevator, up into the icehouse for storage. The ice was kept frozen between layers of straw and saw dust. If stored well, ice may be preserved even during the hottest summer months. Domestic customers might expect a delivery of ice twice a week throughout the year, for use in their own ice box.

A tontine is a financial contract between a group of people. A sum of money is invested either for the benefit of each other as a form of life insurance or for a philanthropic project. Each investor would pay a sum into the tontine and receive annual interest on the capital invested. This could vary year to year based on the number of investors still in the scheme. Depending on the wording of the contact, the interest may be payable on the investors life or they may nominate the life of another individual. This could typically be a child, where there was clearly an expectation of a longer life but could be anyone the investor considered appropriate. These schemes were open to abuse and such fell out of favor early in the 20th century.

Acknowledgements

I would like to thank my beta readers Fliss, Sue and Dick for wading through this text even though this is not their genre.

Also Gin for helping me sound more American.

My editor, Kristina Stanley, for being patient with a still learning newbie writer.

To Michael at *First Editing,* for removing commas where they shouldn't be and for adding them where they should.

Most of all I would like to thank my husband Murray for NOT reading any of my drafts and keeping our relationship sane.

ABOUT ME

Shirley Arnham always enjoyed writing and flirted with fan fiction over the years. Once retired from a career in accountancy, she thought what now? With plenty of stories in her head, why not try her hand at writing a book. Shirley lives in Norfolk, England and is looking forward to traveling the world with her husband.

The Enigmatic Door is her first published novel and is the first in the Outlaw Detective series.

Discover more at:

www.shirleyarnham.com

Other books by Shirley Arnham

Joseph Crane lives a quiet life in a small town in 1880's Wyoming. A genial young man with a successful business, a wife, and a baby due.

Yet all is not as it seems. Previously, he was Florian Fooks, charismatic leader of the Guardian Wall Gang but that wasn't as long ago as he would like.

The shadow of his past looms large when two former associates arrive unexpectedly. Accused of murdering a prominent lawyer, they come seeking his help and Joseph doubts their guilt. Murder was never their game.

If he sets out to learn more, he risks recognition and capture. But his wife needs him here.

If he sends them away, chances are his former associates will hang before reaching trial. He can't have that on his conscience.

Torn between loyalty, self-preservation and a sense of justice, can he uncover the truth behind the lawyer's murder in time without putting himself in danger?

The Enigmatic Door is the first in the Florian Fooks murder mystery series.

In the Pipeline

New life under threat. Suffering amnesia. A killer to find.

Injured in an accident at his store, Joseph Crane doesn't remember turning his life around, being married or becoming a father. In his mind, he is still the notorious leader of the Guardian Wall Gang, Florian Fooks. Things couldn't get much worse, until circumstances force a temporary sheriff on Bronze Canyon.

Jack Priestly is a man Fooks has dealt with in the past and not favourably either. With arrest and a long prison sentence a real possibility, Fooks strikes a deal. With his father-in-law in tow, a man he can't remember, Fooks sets out to uncover who killed the sheriff's brother during a bank robbery.

As Fooks digs deeper, a tangled web of deceit and wrong doing emerges. Under time pressure, he must get to the bottom of it all before the net closes in on him.